# Nate Grisham

## Book 2
### *Renegade Trapper*

WR Benton
Grady Clark

THE BEST IN WESTERN FICTION

**LOOSE CANNON ENTERPRISES**
*Paradise, CA*

*2018 Edition*
*ISBN 978-1-944476-78-6*



Edited by: Bobby La Cour and Daniel Williams
Author images, © 2013 Melanie C. Benton

Cover design and layout © 2013 by www.vim-pearl.com
all rights reserved.
Cover Image:  Clyde D. Lewis, http://www.clydedlewis.com
Interior Images © W.R. Benton, 2013, all rights reserved.
*Mountain Man*, © 2013,
Poem used with permission from Harold Roy Miller

www.loose-cannon.com

# Books by W.R. Benton

*Nate Grisham, Renegade Trapper* (Co-authored with Grady Clark)

*Fur Seekers (Co-authored with Grady Clark)*

*Red Runs the Plain, Book 1 of the Plains Series*

*The Fall of America, Premonition of Death*

*Jake Masters, Bounty Hunter*

*Nate Grisham, Black Mountain Man* (Co-authored with Grady Clark)

*Missouri in Flames, I Rode with Jesse James*

*War Paint*

*James McKay, U. S. Army Scout*

*Blood Money*

*Alive and Alone (Young Adult)*

*Simple Survival, a Family Outdoors Guide (Non-Fiction)*

*Impending Disasters (Non-Fiction)*

*Bubba's Dawg Might be a Redneck (Southern Humor)*

# Books by Grady Clark

*Nate Grisham, Renegade Trapper* (Co-authored with WR Benton)

*The Widow Nancy Buck*

*Nate Grisham, Black Mountain Man*

*The Fur Seekers* (Co-authored with WR Benton)

*A Southern Moon Rising*

# **D**EDICATION

*W. R. Benton*

**T**o all members of our military armed forces, both past and present, I salute your sacrifice. As a retired military member, I know your job is difficult.

**T**o Wendy Hartman, Wendy Gay, Sue Bates, "Cody" Case, and Lynn Marie Gilleran Eisen, my friends on Facebook, and the kind of people who stood strong during the settling of this great country.

*Grady Clark*

**T**o the super voice, Prentis Goodwin and fellow authors, Gayle Gresham, Heidi Thomas, and Teresa Burleson.

**T**o LouAnn Staupe Peterson, a great friend.

# TABLE OF CONTENTS

# Mountain Men

*Poem © 2013 by Harold Roy Miller*

History confirms there has always been
brave and daring adventurous men.
Some are remembered as unfading immortals
while others disappeared through history's portals.

Back when America was growing up strong,
a self-reliant breed just happened along.
An alluring western wind softly whispered his name
and to fulfill his destiny, the mountain man came.

A fearless group of men of whom it has been said
they were born with eyes in the back of their head.
Some are still known today, like Carson, Bridger and Meek;
men who had been "over the mountain and up the creek."

Buckskin-clad with Hawken rifles, masters of survival,
they stood their ground fiercely against enemy or rival.
All were skilled fighters with both gun and knife;
they had to react quickly or forfeit their life.

Longevity dictated they be hard-barked and tough
since the life they had chosen was hazardous and rough.
There was constant danger of sickness or dehydration,
freezing to death or even starvation.

Wild animals and injuries were another threat
as well as savage hostiles they sometimes met.
But it was in their soul's nature to wander and roam
and seldom did they ever call any place home.

They trapped the ponds until the beaver were depleted
and most of the fighting tribes were finally defeated.
The mountain man's role became greatly diminished
and some took jobs as scouts. The era was finished.

The land was settled as pioneers moved in.
It soon grew too crowded for the remaining mountain men.
Though they played an essential part in settling the west
they didn't look back as they rode over the crest.

# Clyde D. Lewis

*A Special Acknowledgment*

The renowned western artist, Clyde D. Lewis, created the original drawing for this book cover.  Clyde is an extremely talented man and the original drawing for this cover is in the possession of the author, who cherishes it very much.  Clyde is a real cowboy and artist from San Antonio, Texas.  He is a member of, and has worked to help sponsor, the Black Cowboy Association and the Men of Color Association of TX.  Additionally,  he is part of the Choctaw Indian Heritage of Oklahoma and he will soon become a member of the New Braunfels, TX Art League.  See more of Clyde's fine work at:

http://www.clydedlewis.com

# Chapter 1

Nate and Cotton Top were sitting in Butterfield's trading post, sipping on whiskey, while they waited for a rough storm to pass. The intensity of the storm was such they figured to leave in the morning. Tonight the trails would be muddy and dangerous to travel, even if the storm stopped at this instant. The door suddenly swung open and a wet man stood unmoving just outside the entrance. With each flash of lightning, the black silhouette of the man was all that showed.

Cotton looked at the man, glanced at Nate, and then said, "Come on in and dry off a bit. Lawdy, yer soaked to the skin."

The man took two steps and then fell to the floor, flat on his face. Water and blood quickly puddled under the man.

An arrow was clearly seen in his upper shoulder and old Butterfield moved toward the man. Squatting, he said, "It's a Blackfoot arrow and this is old 'Possum Thomas. Last I heard he was trappin' up on Baldy Mountain with Johnson, Hanks, Burrows, and a new man named Williams."

Cotton and Nate moved to the downed man and Nate said, "Let me move 'em closer to the fireplace, so we can see to doctor 'em up. We both know 'Possum." The big black man scooped 'Possum up and placed him on a buffalo robe near the flickering flames.

"Let me get my doctorin' supplies and such, and I'll look 'em over." Butterfield moved for his counter.

While Butterfield was gathering his supplies, Nate pulled his knife and cut the back of 'Possum's shirt from tail to the collar. He gave a whistle and then said, "Lawdy, he's been shot three times, too! Two of 'em don't look like much, but one looks real close to his lights."

"Blackfoot will do that to a feller and quick like, too," Cotton said and then moved to the table.  While he could doctor a man as good as most, he figured between Butterfield and Nate, the man would be well cared for.  He poured two inches of whiskey into his tin cup and took a sip.

Butterfield squatted beside the downed man, handed some tools to Nate and said, "Drop these in the boiling water I have in the fireplace.  I was heatin' the water to fix a stew fer tomorrow, but it'll wait."  The old trader rolled the injured man onto his back.  He raised 'Possum's head and poured just a little whiskey into the man's mouth. Once that was down the man, he poured a little more.  When the cup of whiskey was empty, he said, "Pour the hot water on the porch, let the tools cool a bit, and then we'll try to fix ole 'Possum up."

Nate used an old rag near the fireplace to remove the small cast iron kettle and carry it to the porch.  Once back inside, he placed the still hot kettle on a table, and poured enough alcohol in the pot to cover the tools.  Then, he placed the pot beside Butterfield.

"I just gave 'em some laudanum, so we'll start on him in about five minutes.  The arrow ain't in deep, so it's the least of our worries.  The bullet closest to his lights concerns me, but I fed 'em two cups of whiskey and he kept 'er down."

"Any bloody bubbles or blood from his mouth?"  Nate asked.

"None, so I think he was pretty damned lucky."

Nate walked to his table, picked up a bottle and topped off his cup of whiskey.  He then returned to Butterfield.  Taking a small sip, he knelt on the opposite side the old trader was on.  He placed the cup on he floor near his leg.

Butterfield met his eyes and asked, "Ya ready to start the dance?"

"Yep, so I guess ya need the pliers first, right?"

"Uh-huh, and hand me a knife, too.  We'll pull the arrow out first, then tend the gunshot wounds.  I just hope the arrowhead ain't caught in the muscle, or I'll have to cut it out."

"Ya do what needs to be done and don't fret over the small stuff.  Iffen he lives, hell, he'll be in a bed a month, no matter what ya do." Nate replied as he handed the pliers and knife to Butterfield.

Grasping the arrow shaft with the pliers, the old man pulled, and the arrow came out with the head still attached. Grinning, Butterfield said, "Hell, fire, that was easy enough. Now, in the pot you'll see a long thin rod. It's about as big 'round as a pencil and maybe 12 inches long."

As Nate removed the rod, he noticed whiskey dripping from the tool. He extended his hand toward the trader. "What's this used for?" He asked.

"I use it to probe fer bullets and such. I find bullets, broken bone, and all kind of stuff with it." He took the probe and slowly inserted it into the first bullet hole. "Bullet on this one went through the body and it's clean of bone, so let's check the other two."

Nate took a gulp of his whiskey and wiped his mouth off with the back of his hand.

A loud crack of thunder was heard from the storm and Cotton said, "Bad-assed storm out there, so I'm glad as all hell to be in here sippin' panther piss. It'd be poor bull to be in the woods on a night like this." He took another sip of his whiskey.

Nate replied, "Me too, Cotton. It'd be wet doin's fer sure."

"One of these wounds is clean through, but the other ain't. Look in the pot, Nate, and pull out a long and skinny tool that looks like a big pair of tweezers."

Nate chuckled when he pulled the tool out and asked, "Ya got anymore of these tools of yers? Hell, I need these in the mountains with me. Where'd ya buy 'em?"

Butterfield took the instrument and as he inserted it into the wound, he said, "I got a few extra's I'll let ya have, for a low price. I had Abe, my blacksmith, make me up a few sets. I'm thinkin' of selling them here, but don't know iffen any of y'all will buy 'em."

"By God, I want a set, because it sure makes the job easier."

"Got it," Butterfield said and then added, "and it feels like a bullet." A second later the tweezers came up and out of the wound, holding a misshapen 45 caliber ball. The trader dropped the bullet on 'Possum's chest and re-inserted the instrument. "This is near his shoulder, so I'm feeling for any shat-tered bone that may be in the wound."

"Damn, but these tools make doctorin' pretty easy, huh?"

"Yep, I got the idea from an old medical book I saw back east years ago. I've been thinkin' on 'em fer years, but finally got off my ass and had some made. I feel something again, so it's likely bone."

A few minutes later three small pieces of bone and one spent ball lay on the floor beside Butterfield. He poured whiskey on the entrance and exit holes of each wound and then bandaged the man. As he completed the wrapping to hold the bandages in place, he said, "Now, it's up to God if 'Possum goes under or not. We'll move 'em to the bed in a bit."

Throwing back the remainder of his drink, Nate asked, "How much do ya want fer one of those medical tools kit ya got?"

Grinning, the old man said, "Like it, do ya? I can let ya have one fer a dollar."

"Get two of 'em, Nate, 'cause we both should have one fer our possibles bags." Cotton said.

"I'll gather up two fer ya in the mornin'."

Nate and Butterfield moved to the table, where they both sat, and Cotton filled their cups with the rough amber colored traders whiskey. Butterfield knocked his drink back and extended his hand for a refill. After thinking for a few minutes, the trader said, "I hope ya both know it's likely all the men with 'Possum were killed."

"The Blackfoot are a tough bunch, but they have some of the best beaver country in the world on their land. Iffen a feller can sneak in and get out alive, he's made a bunch of money takin' plew. Iffen they catch ya, you'll lose yer hair."

Cotton stood, stretched and said, "I'm goin' to my robes."

"Ya can take an empty room with a bed or curl up by the fireplace." Butterfield said.

"I ain't got much use fer a bed, so the floor over by the fire will be just fine."

"Nate, help me move 'Possum to the last room down the hall and on the right."

Nate gave a loud laugh bend said, "Ya go to the room and pull the covers down, heck, I'll pack ole 'Possum in there on my own hook."

As Butterfield moved down the hall, Nate moved to 'Possum, picked him up in his huge arms and carried the man to his room.  Once in the room, Butterfield said, "I'll stay in here with 'em fer a few hours, until I see how he's gonna do.  We both know he'll come down with a fever, but I don't expect that until tomorrow night."

Nate nodded and said, "I'm gonna have a couple more drinks and do a little reading.  I'll sleep out there by Cotton, so iffen ya need me, just call."

With dawn, three days later, came more rain and it was blowing hard against the windows of the trading post.  It's been raining for four days straight.  Nate opened the door, saw the barnyard was a quagmire of mud, and gave a light chuckle.  *We'll go no place this day and mayhap tomorrow,* he thought.  He returned to the table, picked up his book and began reading.

Cotton return to the building, pulled off his soaked oil cloth and said, "Rainin' like a horse pissin' on a flat rock out there.  I'd be dryer iffen I'd just peed my pants in here."

"Maybe, but the smell would be noticed by the rest of us."

Sitting at the table, where he'd placed a cup of coffee earlier, Cotton asked, "What are ya readin' now?"

"The Holy Bible."

"It's a good book, and more of us need to be readin' it."

"Do ya want to borrow it?"  Nate asked, knowing Cotton disliked reading.

Looking over the rim of his raised coffee cup, Cotton replied, "Maybe later, but not this mornin'."

"Nate!  Come in here!" Butterfield yelled from 'Possum's room.

The chairs under the two men screeched as they stood and moved for the room. Lord, let ole 'Possum live, Nate thought as he neared the doorway.

When they entered, Butterfield was talking to the wounded trapper.  Glancing at Nate and Cotton he said, "Do ya have enough strength to tell Nate what ya just told me, 'Possum?"

"I can talk, and thanks fer the laudanum, Butterfield."

"I gave ya the medicine so ya could tell us what happened. Ole 'Possum has a hell of a tale to tell."

'Possum took a sip of whiskey and said, "Here last trappin' season we met a lone white man up in the mountains, near Dead Squaw Creek. He was a big jasper, close to seven feet tall and well over 300 pounds. Now, the man wasn't fat, it was all muscle, and he had red hair, with a scraggly beard of the same color. He claimed all his partners was kilt by Blackfoot and, by God, where we was at, that was pretty likely. He had close to five hundred pounds of plew with 'em, which meant they'd had a good season."

When 'Possum took another sip of his drink, Nate asked, "Ya doin' okay? I mean is the talkin' wearin' ya out?"

Shaking his head, 'Possum replied, "Nope, I'm fine, thanks to the medicine and this whiskey. Anyway, he went into cahoots with us and we had one hell of a fine season. See, there were six of us trappin'. There was me, Johnson, Hanks, Burrows, and a new man named Williams, along with this new feller named Coon Turner. I ain't sure how many pounds of plew we gathered, but I ain't never seen the like in all my years out here."

"Blackfoot country always has plew." Cotton said.

"Well, the night we were packing to come home, things went to shit. We'd bailed up the plew, packed our supplies, and had it all ready to load on the mules and pack horses. I'd gone to bed, after pulling my guard and fell asleep pretty fast. Something woke me up a little after midnight, maybe a noise or smell or something, so I laid there listening. I heard what sounded like someone choking, so I got up." He took a long pull on his whiskey cup and then held it out for more.

As Butterfield refilled the cup, he continued, "I melted into the darkness and moved toward the sound. When I neared, I saw Coon Turner wipin' a bloody knife off on Johnson's shirt. He then moved toward Burrows, but the man fought 'em and Turner put a bullet in his ass. He killed Burrows with his shot and then giving a loud scream, Coon went absolutely apeshit and started shootin' at Williams and Hanks. I guess he looked fer me, but I'd gone to ground."

"I don't understand." Cotton said and then gave a confused look at Nate.

Nate said, "Hush and let 'em finish his story."

"I shot at the sumbitch, but he moved and it was a clean miss. But, he come fer me at a rush and when I tried my pistol, the damned thing misfired. I moved into the darkness and lost 'em after a few minutes. I stayed hidden fer about two hours, then I moved back to our camp, but saw no sign of the man. I spotted Williams and Hanks near the fire, so I walked into camp."

"Were they both okay?" Nate asked.

"Yep, both were uninjured, but as mad as two hornets in a fruit jar. Coon had loaded our supplies and plew, and then rode off with all the horses, leavin' us to fend fer ourselves."

Nate gave thought to the man's words, but waited to hear the rest.

"Well, the next mornin' at dawn the Blackfoot hit us, and there must have been forty or more of 'em. I figured they must have heard the gunshots when Coon started shootin' at Williams and Hanks."

"Hell, yer lucky ya got away from 'em." Cotton said.

"Cotton, we didn't get away from 'em right then. They took all three of us prisoner and all of us had injuries of one kind or the other. They tied ropes around our necks and walked us a good twenty miles to a village. Williams fell about a mile from the Injun camp and couldn't get up, so a warrior cut his throat right then and there." 'Possum took a long drink of whiskey and I'd heard his voice cracking toward the end.

Cotton started to speak, only Nate held his hand up and he closed his yap.

"Once in the village, them Blackfoot women beat the livin' shit outta me and Hanks. They hogtied us both to a pole, maybe twenty feet apart and then turned rough on Hanks. One old warrior stood near me and he said, 'He will die this day and you will follow him tomorrow. It is the way of the Blackfoot and we will see if you both die well.' I spat on the old man's face, but he just laughed at me and walked off. They gutted Hanks, I mean opened him from crotch to chest and tortured the hell out of the man. I almost lost my mind when they—"

'Possum had a watery eyes and his voice was cracking when he took a long gulp of his whiskey and then held the cup out again. He regained his composure a few minutes later and continued, "Well, they carved on my buddy and did some terrible things to 'em.  Finally, with Hanks all butchered up, but still alive, they piled brush and wood all around him."

"Burned him to death, did they?" Butterfield asked.

"Yep, they did, but by God, my man died strong.  As hard as he died, he kept yellin' curses at the Blackfoot, along with the Lord's prayer, until the flames grew so high I couldn't see 'em anymore.  The Injuns yipped and yelled as Hanks went under, but I'm here to tell ya, he had the bark!"

"How'd ya get away?" Cotton asked.

"Well," 'Possum took his hand and wiped tears from his eyes, "About two hours later, there was nothing to see near Hanks' pole but a smokin' shriveled black form in the dirt. The smell would have knocked a fly off a shit wagon a hundred yards away, and I'd worked my left hand free from the rope. This woman came near, holding a knife in her right hand and I knew she was out to cut on me a mite.  I let her get close, glanced around and saw we were alone.  I grabbed her, took the knife away, and cut her throat and just about that quickly, too.  I was scared shitless and knew my turn was comin', so I had nothing to lose."

He took another drink, closed his eyes and continued, "I moved toward the horses, killed three kids they had guardin', but the last one screamed when my knife entered his kidney.  I threw my ass on the closest horse and rode like hell.  I took two gunshot wounds as I broke from the village.  For the next five days I got by with an hour or two of sleep a night and no food at all.  The only water I had was from streams and rivers I crossed.  And, to be honest, I don't remember much after that, until I woke up in this bed this mornin'."

It grew quiet in the room, as each of us gave thoughts to the words spoken by 'Possum.  Finally, Butterfield said, "Here, drink the rest of this whiskey and get ya some more sleep.  You're healin', but rest is the best thing for ya." The old trader then nodded his head toward the door.

The three of us gathered at the table, as Butterfield brought a quart of good whiskey and added a good inch to our coffee. "Now, normally, I ain't much of a drinker, but I do like it when I have some serious thinkin' to do."

"I hear ya." Nate replied, still hearing 'Possums words in his mind.

"Boys," Butterfield said, "we've a real problem on our hands."

Cotton looked over the rim of his cup, raised one eyebrow, and asked, "How's that?"

"We've a renegade trapper and he must be brought in for justice."

"Yep, Coon Turner is in a world of hurt, but it's likely he doesn't know it yet." Nate said and took a sip of coffee. "He likely thinks Hanks, Williams, and Possum died in the woods. Hell, even without the Blackfoot attack, it's unlikely the men would have made it to safety, not without horses."

"So," Cotton asked, "what do we do?  We don't even know where the man went."

Butterfield said, "Cotton, use yer head fer something besides a place to put yer hat.  Hell, he had a full load of prime plew and he didn't come here, so that leaves Fort Atkinson or Saint Louis."

"Yep, he'll be wantin' cash money or my name ain't Nate. So, Butterfield, I need some supplies, because Cotton and I have a cat to skin."

Moving behind his counter, Butterfield said, "Ain't no charge fer the supplies, since yer goin' after that worthless bastard.  Tell me what ya need, Nate, and it's yers."

# CHAPTER 2

Coon Turner was concerned, and had been for the last three days. The weather had turned wet and he'd been forced to seek shelter. The first river he'd come to was swollen and overflowing its banks, and he knew he'd go nowhere until the water level dropped. He had six mules and pack horses loaded down with plew, as well as two horses with supplies and gear, so he had what he needed to survive, but the fact he'd left at least three of the trappers alive worried him. He knew that even without horses they were still a dangerous bunch. *If the word gets out I killed for plew, they'll come for me*, he thought as he spooned beans into his mouth. *But, they won't come until this weather breaks. Ain't a man or beast out in this mess.*

Lightning flashed across the sky and exploded into many small fingers of light, followed by a sharp *crack* of thunder. The horses danced on the picket line, but they'd all been double tied and were secure enough. The runoff suddenly overflowed from behind his shelter and two small streams moved across the ground in the center of his canvas structure. Cursing, he moved some supplies and turned a bucket up-side-down to sit on.

Spooning more beans into his mouth, as he chewed he thought, *I'll bet ya Mary will want me now. Hell, the furs I got are worth thousands of dollars and all women love money. But, iffen she doesn't want me, I'll head to New Orleans and buy me a couple of women there. They're pretty too, and while they'll be whores, it doesn't matter much. All women are just whores when ya think on it a spell. The only difference is a soiled dove charges a man everyday, where a wife spends a lifetime milkin' a man dry.*

He finished his simple meal, wrapped up in his robe and went to sleep.

It was a little after midnight when he heard a horse nicker and he sat up, pulling his Hawken rifle in close. He cocked the long gun and then stood. The rain had stopped, but he could still hear drops hitting the stretched canvas of his shelter as it fell from the leaves. *I wonder when the rain quit?*

He moved toward the animals, knowing any Injun would try to steal his horses. He saw and heard nothing, but felt something in the darkness. His warning system had never been wrong and many times in the past it'd saved his life. He squatted next to a large oak tree and waited.

Two hours later, he spotted movement, as an Injuns silhouette was seen against a lighter sky.

He lined the sights up on his Hawken, took a deep breath and then squeezed the trigger. His shot was loud and it was followed by screams. He moved about ten feet closer to the horses and started reloading his rifle. Two warriors, seen against the gray sky, suddenly ran for his mounts.

His rifle fired once more and a man dropped, but when he pulled his pistol, all he heard was a *snap* as it misfired. He pulled his second pistol, but the brave had gone to ground. Once again he moved to the right and waited, his pistol cocked.

*Come on, move, ya red bastard!* He thought, but knew the brave was taking his time and moving toward him.

Suddenly, almost right at his feet, the warrior sprung from the ground and almost instantly the mountain man felt the sharp bite of a blade against the side of his head. When the brave raised his hand once more, Coon pushed the pistol against the man's belly and pulled the trigger. The Indian stiffened, screamed, and then fell to the ground jerking and twisting. Wiping something wet from his eyes, Coon picked up a dropped tomahawk and buried the blade in the top of the warrior's head. All movement ceased.

Rising slowly and in pain, Coon moved for his fire. Once there, he added some kindling and waited for the flames to grow larger. His hands were covered in blood and his head was throbbing. He wiped his hands off on his pants and then felt his head. He could feel a long cut to the side of his head, but it seemed shallow, and the lobe on the ear was missing. Lowering his hands, he saw they were covered in fresh blood. He pulled his possibles bag near, removed a bottle of whiskey and a roll of cotton material.

Pulling his knife, he cut about a 12 inch piece of material from the roll and poured whiskey on it. Once it was saturated, he placed it against his injured head. A sharp burning pain was felt and his feet kicked wildly at the mud. He gave a loud gasp and then pushed the cloth tightly to his head. Tears ran down his cheeks, but he gritted his teeth against the anguish. A few minutes later, the pain was less and he suddenly felt weak.

He pulled the rag from his head, poured more alcohol on it, and applied it once again. It was painful, but not nearly as severe as the first time. He ripped more cloth from the roll and tied the crude bandage in place. He stood and made his way to each warrior, cutting their throats one by one.

Returning to the fire, he gulped down about a fifth of the bottle of alcohol and then leaned back against his saddle. *Sioux, and they must have spotted me before the rains started and waited for a break in the weather to attack. I'm one lucky man to still be alive.*

As the alcohol started working against his pain, he thought, I need to move tomorrow, even if the rivers are still high. If nothing else, I can move south and keep the watercourse in my view. Damn, my head hurts like a sumbitch. He took another long slug of whiskey. I ain't sure I killed all the warriors and iffen not, they'll go for help. I need to make tracks come first light. I should have waited until later, after 'Possum and the boys were ready to take the furs in to trade before I killed 'em all. But, they'd been talkin' about goin' to the rendezvous and then I'd been shit out of luck. No, I killed 'em at the right time. I'll rest an hour, then take some laudanum and load the horses.

Two hours later Coon was moving parallel to the river and keeping his eyes open for any spots of light in the distance. He knew from experience that a campfire could be seen for miles off and the last thing he wanted was company. He kept the whiskey near, and off and on he'd take a snort. While he knew drinking was a good way to end up dead, he had no choice if he wanted to move. The pain was just too much for him not to drink. He'd only taken the one sip of laudanum, because he'd seen women who used it everyday and they had to have it after a short spell. He figured any habit like that, he didn't need.

By mid-morning he was having a hard time staying in the saddle and as he moved toward a large oak tree, his world grew gray and then slowly faded into black.

He awoke under a sheet of canvas and could clearly see the gray material stretched tightly over his head.  He was wrapped up in someone's buffalo robe and he could smell a fire.  He raised his head, but was immediately attacked by pain, so he called out, "Whiskey?"

A couple of minutes passed before a young mountain man squatted beside him and said, "Here, drink this.  It's a mixture of laudanum and whiskey.  It'll help yer pain."

Raising a trembling hand, Coon threw the drink back and extended his cup again, "More, I hurt."

The young man chuckled, refilled the cup and said, "Hell, I guess ya do, old timer.  You've a cut to the skull on your noggin, one ear cut in half and gone, and a cut to the side of yer face.  What in the hell did ya tie into lately?"

"Sioux attacked me early this mornin' and I killed two of 'em."

"It might have been the Sioux, but it wasn't this mornin', be-cause ya been here for three days."

Taking a healthy gulp of the whiskey, Coon said, "Three days?  Are ya sure?"

Laughing the young man said, "Yep, Blake and I found ya layin' in the mud by a horse, and ya had six others loaded down with plew."

"Sioux killed my trappin' partners, and I made a run fer it.  I guess I got as far as pure grit would take me."

"Ya said the attack happened at night and we found ya near noon, so ya couldn't have come far."

"I think that's right, but I ain't thinkin' clearly.  Can I have some more whiskey?  I don't want no more laudanum, because it ain't good fer a man."

"Sure, here's the bottle.  My name is John Morris and my partner in James Blake, and we're both free trappers.  We're headed to Saint Louis to unload our plew."

"Thank ya kindly fer the panther piss.  We were headed to Fort Atkinson, but I ain't sure what to do now."

"Well, if we can get your plew sold, you'll have a bunch of cash money.  I think you'd get more fer 'em in Saint Louis than at the fort."

"I feel I need to send some of the money to families of the men killed, but I don't know much about none of 'em.  Hell, I spent years with 'em and we never talked much about home." Coon lowered his head.

John gently touched his back and said, "The money ain't important.  I've been ridin' with James for years and I don't even know where he's from.  I think those men would want ya to keep the money."

An old mountain man entered the lean-to and said, "I thought I heard ya talkin' over here." Extending his hand he said, "My name's Blake, James Blake."

As they shook, Coon said, "I'm Thomas, Coon Thomas.  I was with a bunch that got rubbed out by the Sioux."  He lied easily when it came to his name.

"By God, they can do the job, let me tell ya.  We almost lost ya a couple of days back when ya come down with a fever coma.  John treated ya with some willow bark and yer fever finally broke.  When we first found ya, well, I thought fer sure ya'd go under on us."

Pulling the cork on the whiskey bottle, Coon raised it to his lips and took a long drink.  His vision was blurry and thanks to the strong drink his headache was gone, but these two men just opened up a bunch of possibilities for him.

Shaking his head a few times he said, "Blurred vision. Listen, I appreciate what the two of ya have done for me, and I'll make it up to ya both one day."

"Trappers need to help each other, because it's a rough life we live." John said.

Looking the men over, Coon saw they were of average size, but James was the older and stronger of the two.  John seemed the smarter, but neither of the men were good looking or even close to handsome.  Both wore long brown hair and matching beards, with James' being streaked with a few strands of white. John had blue eyes and he was constantly smiling, as if he found the world humorous. James had serious cold gray eyes, and his personality seemed just the opposite of the younger man.

"How long do ya think before I can travel?  I ain't real comfortable bein' here, not after what the Sioux did to us." Coon asked.

"Mornin' at the earliest.  The rivers have finally gone down, but I think ya need another night of rest.  As fer ya feelin' uncomfortable, hell, I'd guess so." James said and then asked, "Do ya think ya can sip a little broth?"

"I ain't hungry, but if you'll bring me some I'll drink a cup or two."

"I'll get ya a cup and that's it.  Ya drink too much and you'll throw up.  Take it slow and easy like when ya drink it, too.  Ya ain't had no food at all since we found ya, and I ain't got no idea the last time ya ate anything." John said as he moved out of the shelter and stood.

Looking around the raised bottle, Coon replied, "I ate, from what I remember, four days back, iffen I've been here for three days."

As he sipped the broth a few minutes later, he watched the other two men repairing gear and cleaning their guns.  Picking up the laudanum, he took a swig and then asked, "Did y'all have a good trappin' season?"

"Pretty good.  I suspect we've a couple thousand dollars in plew, but we ain't got even close to what ya have.  I'd not be surprised iffen yer plew don't bring much more than five thousand in Saint Louis." John replied without looking up from the harness he was working on.

"Yep, yer boys had a good season from what I see." James added.

"I'm gonna get some more sleep, but I'll keep the whiskey near me today and tonight.  That way iffen I get some pain I won't have to bother either of ya."

"Whiskey we have, so I'll bring another bottle over to ya in a bit.  I'll just lay it beside the other bottle.  Coon, yer lucky to be alive, but iffen ya start to feel faint or dizzy when we ride tomorrow, let us know, because ya mighten need to stop fer a spell."

"No, I want ya to tie me to my horse in the mornin', because I'm worried about them Sioux.  I ain't never been as scared in my life as I was durin' that attack.  They was all over us and in just seconds, too.  No, we need to move and do the job as quickly as we can."

"Iffen that's what ya want, I'll do it.  Now, ya get some sleep, because tomorrow will be a long day for ya."

An hour before dawn this morning, Coon was tied to his horse and was moving down the trail.  His legs were tied under the horse and his left hand was tied to the saddle horn.  His right hand was free and held a new bottle of whiskey.  While he felt little pain, his vision continued to bother him.  He knew he wasn't sitting straight in the saddle but honestly didn't care.  To move away from the shining mountains was his only goal, be-cause if even one of the mountain men lived, they'd come for Coon, and he knew it.

Near noon they stopped for a quick meal and John asked, "Can ya ride without the ropes the rest of the day?"

Grinning from the alcohol, Coon replied, "I can do that, as long as I don't have to sit square in the saddle.  I figure iffen I stay drunk the pain will eventually leave, and then I'll deal with the hangover."

James said, "I know the feelin' well.  Here about two years ago I took a Comanche lance in my right thigh.  I guess I stayed drunk fer a month before the pain finally disappeared, but the hangover was nothing compared to the hurting I had."

"Have ya decided iffen you'll take yer plew to Saint Louis, or get rid of them at Fort Atkinson?"

"Well, I'm a Missouri boy born and bred, so I guess Saint Louie will be the place.  I think my beaver days are over."

"Waugh! Ya gonna be a flatlander after seein' the shinin' mountains?  Not me.  They'll bury me in my mountains." John said with disgust.

*It's more likely I'll kill ya near Saint Louis,* Coon thought but said, "I ain't sure yet.  Hell, those Sioux scared the shit outta me and I mean they did the job good, too.  I never heard of Injuns fightin' at night, but they damned sure did."

"Injuns will fight when the notion hits 'em," James said and then added, "if they think they can win the battle. Me and John here, why we've fought 'em at night before and not just the Sioux, either.  No, Injuns are born fighters, and some of the best men in the world to ever crawl on top of a horse."

Coon shook his head and replied, "I don't know, really, but they're deadly on foot.  I've never fought one on horseback, and don't think I want to try now."

John lighted his pipe, puffed a few minutes and then said, "Don't let that one attack turn ya yeller or make ya think ye ain't tough enough. By God, ya survived and that's all that counts. Out here ya need—"

"I ain't yeller!" Coon replied brusquely.

"Ya misunderstood what I meant, Coon, and I wasn't callin' ya yeller. I just meant an attack like that can scare any man, but don't let it scare ya so badly ya give up the mountains. That's all I mean by it and that's the truth. Pull in yer horns."

"That sounds a lot better. But, I am scared of what happened. Hell, I still cain't see right most of the time, but maybe by the time we get to Saint Louis I'll change my mind."

Handing him a plate of beans and deer meat, James said, "Eat this and let's ride. We have a long day ahead of us."

Days turned into weeks and weeks into months. After almost three months, the three men were camped in the Ozark Mountains of Missouri and Coon was back in his old childhood stomping grounds. The weather was cool overnight and blazing hot in the day, so summer wasn't far off. The camp, selected by John, was was surrounded by high bluffs and to the left the Little Piney River flowed. The men were much more relaxed now, knowing the biggest tribe around, Osage, were known to be friendly. They still had a guard at night, mainly because of what John said, "Even friendly Injuns will steal a man's horses."

As they sat around the fire over supper, Coon asked, "How many more days until we get to Saint Louis?"

"Nigh on four would be my guess, barrin' any bad weather. This is good twister weather, with the days hot and nights cold. Lawdy, we don't need one of 'em either. Hell, I saw a hay straw drove right through an oak fencepost once, just from the wind. Twisters here are serious business. But, yer from 'round here ain't ya, Coon?" James asked.

"Yep, my pa had an old rock farm 'bout eight miles south of here, but it wasn't worth a shit.  All we ever grew was snakes and rocks, with both of 'em bein' good size.  My pa was a hard man, so one mornin', when I was about fourteen, I left home and ain't never been back."  Coon replied, but thought, *and I killed the mean sumbitch with his own shotgun, and ma, too. All they ever did was beat my ass and make me slave in the fields like a damn black man.  Best thing I ever did was kill them two.*

John poured some coffee and asked, "Do ya want to stop a spell and see yer family?"

Coon faked a loud laugh and said, "No, I ain't got an urge to see either one of 'em again.  Pa beat my ass all the time with whatever he had in his hands.  Besides, I been gone fer over ten years and they'd both be in their 50's iffen they're still alive."

"Well, it ain't likely they yet live.  Most folks die before they ever get that old, but I did have a grandpap that lived to be in his seventies.  He was the meanest bastard God ever placed on this earth.  I've always wondered why some men and women are so damned mean and mad at the world." James said.

John grinned and replied, "I think many folks have big dreams of riches and fame, but when it doesn't happen, they turn angry.  They expect the world to bow to them and give them what they want.  Only, life ain't like that."

Coon said, "The world ain't gave me nothin', but a hard time."

"Well," John said as he stood and stretched, "time fer me to hit my robes.  We need to be on the trail an hour before day-light."

"Same shifts of guard as before?"  Coon asked.

"Yep, me, then you, and finally John.  Do you want to change or something?"

"Huh-uh, just wantin' to make sure."  Coon spoke and then stood.  With a slight grin on his face, he moved toward his robes.  *Tonight, on my shift, I'll make my move,* he thought as he pulled the buffalo robe up against the cool night air.  *And, tomorrow I'll be a couple of thousands dollars richer.*

Shortly before midnight Coon was up and sitting under a large cedar tree.  It was chilly, so he wore his old wool capote. He glanced at the sky overhead and saw millions of stars twinkling and shining brightly. A full moon was out, so the area was almost as well lighted as during the day. James had been in his robes for about two hours, when Coon stood and pulled his knife.

The two mountain men shared a shelter and Coon knew he had to be quiet when he killed the first man, or he'd wake the other. He moved to James, figuring he'd be in a deep sleep, and the easiest to put under. Squatting beside the young man, Coon placed his hand over the mountain man's mouth and quickly ran the sharp blade of his knife over his throat.

James quivered and jerked violently as his blood spurted into the air with each beat of his heart. John, being a light sleeper, opened his eyes, glanced at James and then Coon.

"Ya sumbitch!" John yelled and his horse pistol came up and spat fire.

Knocked on his ass by the impact of the bullet, Coon pulled his pistol, fired in the direction of John and heard a loud grunt. Then, pulling his second pistol, he stood and looked for the man. He wasn't seen. Circling the camp, Coon searched, but lost him in the dense brush. *Sumbitch, iffen he lives and goes to the law they'll string me up!* He thought as he started gathering gear. *Iffen I can get to Saint Louis and sell these plew, I can move east and they'll never find me. Money will buy me protection.*

Then, taking a burning log from the fire, he moved to the canvas shelter. The blood on the ground was bright red, so he knew John had a serious injury. *Mayhap the sumbitch will die on me and take care of that problem. I don't reckon he'll live long bleeding like that.*

An hour later, Coon Turner was moving toward the big city beside the wide Mississippi River, leading horses piled high with beaver plew.

# Chapter 3

Nate rode his horse at a walk down the old trail that led to Saint Louis, with 'Possum and Cotton Top bringing up the rear. Cotton and Nate had their plew from the season, figuring to unload them in the big city. They'd discovered at Fort Atkinson that Coon Turner had not stopped there to sell his furs, so the only other place to do the job was Saint Louis.

Cotton rode up beside him and asked, "Do ya think Coon will stay in the city or move east?"

Nate thought for a minute or two and then said, "Hard to say what he'll do, once he has money. Money will hide a man and do the job well, but I have friends there."

Cotton nodded, but didn't respond.

"I figure you and 'Possum can check the saloons and stables where white folks go, and I'll check the dives down on the riverfront. Some of my friends work in the stables or on the docks. Black folks will know more about Coon than whites will, or so I'm thinkin'."

"Why's that?"

"Well, it's pretty simple really. See, Coon looks pretty typical for most men, except he's big. Now, once in the city, I expect him to buy some good clothes, clean up nice, and then he'll be harder for white folks to remember, unless he's a ladies man. Soiled doves will remember him, so that's who I want ya and 'Possum to talk with the most. Now, bartenders might remember him, but it all depends on how he acts in a saloon. His size won't help him, but it won't hurt 'em much either in a place this big."

Cotton twisted his head to the side, spat a brown stream of tobacco juice, and then asked, "What do ya mean by how he acts in a saloon?"

"Iffen he's mean, a big tipper, flashes money, or loud, they'll remember him.  Don't forget that most saloons have free food for those who are drinkin' too.  I figure a big man like Coon, after months on the trail, will eat like a starved dog.  A thing like that might standout to a bartender, so he'll remember it."

"Well, them soiled doves will want money to talk and I ain't got none right now."

Nate laughed and said, "Ya will have once we get rid of our plew.  I suspect we'll get top dollar fer our furs in a big city like Saint Louis.  We'll split the money fifty-fifty, like we always do, but whatever ya have to spend talkin' with whores, I'll make up half of it to ya. We're in this together."

They rode in silence for a few miles, then Nate said, "I've been thinkin' of askin' 'Possum to go into cahoots with us once this is all over.  How does that make yer stick float?"

"Hell, I like 'em and I've known 'em fer years.  He's got bark, 'Possum does, so I vote yes.  I hope he don't think he'll recover any money off of Coon's body.  It's likely he'll drink and party that money away."

Nate stopped his horse, gazed into Cotton's eyes and said, "It ain't about money, but we'll look fer that too.  It's about rightin' a wrong and seein' justice served.  Whatever money Coon has on 'em we'll take off his cold and dead body, then give it to 'Possum.  A renegade trapper is about the lowest form of life on this earth, next to a woman killer.  I don't think he'll have the time to spend over five thousand dollars before we corner his ass.  Now, if possible, we'll take 'em back to Butterfield's fer a hangin', but I won't go out of my way to take him alive."

"I hear ya, but what if he puts some of the money in a bank, hell, we'll never get to it."

Nate laughed and said, "The Crow and Shoshone were nice enough, in my younger days, to demonstrate the fine art of torture and, as ya know, I'm very capable of causin' pain to trash like Coon.  I could cut on the big boy all day and then not miss a minute of sleep later.  I'm sure with a few twists and turns of my sharp Green River knife, Coon will be more than willin' to sign a big bank draft for any one of us—but the draft may be written in blood instead of ink."

Cotton felt a shudder go through his body at the thought of Nate with his big knife.  He considered the situation for a minute and then said, "Should we go to the law for—"

Nate instantly raised his left hand and said, "Hush. We've a man down about a hundred feet from us on the right side. See 'em?"

"Uh-huh. How do ya want to do this?"

Motioning 'Possum forward, Nate gave the situation some thought. Once 'Possum was beside them, he said, "I'll move to 'em on foot, while the two of ya cover me. Cotton, ya cover the left side and 'Possum, ya cover the right. I'll keep an eye on the man as I approach him. If he makes any sudden moves, I'll kill his ass. Any questions?"

"Nope," replied 'Possum, "but we should all dismount, so we're less of a target."

"Yep, we should." Nate agreed.

Once on the ground, the big man said, "Okay, I'm movin', so keep yer eyes peeled in the event things turn to shit. Cotton, tie all our horses to a limb in case this turns to shootin'. While we're close to the city, I don't want to spend four days walkin' there."

Nate moved forward cautiously, scanning the countryside as he approached the man. He saw blood on the man's back, but no movement. *His hands are clean of weapons and away from his body, so he's not a threat right now*, Nate thought. *Dressed in skins, so he's a mountain man.*

Once beside the injured man, Nate used his right foot to turn the man over, as he held a cocked pistol in his hand. *Sumbitch, it's John Morris*, the big man thought and then squatted. *He's breathin' and took a slug high to his shoulder. He's lost a lot of blood though, so he might go under.*

Standing, Nate called out, "It's John Morris, so bring the horses up. He's taken a bullet, so we have some doctorin' to do. Move off to the left, near the oaks and make camp."

Nate, with Cotton's help, soon had John on a buffalo robe and treating his injury. He used the probe and long tweezers he'd purchased from Butterfield to remove a ball from the injury and cauterized the wound. John had not regain consciousness during the whole process and that worried Nate. *Well*, he thought, *if this alcohol gets no response out of him, he's in pretty sad shape.*

When the rough traders whiskey hit the wound, John gave a low moan and his body twitched, but he soon lay still again.

Pouring more whiskey into the man's mouth, Nate wondered what had happened this close to Saint Louis. It was likely some scum from the city robbed John, but he'd have to wait and see if the man survived before he'd know for sure. *This is why we keep a guard all the time*, he thought as he poured a cup of whiskey and then wiped the blood from his hands on an old rag.

Cotton, who'd circled the area looking for others or a camp walked to the small fire and sat in the dirt. He met Nate's eyes and said, "I just found Blake over in a camp with his throat cut. From the sign, I made out three men made camp and one turned killer. All the horses and plew are gone."

Nate gave the words some serious thought. Finally he said, "We may have another trapper that's turned killer or it might just be we've found fresh sign of Coon. Ain't no way to tell unless John comes around in a day of two. Right now, I want ya to go make some meat. I'm sure this place is alive with deer or turkey."

"What about Blake's body?"

"I'll take care of him and do the job directly. I figure by the time I dig a grave and bury him, ya should be back with some meat. I'll keep 'Possum on guard." Nate stood and wiped his dusty hands on his trousers. "Now where is the camp from here?"

"Maybe two hundred feet, north of the trail."

Just after a supper of deer steaks and beans, John opened his eyes and whispered, "Wa . . . water?"

Nate move to the man's side, gave him a little water laced with whiskey and asked, "How ya feelin', John?"

"L . . . like hell warmed over."

Pulling a half-pint bottle from his possibles bag, Nate pulled the cork and said, "I'm gonna feed ya a little laudanum for yer pain. Once the drug kicks in, we need to talk a spell."

John nodded and opened his mouth for the drug.

Nate gave the man about a teaspoon of the medicine and then waited.  As he sat, he poured himself a cup of whiskey and scanned the area.  Seeing nothing, he took a sip.  Glancing at the other two men, he saw Cotton licking his lips, so he said, "Cotton, come and get this jug and pour ya both a cup of panther piss.  Now, one is our limit, even iffen we are close to the city.  Ya can let yer hair down after we get Coon."

As Cotton stood, John suddenly said, "Coon?"

"Yep, we're on his trail because he turned renegade and killed some trappers.  How well do ya know the man?"

"Well enough to know he killed James and stole our furs.  He's the bastard that shot me."

"Tell me all about what happened, John, I have an interest."

When the man finished, Nate fed him a bit more whiskey and said, "Ya get some more sleep; we'll talk about Coon again in the mornin'."

Once the wounded man was sleeping, Nate made his way to the fire and said, "It'll be weeks before he's able to ride and it puts us in a bad position.  Iffen we wait too long, Coon will fly the coop, but I ain't sure how to handle this."

'Possum said, "Let me stay here, while y'all go into the big city.  Hell, Nate, I ain't lost nothin' in Saint Louie I need to go get.  While I'd like to have a hand in killin' or capturin' Coon, one of us needs to stay here with John."

Nate grinned and said, "Ya sure?  After all, ya have first call on the man."

"Justice is what I want, and it matters little to me who gives it.  Iffen ya take 'em alive I'll see 'em swing at the tradin' post."

"Okay, that's how we'll do it then.  I'll leave the medical supplies with ya and the meat, so you'll do fine until we get back.  I'm sure in about three days John will be up and about, but he'll still be weak.  Do ya need anything from the city?"

"Just some chewin' tobacco and three bottles of good whiskey.  There may be a problem though, because I ain't got no money."

"Sure ya have money, once Cotton and I sell our furs.  We'll spot ya some so ya can trap with us next fall, iffen ya want."

"By God, that's a good idea, 'cause I been wonderin' what I was goin' to do.  It was rough on me to lose all my trappin' buddies like that."

"Okay, now listen to me closely. We'll be gone for at least two weeks. I figure the ride there and back will take us eight days, then five or six to find the man. I can't promise we'll find 'em, but iffen he's still in the city we'll get wind of it. Now, iffen he's move east, we'll come back for the two of you. By two weeks John will be able to ride short distances."

'Possum nodded, but Cotton asked, "When do we leave?"

"Two hours before first light in the mornin'. We'll travel hard and fast, because I ain't sure how long Coon will stay in town. Iffen he suspects we're on his ass, he'll go to ground and we mighten never find 'em."

"Yep, it's a big place." Cotton said.

"Not just that, but from the city he can go any direction you can imagine. He can hop a boat and go up the Missouri River, or down to New Orleans. From New Orleans he's just a hop, skip, and jump from the east coast of America. Hell, iffen he gets to New York or Boston, we might as well just go home."

"Well, I draw the line at Saint Louis or within a hundred miles of the place. Iffen he hops a boat, I'm callin' the hunt off." Cotton said, and Nate knew the man was serious.

Morning was cold, or so Cotton complained as they moved along a well traveled trail leading to the city. It was mid-morning when they met a group of trappers heading west after unloading their plew. Both men kept their guns pointed in the general direction of the men until they drew near and were recognized.

"Ty Fisher, is that yer ugly ass over there mounted on that homely horse?" Nate joked.

"Well, iffen this ain't a damned fine howdy, it's Nate Grisham. How in the world have ya been?"

"Doin' fine. Who's the other yahoo's with ya?"

"Jarel Wade, Deacon, and Bear, hell ya know 'em all."

"Deacon, ya look like you've fill out a bit, son. I guess mountain life is agreein' with ya."

"It has agreed with me, and the good God has blessed me with much more than I deserve."

Nate smiled and replied, "As he has all of us, Deacon. Listen fellers, I hate to turn serious, but we're on a tramp and have blacken our faces against one of our own. We're lookin' fer Coon Turner. Ya mighten not know the man, since this was only his second year in the mountains, but he's turned renegade and killed some folks."

"Hell, I know 'em and just passed him about four hours back, and he was headin' east." Jarel Wade said.

"That boy had a line of pack animals and every single one was loaded down with plew. When Ty asked him about it, he said his partners was killed by Blackfoot." Deacon added.

"They was killed alright, only he did the killin'." Cotton said.

"Well, we didn't question the man, because we all know death well in the mountains. Accordin' to Coon, the Blackfoot did the killin' and he just barely got out alive." Ty said and then grew quiet in thought.

Jarel said, "I didn't think the story was right at the time, but hell, Coon is one of us. I was wondering how the man got away with all the plew, iffen everyone had been butchered like he claimed. I've yet to see the Blackfoot let a man take his furs and just leave. They usually hound a jasper until they kill 'em or he reaches safety. And, most of the time, all he manages to save is his own ass."

"Nate, do ya want some help? Iffen so, me and Jarel can lend a hand." Ty said and glanced at Jarel.

"What I need most is for a couple of ya to meet with 'Possum, he's down our back trail a ways and give 'em a hand. John Morris was shot in the shoulder right after Coon killed James Blake."

"How about Bear and Deacon go to 'Possum while me and Ty help ya look fer Coon? He ain't gonna be easy to find in the city, once he cashes in those furs. I'm tellin' ya right now, he's got well over five thousand dollars in plew. With money like that, hell, in Saint Louis you'll never find 'em, unless he wants found." Jarel said, and he looped a leg over his saddle horn.

"Okay, that's what we'll do then," Nate replied and then added, "Let's ride. I want to get to the city before we lose his ass. He owes us for the lives of our friends."

Nate and his small group moved east and just after dark they pulled into some trees for the night.  Camp was quickly established and supper of beans and fatback was placed on the fire.  Later, as they ate the simple meal, Nate asked, "Do any of ya know Coon well?"

"I met 'em his first year out and it was at the roonyvoo in '24.  He was pretty roostered the night I met 'em and pissed.  It seems he lost a heap of money on a horse race earlier in the day." Ty said.

Jarel smiled and said, "I met 'em the first time at Butterfield's, but he seemed like a typical trapper to me.  He had a good sense of humor, was quiet, and looked like a deep thinker.  I never would have thought he'd turn against us."

"Well, he damned sure did." Cotton said, and then added small log to the flames.

Nate asked, "Do either of ya know where he's from?  I didn't know 'em that good."

"The night he was drinkin' he said he'd grown up in Boston and that his daddy was a rich businessman, but it mighten have been just the whiskey talkin'."

"It doesn't matter.  I'll try to find his ass in Saint Louis and iffen we miss 'em, I'll head back to the mountains.  We'd never find 'em in some big city like Boston or New York City.  I'll tell ya one damned thing, before I leave, iffen we don't get 'em, I'll report the killin' to the law." Nate said.

Ty chuckled and said, "Nate, the United States doesn't have jurisdiction over the west, not yet anyway, so reporting it will be a waste of yer time."

"I don't understand what ya mean."

"It means the west ain't part of the states and American law doesn't apply out there.  To kill or rob in the west is not against the law, since there are no laws established to govern the land.  If we want justice served, then we'll have to see the job done."

"Sumbitch," Nate exploded, "ya mean to sit there and tell me it's legal to kill other men in the mountains?  I was hopin' to have the law put a poster out on the bastard iffen we missed 'em."

Jarel nodded and said, "We've had the problem before.  Once he reaches the city, he's a free man, because ain't no law dog gonna touch 'em."

# CHAPTER 4

Coon sat on a rise and looked down on the city beside the big muddy river, and smiled. All he wanted to do now was get rid of the furs, find a nice hotel, and have a few drinks. He kicked his horse gently in the ribs and wondered how much his furs were worth. He also gave thought to where he'd be safest and finally decided to stay in a nice, but not expensive hotel. The last thing he wanted was to sleep on the riverfront and worry about being killed or robbed. *I need some new clothes too*, he thought, *or I'll stand out dressed in skins.*

As he entered the city, no one seemed to notice him, but folks were used to mountain men coming and going, so Coon's arrival was unnoticed by most. Stopping in front of a saloon, he asked a man sitting on the steps, "Where can a man take beaver pelts?"

The man stood and said, "Down on your left you'll see a place that'll buy 'em, and keep an eye on 'em when they grade the furs, because I've heard they'll cheat a man."

"Thank ya for the information." Coon said and kicked his horse into a slow walk. A few minutes later, he spotted the place and tying his horse to the hitching post, he entered.

"Ya got furs?" A portly man asked from behind a counter.

"Yep, I do and a shitload. Get some of yer men to unload 'em and bring 'em in."

"Ya got that many?" The fat man moved from behind the counter.

"Take a look out yer window."

The man moved to the window, glanced out and yelled, "Jones and Franklin, get yer asses out here and unload this man's furs! Let's hop to it boys, he's got a bunch too! My name is O'Brien, James O'Brien."

"Now, Mister James O'Brien," Coon said, "I heard ya don't always grade furs fairly, so I'll stay by yer side as ya grade mine."

The man sputtered a bit and replied, "I don't know who told ya that, but by God, they're a damned liar.  I treat every man I trade with fairly."

"Mayhap ya do and mayhap ya don't, so I'll stay with ya.  More than one good man died to get those furs, so I'll see top dollar for my effort to bring 'em in."

"Injuns?"

"Yep, Blackfoot and mean sumbitches, too."

"I've heard that before." Seeing his men bringing in the first bundles of furs he said, "Place 'em on the floor, boys, and get the rest."

Two hours later, the grading done, O'Brien said, "You have a lot of prime plew and I can't pay you what they're really worth."

"How much less are we talkin' about here?"

O'Brien did some figuring on a piece of brown paper and then said, "Your furs are worth a little more than $6,000.00, but I can't pay that and no place in town will either.  I can give you $5,000.00 in cash and a thousand in trade.  That's my top offer, too."

*Well, they were easy enough to get, so I ain't losin' any money,* Coon thought and then said, "I'll take it, but I want the trade in guns, Hawken's, every last penny."

*Hell, Hawkens I have and get 'em wholesale from the brothers, so I can come out on top with this trade,* thought O'Brien.  "Deal, but what in the hell are ya going to do with that many guns?"

"Why, I'll trade 'em to the Injuns." Coon said and then broke out laughing.

Shaking his head, O'Brien said, "Yeah, right.  Let me get a bank draft and your guns will be ready in the morning, any time after first light."

An hour later, Coon was in a nice but not classy hotel room sipping on rye whiskey.  He sat by an open window that overlooked a busy side street and from what he could see, everyone was in a big hurry.  He fought down a bit of panic when two lawmen walked by, but knew he'd committed no crimes in the states.  He threw back his drink and poured another one, not noticing how his hands trembled with fear.

*I need to get those guns in the mornin' and then get the hell out of town. If any of those men I shot survived, I'll have mountain men on my ass and they'll be hard men to lose, city or not. There are two, I never saw their bodies and that's two too many. I suspect 'Possum went under, but John, I have no idea what happened to him. If the word gets out I killed in Missouri, I'll have the law on my ass, too. Maybe takin' those guns to the Injuns ain't such a bad idea after all,* he thought, and then downed his drink.

He poured another and thought, *I can move out west a bit, find some saloon scum and ride into the mountains to do my trade. I'll bet I can get furs and never have to work at the job. Hell, furs don't mean much to an Injun, but a good rifle does. With Hawkens costin' forty dollar a piece, I should have at least twenty-five in the morning. Then, I can swing by the Hawken company and pick up another thousand dollars worth. Iffen I work it right, I can make a pretty penny off this deal.*

*Right now, I need to find some decent grub and new clothes.* He left his glass of whiskey on the table and walked from the room.

At the desk the clerk gave him directions to a general store, and Coon made his way for the clothing first. As he walked, he saw no one he knew and he was sure anyone behind him wouldn't arrive until the next day at the earliest. He'd traveled long and hard after taking the furs from John and James.

A bell above the door to the general store tinkled as he entered. A thin man wearing wire-rimmed glasses looked up from a ledger he was writing in and asked, "May I help you?"

"Do ya have any ready-made clothes? I need to get out of my buckskins."

"I sure do and if you'll follow me, I get you taken care of and quickly, too."

Less than thirty minutes later, Coon exited the store wearing his new clothes and carrying his buckskins. He'd bought new canvas pants, a navy blue shirt, boots, and a gray felt hat. Also wrapped with his old skins he had a new neckerchief, a brown vest, and two pairs of long john underwear. He still carried his pistols, but he'd left his rifle in the room, because few men in town were armed with long guns.

He spotted a restaurant across the street and made his way to the place. Once inside, he sat at a table and placed his order with a beautiful young woman in her early twenties.  He'd ordered the special of the day, roast beef with vegetables, biscuits, and coffee.  At first he'd almost left, because he thought the price of fifty cents for a meal to be a bit steep, but realized he had money.

Quickly finishing his meal, he stood, placed a dollar on the table and left.  Outside he realized he was content, now that his belly was full and growing sleepy.  He glanced at the sun, saw it was yet a couple of hours from dusk, but decided to grab a short nap.

Back in his room he finished the whiskey in the glass he'd left on the table and stretched out on the bed.  In a matter of seconds, he was asleep.

Coon awoke late and wondered if any of the eatin' places would still be open.  At the desk, he asked a stout clerk with little hair where he could find a place to eat.

"Sir, there aren't many places open this time of night, if any, so I suspect your best bet would be to try a saloon that has free finger food.  The Blue Bull has ham, pickled eggs, fish and such, and the drink prices are very reasonable."

"Where do I find this place?  I'm new to the city and have no idea where things are located."

"Go out our door, take a right, down two blocks and turn left.  About halfway down the block you'll see the saloon.  I don't drink often, but that's where I drink, and a beer will cost ya nickel."

Coon gave a quick "thanks" and made his way out the door and down the street.  He found the saloon easily enough and it had a fair crowd when he entered.  Making his way to the bar, he said, "Double shot of bourbon and beer chaser."

The bartender was a tall thin man with long black hair and cold gray eyes, but his smile seemed genuine as he said, "Fifteen cents.  And, help yerself to the food."

Coon looked at the end of the bar, near the wall, and saw all kinds of finger food, from smoked ham to beef jerky.  *This is a smart man.  All of those foods are salty, so his customers will want more beers after they eat.*

He moved to the food, picked up a small plate and loaded it down with ham, boiled eggs, biscuits, and smoked fish.  *They can keep the damned jerky, I've had more than my share of the nasty shit in the mountains,* he thought as he made his way back to his drinks.

Coon was about half finished with his plate when a man in the back of the room stood and called out, "Floyd Kramer, yer a no account back shootin' sumbitch!"

Since the confrontation didn't involve him, Coon continued eating, and just as he took a sip of his beer, a rough hand jerked him around. His beer, being held near his lips, spilled and soaked the front of his new shirt.

"I knowed it was ya, Floyd, ya filthy bastard!" A man of average size, long brown hair and scraggly beard yelled.

Angry, but wanting to avoid trouble, Coon said, "My name is Coon Turner and I'm not Floyd. You've mistaken me for someone else." *I don't need the law near me, not on this day.*

"Damn Coward! Ain't a one of ya Kramer's with any sand in yer gizzards."

"Look, I don't want any trouble with you. I'm just a mountain man from out west in town to unload my furs. I'm tired, hungry, and just want to eat and have a beer or two." Coon turned his back on the man. Meeting the bartenders eyes, the thin man shrugged, so he kept an eye on his back using the big mirror behind the bar.

"I'm givin' ya to the count of three and then I'm goin' to shoot ya down like the no good damned  dog ya are! One, two, —"

In the mirror, Coon saw the man moving for his pistol, so he turned, pulled his gun, snapped the hammer back, and pulled the trigger, all in one smooth act. The big 54 caliber ball struck the man in the belly, knocking him on his butt in the middle of the floor. Down, but not yet out of the fight, he fired and his slug knocked a big chuck from the bar beside Coon.

Pulling his second pistol, Coon pulled the hammer back and watched as the man raised his second pistol slowly. As the gun came up, Coon yelled, "Drop it, or I'll kill ya!"

When Coon heard the hammer lock on the man's pistol, he fired and there came a loud scream. The man fell make to the floor and began to jerk and twist as he squalled. The bartender moved to the injured man, kicked both pistols out of reach, and then squatted. Glancing at Coon he said, "The second shot hit his lungs, so he's not long for this world."

Standing, the bartender glanced at a man sitting near the wall and said, "Frank, go fetch a doc, but there ain't no real hurry. While yer out, bring an undertaker back with ya too, because the doc won't be able to do much."

When the bartender moved back behind the bar, Coon said, "Give me another double bourbon, while you're back there."

Pouring the drink, the bartender asked, "Don't ya think I should bandage the man before he bleeds to death?"

"No, I really don't think so. Bleedin' to death will be a much quicker outcome of what usually happens with a gut and lung shot man. Hell, iffen the doc gets his hands on the man it might take 'em days to die and he'll be in some serious pain, too. Do ya know 'em?"

"No, I ain't never seen the man before."

"I don't know who Floyd Kramer is, but it looks like the man has some serious enemies." Coon threw his drink back.

"Ya must look like the man, 'cause he was damn sure ya were that Kramer jasper. Here," the bartender said, "this drink is on the house." He poured another double.

Right at that point a lawman walked in, glanced at the dying man and asked, "Who did the shootin'?"

"Me," Coon replied and made sure his hands were both on the bar.

"The man on the floor wouldn't leave this feller alone and started the whole mess, Bill. Actually, he even drew first, after he pulled this man around and spilled his drink. He thought this man was somebody named Floyd Kramer."

Bill looked at Coon, pulled out a stub of a pencil and small pad and asked, "What's your name?"

"Thomas Turner and I'm in from the mountains to get shed of my skins. I came in here to eat, since the restaurants are all closed, and to have a few drinks. I've never seen the man on the floor in my life."

"Bill," the bartender said, "the injured man just would not let it go. He gave Turner to the count of three and then pulled his pistol."

After giving the lawdog his local lodging information and a bogus mailing address to Butterfield's trading post, Coon relaxed. He knew there were no wanted posters on him and he was clean, except for what he'd done recently and it was un-likely that had been reported.

The sheriff said, "I'm gonna take a few statements from others in the room, but I don't see where you had much of a choice, except to defend yourself, so you're free to go. However, if I have any questions, I'll look you up at the hotel in a few days. How long do you intend to stay in the city?"

"I'll be here for at least ten more days, because I'm to meet some friends before we head out west to trap another season." Coon lied easily.

"Ya mighten want to look up that Floyd Kramer and see who in the hell he is, Bill. He seemed to think this Mister Turner was him."

"I'll do that. That's all I ne—"

The batwing doors to the saloon suddenly swung open and in walked an old doctor, his black medical bag in his left hand. As he passed Coon, the mountain man noticed he reeked of stale whiskey.

Squatting and pulling the moaning man's hands away from his injuries, Doc said, "Hell, I cain't help this jasper. With his gut and lungs shot up he'll die on me eventually." Opening his black bag, he removed a pint of laudanum, poured a little in the wounded man's mouth and continued, "Does this man have any money? I'll need to keep 'em at my place until he expires, only, hell, that might be in a week."

Bill, the sheriff, squatted beside the injured man and went through his pockets. He found a pocketknife, a key to the Western Hotel, fifty dollars in cash, a twist of chewing tobacco, and a wanted poster. "How much will it cost to keep an eye on this feller until he dies?"

"Two dollars a day and then the cost of any drugs I have to give him."

Peeling off a twenty, Bill handed it to Doc and said, "Keep a record of what the cost is, so I can forward what money re-mains to his kin."

Coon knew there'd be little money, if any, remaining from what the doctor now held in his hand.

"Sure, Bill, ya know me, so I'll list the expenses by the day. I'd suggest ya keep the rest of of the money to plant the man nice."

Bill unfolded the wanted poster, read for a few minutes, glanced at Coon and then back at the poster and said, "Son, yer a dead ringer for this Floyd Kramer on the wanted poster. I need you to pull your shirt off."

"Huh? Pull my shirt off? Why?"

"This Kramer has two long knife wounds on his back. According to this paper, the scars are about a foot long each. He also has a scar from a bullet about eight inches up from his left nipple."

Coon laughed and said, "Not a problem for me, because I have no bullet scars or knife wounds like that on my body." He quickly undressed and stood which his shirt off for a few minutes as the copper looked him over closely.

"I'm sorry I had to do that, Mister Turner, but it's my job. Listen, I'm going to write on the back of this wanted poster that I checked you out in Saint Louis and you're not Kramer. I'll sign and print my name, badge number and mailing address. If you run into any problems, it ain't likely to help you much, but it might help at some point. If you can keep men off your ass long enough to show the paper."

"How much is this Kramer worth?" The bartender asked.

"Five thousand dollars and it's for murder and robbery in Boston."

"D . . . damn me," Coon stammered, "I need to take good care of that paper when you give it to me. Hell, somebody will shoot my ass in the back for that kind of money."

"If you're heading back out west, Mister Turner, I'd not worry about it, because the law stops at the western boundary of Missouri. Hell, even if you were Kramer, you'd be safe out west." Bill handed the wanted poster to Coon.

"I guess so, but I don't like this at all." Coon said and then turning to the bartender he said, "Pour me another double." He began to dress again. Once dressed, he placed the wanted poster in his coat pocket.

Doc stood from where he'd bandaged the man, looked around and asked, "Do any of ya men want to earn two bits? Help me get this feller back to my office and you'll have some beer money."

As the men moved out the door carrying the dying man, Bill was now sitting at a table going through the papers and letters the man had on him.  Finally, he said, "The shot man is named Homer Poor and he's a bounty hunter out of New York City."

"Hell, no wonder he wanted ya, Turner," the bartender said, "ya were money in the bank for the man.  I ain't got no use for a man hunter, none a-tall.  It's different for the police, but not a bounty hunter.  Hell, they're just like a gun slick in my mind and hire their guns to look for the man with the most reward money."

Bill said, "He has a ledger here that I'm lookin' over.  Looks like he was expecting a payment for two thousand dollars from the Federal Government and it's being sent by wire to the telegraph office.  He was in room 14 at the Western Hotel, his horses are at Baileys Livery Stables, and his full mailing address is written on here, too." Turning the pages of the ledger the lawdog laughed a few minutes later and said, "Seems Mister Poor was a big spender and kept a list of women he'd met during his travels.  The man has stars beside each name, too."

"When's that money to be at the telegraph office?" The bartender asked.

Glancing at the ledger again, then flipping a few pages, Bill said, "It should have arrived here this morning, but I don't think he picked it up yet.  See, Poor kept very accurate records and he has a date and time for each of the previous money transfers he picked up.  This last entry is blank."

Coon suddenly getting an idea, asked, "Am I free to leave now?"

"Sure, Mister Turner, I've got all I need from you.  If you change hotels or leave suddenly, just let me know."

"Sure, not a problem." Then turning to the bartender he said, "Give me a good bottle of your rye whiskey.  I think I'll have a few drinks later in my room."

Pulling a bottle out from under the bar, the man said, "Two dollars.  Listen, I'm sorry this happened in my place, so if ya come back tomorrow, the first couple of drinks are on me, okay?"

Coon gave a false chuckle and said, "Sure, I'll be back." *I'm gonna hit the telegraph office and pick up some money.  Then I'll load my gear, get another hotel room, and pickup my new guns in the morning.  After that, I'm goin' to catch me a steamboat goin' up the Missouri.*

# CHAPTER 5

Nate and his small group stopped on the same rise Coon had and viewed the busy city streets of Saint Louis. It looked like an anthill to Ty, and he said as much.

"We're here lookin' fer a killer, not a place to live," Jarel said and then laughed loudly. "Come on, we're wastin' daylight."

As they entered the big city, Cotton asked, "Where to first? Hell, the size of this place confuses me."

Nate said, "The first place to unload furs is our best bet. I'm willin' to bet ya he's been there, too."

"Likely," Ty said, "because he wanted to unload and be gone quick like. But, the quality of the plew and the weight will make him a well remembered man."

Nate said, "Off the near side I see a place."

As the men rode up to the hitching post a fat man with a red face exited the building and said, "My name is O'Brien, James O'Brien, and how may I help ya fine gentlemen?"

"First, who are ya? Do ya work here?" Nate asked, because he had furs to get shed of, too.

O'Brien laughed and replied, "My man, I own this business. Do ya have beaver plew?"

"I got a few, but first, we're lookin' fer a man and he would have had a shitpot full of furs and all were prime or close to 'er. He'd have been here within the last day or so. Big man, reddish hair and beard, packin' a Hawken rifle and wearin' skins."

O'Brien cleared his throat and then asked, "And, why are ya lookin' for him?"

"He's a killer and a thief. All those furs were stolen, after he killed the men who took 'em."

"Well," said O'Brien, "the man was here and I bought his pelts, but I had no idea they were stolen. He informed me his partners had been butchered by the Blackfoot.  He has a con-siderable amount of change on 'em now, and I've no idea where he's gone."

The group was silent for a few minutes and then Ty asked, "When was the last time you saw the man?"

"Nigh on an hour ago.  He come by with a wagon to pick up his rifles, had the thing loaded down with trade goods, and said he was going to have a few drinks.  I'd imagine, from the way he talked, he's still in the saloon."

Ty scratched his beard and than asked, "Rifles?  How many did he have?"

"He placed an order for 25 Hawken earlier and then this mornin' cleaned me out of another 25.  I ain't got no idea what he plans to do with 50 Hawken rifles, and don't care, since he paid in cash."

"Hell," Nate said, "That's close to two thousand dollars, since those big guns are going fer forty dollars a pop."

O'Brien grinned and said, "It's exactly that amount, to the penny.  Now, which of ya has furs?"

"Where's the closest saloon?"  Ty asked.

"Down the street a bit, why?  Don't ya want to unload your furs?"

"We've a cat to skin first, but Mister O'Brien, I promise ya I'll be back in a bit to sell ya my plew, iffen yer payin' top dollar." Nate said.

"That I am, son, and I can pay in cash if ya have less than two thousand dollars worth," O'Brien said and then followed it with a small chuckle.

"Let's go fellers, mayhap we'll get lucky."  Jarel said as he pulled his horse around.

The saloon had two dockworkers sitting in chairs just out-side the door and as the small group entered, they nodded at the rough looking men.  Inside, there was no sign of Coon, so Nate walked to the bar and said, "Give me a bottle of good rye and five glasses."

The bartender gave a sneer and said, "We don't serve yer kind in here, boy.  Ya need to do yer drinking down on the docks, with the rest of the Nig—"

Nate's pistol came up and was cocked in one fluid motion and with the barrel in the bartenders face he said, "Finish the word and I'll kill ya.  See, I don't like the name much, never have, and if ya say it, I'll turn real mean on yer ass.  Ya know how much us colored men enjoy spillin' a white man's blood, now don't ya?"

"Mister, I ain't the owner and I don't make the rules.  The boss says, all Nig— black folks are to be turned away.  But, iffen ya get that gun outta my face, I'll get ya that bottle and some glasses."

"I'll lower my gun, but I'm warnin' ya, iffen yer hand comes up with anything other than a bottle or glasses, I'll pull the trigger."

"H . . . honest, Mister, I ain't gonna try nothin'."

The bartender pulled out a bottle of rye and five glasses, and giving a loud gulp, he said, "Two dollars fer the bottle."

Ty tossed the man two dollars in coin and said, "Now, I need answers to some questions.  We can do this the easy way," he pulled his skinning knife and sunk the blade tip deep into the bar, "or the hard way.  It don't matter to me which way we do this."

"W . . . what kind of . . . questions?"

Nate poured the drinks and took a sip of his before he asked, "Ya had a big white man in here, reddish hair and beard, within the last two hours?" All but Cotton picked up a glass.

"Yep, I did." *I cain't lie to these men, they're killers.*

"Did he say anything about where he was headed or anything unusual?"

Slowly pulling another glass from under the bar, the man poured himself a triple rye, knocked it back and said, "He gave me twenty dollars to not say anything, but he hired six fellers to ride with 'em.  He said he was heading out west to make his fortune.  Now, I know he had money, because he paid them jaspers their first months pay, at two dollars a day, up front.  He said iffen I told anyone, he'd come back and kill me."

Nate moved to the bar, picked up his drink, and then knocked it back.  He extended his hand and said, "Give me the twenty dollars he gave ya.  Ya didn't keep yer word and I'll make sure the man gets his money back."

"Do ya take me fer a fool?"  The bartender asked.

Nate laughed and said, "No, sir, and I'm not out to steal the money.  Unlike ya, I'm a man of my word, so ya can bet yer ass

I'll hand the money to him or bury it with 'em. It doesn't matter much to me either way, but he'll get 'er back."

The bartender pulled a double eagle from his pants pocket and tossed it to Nate. *I think he'd kill me fer a hell of a lot less than twenty dollars, the man thought.*

Catching the money, Nate said, "Thank ya kindly and I'll let him know ya returned it, iffen I can. Now, how was them jaspers gonna leave Saint Louis?"

"By boat was all I heard. They was goin' up the Missouri and that's all he said, I swear it."

"Now," Nate said, "I'm gonna join my buddies at a table in a few minutes. Do ya have any problems with that?"

"No, no, not at all. Y'all enjoy yer whiskey."

Fifteen minutes later they realized they'd never catch Coon as things were. They decided to head back to the mountains and wait for the man. They all understood he'd purchased guns for Injuns, but which tribe? They knew if they visited a few tribes in a few months, it'd all come together.

Standing as a group, Ty picked up the bottle and headed for the door. Nate grinned at the bartender and said, "Yer a damned lucky man and I hope ya know that. Hell, I ain't turned mean in over a week and I need to blow off some steam."

Just outside the door, Ty tossed the bottle to one of the men loafing in a chair and said, "Here ya go, a little panther piss to brighten up yer day."

As they mounted, the two men pulled the cork and began to take long swigs from the bottle of rye. The one on the right waved as the small group moved back toward O'Brien's Fur Company.

Four days later, the small group rode to 'Possum and explained the whole thing to the man. He was upset, but as he said, "By God, iffen I see the man I'll kill 'em on sight. Killin' partners ain't something I have much use fer and I'm still goin' after the man. Are ya in or out, Nate?"

Nate laughed and said, "'Possum, we started after the jasper and I ain't quit nothin' yet I've started. We'll see 'er through with ya. Won't we, Cotton Top?"

Cotton sent a long stream of brown tobacco juice to the fire, wiped his mouth off with the back of his hand and replied, "Yep, I ride where Nate rides. Onliest problem I see is, where do we start?"

Ty shook his head and said, "Good luck fellers, 'cause me and the rest are movin' up by Baldy Mountain fer the comin' winter. But, understand right now, iffen ya need us to ride with ya, we'll do the job."

"No, Ty, hell, there are four of us and only seven of them. We'll make out with what we got easily enough. Ain't a one of 'em, except Coon, a mountain man, so they'll be useless to the man in the woods. I'll bet a dime to a bear claw ain't a one of them boys anything other than dockworkers or city trash out fer an easy buck." Nate said and then asked, "So, when do y'all leave?"

"We'll head back in the mornin', likely a couple of hours before first light. How about ya?"

"John won't be ready fer a horse for another week or more, so we'll meet ya sooner or later in the shinin' mountains."

Jarel looked over at John and asked, "Ya gonna ride with these men?"

"Damned right I am. I have revenge on my mind and I'll see this played out."

"Son," Bear said as he thought of his dead wife, Falling Leaf [1], "revenge don't change a damned thing, except keepin' the bastard from killin' again. I know all about revenge. If ya expect to feel better after Coon's dead, it won't happen."

"The Bible says, an eye fer an        "

"Eye." Deacon said and then added, "Son, make sure ya have an honest heart when ya go after the man and that yer after him for the right reasons. Sure, he deserves to die, ain't a man here that doesn't know that, but don't let anger spoil yer soul."

John looked confused and then asked, "What do ya mean, spoil my soul? I've lost yer trail and fail to see the sign."

---

1 *See "War Paint" by W.R. Benton, released 2013.*

"Some fellers get so hungry to extract revenge they'll do anything to see they have it. They start to live only for blood and that's not good fer any man. It becomes a disease to them and it's killed more than one feller. Ain't a man here tonight, not a single one, that hasn't been on a revenge trail at least once in their life. But, I hope ya paid attention to Bear, because revenge won't bring yer dead partner back or remove the scar from the bullet hole in your shoulder. Now, I don't preach religion out here like I should, maybe, except I'm only going to tell ya this once. Don't let your hate destroy ya and grow to the point it's all that matters in yer life. Pray and ask God's help. He'll help ya and He knows yer heart. That's all I have to say on the matter."

John looked into the flames as he gave Deacon's words some thought and then he said, "I'm a God fearin' man, but don't usually act like it. I guess I'm a pretty poor Christian, but my life is hard and I don't pray as often as I should."

Deacon smiled and replied, "Then, John, yer a normal man and God understands. As long as ya speak to him and live the best life ya can, you're closer to being a better true follower. Now, I don't know if ya have a Bible, but get ya one and read 'er when ya can. Study it and mold yer life after God's word."

"Ain't no church in the mountains."

"I disagree, because we live in God's own home. No, ain't no preacher man or choir singin' takin' place on a Sunday, but God is close to us and all ya have to do is look around. Now, let's talk on something else before Ty gets mad and accuses me of preachin' again." Deacon broke out laughing.

Ty shook his head, grinned, and said, "Deacon, ain't a man here that ain't a sinner or that doesn't believe in the Good Lord. We're just hell-raisers and it's a rough life we live. But, yer right on the money with the Bible and I never go into my mountains without mine. Me and God have been friends fer years."

Cotton stood, stretched and said, "I'm hitting my robes. Dawn comes early in these parts and I'm just plain beat."

One by one the men retired for the night until all that remained was John by the fire and Jarel guarding the horses. Finally, after some powerful thinking, John stood and made his way to his blankets.

A week later, Nate, John, Cotton and 'Possum rode from the camp heading west. This morning is clear, with just a few cotton balls of white clouds hanging on the western horizon, and the weather warm. 'Possum was riding a hundred yards or so in front of the group, while Cotton rode drag behind the group. Nate didn't expect any real trouble while still in Missouri, but he'd take no chances. More than one man had lost his horses or been killed in the state and while it was semi-civilized, there were still bad men around.

John was quiet and had been for the last few days, so Nate tapped his horse lightly in the ribs and moved up beside the man. "What's on yer mind lately?"

John grinned and replied, "So, ya could tell I've been thinkin', huh?"

"Yep, but iffen ya want to talk about it, I'll listen."

"Not much really important, but I've been givin' Deacon's warning about how hate and revenge can ruin a good man. And, Bear said getting his revenge didn't changing anything at all in the long run. I'm startin' to think I was a damned fool."

"Revenge has its place, except it's more important to see justice served than to go on a personal killin'. Just killin' to avenge a wrong is not the right way to do this sort of thing. The dying man must understand why he needs to die. We'll try to bring Coon in for a trial, but he'll likely die before that happens."

"Why a trial? Hell, 'Possum said that he saw the man killin'."

"Young pup, we'll have a trial to show others Coon was treated fairly. We'll not have a trial for Coon, hell, he'll stretch hemp anyway. We're doin' it because it's the only fair way to kill 'em."

"I see the why, but it seems like a waste of time to me, iffen he'll die anyway."

"I don't think we'll take 'em alive anyway. So this whole conversation might be a waste of time, huh?"

"Yep, I hear ya. I guess we'd better stop the naybobbin', because we're on a tramp, and it ain't very smart to talk while movin'."

Nate allowed his horse to slow, so John could move ahead of him. He then fell back to where he'd been riding earlier and scanned the countryside.

The day was uneventful and by nightfall they'd covered another thirty miles or so. Camp was quickly established in an oak grove, a meal of beans and bacon placed on the fire, and the horses watered and wiped down.

After supper, Cotton asked, "So, Nate, have ya given much thought to where we're goin' to start lookin' fer Coon?"

"Yep, I have, old son. We'll ride to the Sioux and speak with Hump about Coon and see iffen he's tradin' rifles with The People. Iffen he is, we'll know soon enough."

"Why the Sioux instead of another tribe?" John asked.

"The Sioux are about the friendliest of the tribes and a smart man would deal with them. Hell, the Ree or Blackfoot would kill Coon and his men before they let 'em say a word. The Comanche might trade, but it all depends on their mood at the time. The Shoshone are up in the mountains and I don't see Coon goin' any further than he has to go to complete the job."

"Do ya think he'd get off the boat at Fort Atkinson?" 'Possum asked.

"Yep, I do, but I'd not given that any serious thought. See, Coon will need some gear and horses before he moves into the plains. He'll also need some pack animals to carry his guns."

"Are we stopping at the fort?" John asked.

"Maybe, I ain't decided yet, but we need supplies as well. Only, if yer thinkin' we can catch Coon there, it won't happen. See, by boat he'll be there weeks before we arrive and he'll already be out on the plains by the time we ride through the gates. Those boats are much faster than we are."

"Damn," Possum said.

Nate chuckled and then said, "We ain't in no hurry. Once he gets there, he'll move onto the prairies to move his guns. All we have to do is find which tribe he's dealin' with. He'll still be there by the time we arrive, because when it comes to tradin', the Injuns take their sweet-ass time and don't rush the job."

Cotton pulled his pipe from his mouth, "Ya know we cain't just ride into any village and take the man, hell, he's protected as long as he's their guest."

"There are two ways to get the man. We can wait for him to leave a village, then confront him or we can ride into a village and I can challenge him."

"Challenge is pretty serious stuff, because only one of ya will stay alive. By most tribal law one man must die. Ya sure ya want to do that?"

"Well, I ain't afraid of the man and don't really want to do that, but left no choice, that's what I'll do."

"I've only seen one challenge and it was with the Comanche. They tied a rope on each fellers left wrist and it was mayhap six feet long. If either took the rope off, the Comanche would have killed the man instantly. They was two pretty good sized fellers, too." Cotton said.

John asked, "Well, how did it end?"

Cotton gave a faint smile and replied, "They ended up killin' each other."

# Chapter 6

Coon and his men got off the boat at Fort Atkinson, tired and hungry, but they'd made excellent time, arriving almost a full day earlier than scheduled. While not overly impressed with the men he'd hired, Coon knew they would do the job, as long as there was no serious physical labor involved.

"Where are we goin' now, Coon?" Shorty asked as they walked down the plank to shore.

"We need to get to the sutlers, order some supplies and see about horses. Ya can take all the men, except Clyde with ya, and find a saloon, iffen they have one. The last time I was here all drinkin' was done at the sutlers. Leave Jones here to watch over the crates. Ya can bring 'em back a bottle so he can have a few drinks later. Me and Clyde will see about supplies."

"If there's a saloon around, me and the boys will find 'er. Come on boys, the first drinks are on me."

*Yep, that's about all ya can do real good is drink,* Coon thought, but kept his mouth closed.

As soon as the men walked away, Clyde said, "Yer a-gonna have trouble with some of the boys before too long. They're a lazy bunch and ain't a one of 'em that knows shit about the plains or the mountains."

Clyde was an average sized man, on the high side of his forties, who was a no nonsense kind of man. Both his hair and beard were long and unkempt. When angered, his eyes spoke for him. He'd spent a couple of years trapping plew, but got tired of fighting Indians, so he'd gone back east. Besides Coon, he was the only man with any experience. He spoke Sioux, some Shoshone, and a little Comanche, but wasn't fluent in any of them. Of course, he knew how to communicate using sign language, so he'd do if things turned rough. He'd signed on to return to the mountains and he was desperate for a job.  When hired by Coon, he was down to his last dime.

"I'll handle the men, so don't ya worry about 'em. Ya get paid to be my second in command, but I run this show—understood?"

"Shore, Coon.  Yer the boss and I can live with that.  There's the sutler straight ahead."

A cowbell gave a loud *clang* when the two men entered and a thin man wearing an apron asked, "What can I do ya fellers out of today?"

"Here's a list of supplies I need as soon as ya can gather 'em up."  Coon handed the list to the clerk.

"This a lot of stuff, so do ya have a letter of authorization from one of the fur companies?"

"Nope, I'm a free trapper.  Ya do take cash, don't ya?"

The clerk smiled and replied, "Why, yes, of course.  However, the expense will be close to a thousand dollars."

"Ya just gather it all up and I'll pay ya when yer done.  Oh, do ya know where I can get some good horses at a reasonable price?"

"Hance Patterson has some good horses, and he's due in today to pick up some gear."

Coon thought for a moment and then said, "Let me have a bottle of good rye and we'll take a table and wait on this Patterson feller."

Coon and Clyde moved to the closest table and within minutes the clerk placed a quart of rye whiskey and two tin cups in front of him.  Pushing one cup to Clyde, Coon pulled the cork and poured the drinks.  He'd just took a drink when the cowbell clanged and when he look over, a short man with long red hair entered.  He was wearing canvas trousers, homespun shirt, and a leather cowboy hat.

"I'll be right with ya!"  The clerk yelled from the back.

"Take yer time, Tom, it's me, Patterson."

Standing, Coon walked to the man and said, "Mister Patterson, I couldn't help but hear your name.  I understand ya have horses?"

"Yep, I do, and each is broken."

"I need about twenty of 'em, so what kind of price can ya give me for that many, if ya even have that many?"

"Whoa, that's a lot of ponies.  I got 'em, but I only take cash.  If ya have that kind of cash, well, I can let ya have 'em fer, oh, I guess ten dollars a head."

"Will ya deliver 'em or do I need to come to yer place?"

"I'll deliver 'em here, if that's what ya want.  I have a couple of hired hands and the army usually takes a few each month, but they don't need any right now."

"How soon can ya deliver?"

"Is dawn tomorrow a problem for ya?"  Patterson hoped it was okay, because times had turned rough for him over the last few months.  The army hadn't been purchasing like they had in the past.

"No, that's fine.  Do I pay ya now or when ya deliver?"

"Hell, ya want to see 'em first don't ya?"

"Join us at the table for a few drinks, iffen ya have the time." *Slow down, ya are starting to sound like yer in a big hurry.  Do this right and get the horses ya need.*

Patterson grinned and said, "I always have time for a double shot of rye."

Pulling up a chair, as Coon sat, Clyde extended his hand and said, "I'm Clyde, I work with Coon."

"Yer wantin' a lot of horses, Coon, but you'll find mine are good critters, every single one of them."  Patterson threw his drink back and poured another one.

"We're trappers and need the mounts for us and our supplies."

"Mine are all young, so they'll last ya some years yet."

The clerk stuck his head out a door and said, "It'll be a bit before I get yer supplies ready fer ya, but Hance, yer's is just outside the back door."

Knocking his second drink back, Patterson stood and said, "I'd stay and beat my gums with ya, but I've work to do.  We'll be here in the mornin', right at sunup."

Coon and Clyde stood, shook the man's hand and then sat back at the table.  Silence filled the small room for a few minutes, then Clyde asked, "What's in the crates we have?  Now, don't tell me it's some Injun trade trinkets, because I know better.  Each of those crates weighs a ton."

Coon smiled and said, "Guns."

"Sumbitch, Coon, ya like to live pretty dangerously don't ya, son?  If the Federal Government finds out they'll hang yer ass, and us right along side of ya."

"Ain't no law out here."

"Yer wrong.  The only two laws I know of are both Federal. It's against the law to sell whiskey or guns to the red man.  Ya ain't planning on give 'em whiskey too are ya?"

"Nope, but that's a damned fine idea.  We'll get about fifty gallons to take along, and I'm glad ya brought it up."  He made his way near the door to the backroom and asked, "Can ya add fifty gallons of traders whiskey to that order?"

"Uh, well, sure, but why in the hell are ya needin' that much?"

Thinking quickly, Coon replied, "I'm gonna take to a trader in the mountains named Butterfield.  Do ya know 'em?  He asked me to pick it for 'em on my way through here and I forgot."

"Yep, I know John Butterfield, so I'll have the whiskey ready too, fer a dollar a five gallon jug."

"Sounds good to me.  Listen, we're getting horses from that Patterson feller here in the mornin', so can I pick up these supplies and pay ya then?"

"Sure, not a problem.  I'll have it stacked by the back door when ya get here."

"I'll be back right at sunrise.  Do ya have a saloon here now?"

"Sure, go out the west gate and you'll see it on the right.  It's just a tent with a fake wood front, but he gets the business. Just opened a couple of weeks back."

"See ya in the mornin'."  Coon picked up the rye and they left the sutlers, heading to the saloon.

They entered the saloon, made their way to the bar, where Coon ordered two beer chasers for the whiskey.  They spotted Shorty and boys at a far table and moved toward them.

"Howdy, boys, how are the drinks?" Coon asked.

Shorty looked as if he'd just been slapped and said, "After the way ya treated me a few minutes ago, now yer wantin' to be friendly?  What in the hell is wrong with ya, Coon?"

Coon gave a blank look and said, "What are ya talkin' about. I ain't seen ya since we got off the boat."

"Bullshit. At the bar, not twenty minutes ago ya threatened to beat my ass iffen I didn't leave ya alone so ya could finish yer drink."

Clyde laughed and then said, "That ain't possible, Shorty, because twenty minutes ago we were still at the sutlers."

Shorty blinked his eyes rapidly a few times and said, "Now, I know I ain't the smartest man around, but I know my boss when I see 'em. Ask these other fellers, 'cause they saw ya, too."

All of the men agreed and a shudder went down Coon's spine as he thought, *Floyd Kramer is out here and that can either help or hurt me. Iffen I work this right, I might be able to put the blame on what I'm about to do on him. Hell, I can't go back to Saint Louis, not after collectin' Poor's bounty money at the telegraph office.*

Suddenly, Wild Bill said, "Maybe it was a twin of Coon's. My momma used to say we all have a twin in this world, so mayhap that's what happened."

Turning to Shorty, Coon asked, "Did this man really look like me?"

"His clothes were different, but he was dressed sort of like ya. He had on buckskins, but now that I think on it, he had a black hat, not gray like yers. I'm tellin' ya right now, he's a spit-tin' image of ya, no matter how ya look at 'em."

"Was he carryin' guns?"

"Yep, had two just like ya do all the time. Coon, this is some scary shit in my mind."

Coon faked a laugh and replied, "Let it go. He most likely thought ya were somebody roostered that wanted to mess with 'em. But, by damn, it wasn't me."

"Hell," said Jonas, "I'm surprised ya didn't run into 'em, Coon. He couldn't have left but minutes before ya walked to the bar."

Grinning, Coon replied, "Well, we didn't. I passed a sleepin' place just before we found this place so here in a bit let's head there and get rooms for the night. It's a big tent, so don't expect a reg'lar hotel room. More than likely, we'll have a cot with a blanket between 'em for a room, but we leave in the mornin' at first light. Now, y'all can stay here and drink all ya want, but iffen ya can't ride in the mornin', yer fired."

Morning arrived clear, but chilly, and the men were moving the horses and supplies from Fort Atkinson to the north-west. All of the men were at the sutlers on time, except a couple looked like hell, and they weren't exactly sitting straight in their saddles. Shorty leaned over and puked as he followed Coon. Finally, pissed and angry, the old mountain man stopped the group and made each rider drink a full cup of whiskey.

"By God, the hair of the dog should cure every damned one of ya. But, no more drinkin' like that until we return or we'll all end up dead. I'm warnin' each of ya right now. Iffen I catch ya drinkin' I'll leave ya on foot no matter where we are."

Shorty almost spat his whiskey out. He turned to look at Coon and asked, "Are ya serious? Hell, I'm a grown man and iffen I want to drink, I'll do it."

Coon pulled his pistol, aimed at Shorty and said, "Dismount right now and leave."

"What?"

"I no longer need ya, Shorty. Now, ya have to the count of three and then I'll shoot ya off of my horse, 1."

*Damn me, he's serious,* Shorty thought, but replied as he swung out of the saddle, "Pull in yer horns, I'm leavin'. Keep in mind, Coon, I never forget when someone wrongs me and one day you'll pay for this."

Coon's shot was loud and Shorty was knocked backward, to land on his back. There was a bullet hole where his left shirt pocket button used to be. He jerked a few times, gave a loud sigh, and rolled over on his side—dead.

Gazing into the eyes of the other men, one at a time, he asked, "Anybody else want to threaten me or try to drink on this trip?"

Silence.

"Let's move, we're wasting daylight." He ordered.

"Ain't we gonna bury Shorty?" Jonas asked.

"Hell no, son, the critters have to eat, too. Now, let's move."

That night after supper the men turned in early, after Coon assigned guards for the night. It remained cool, but not cold, and the earlier winds had died down. It was on Jonas' shift when the old mountain man felt a light touch to his ankle.

He opened his eyes to see Jonas squatted beside him with his hand cupped around his ear. Listening, Coon nodded, got up and made his way to each man. After they were awake, he whispered, "Find cover and stay awake the rest of the night. Something is out there, the night sounds are gone."

An hour later the horses began to dance and prance on the picket line, so Coon and Clyde move to the animals. Whispering, Clyde said, "It ain't Injuns, but I hope to hell it ain't what I think it is."

"It could be a griz—"

"Bear!" Screamed one of the men as the huge beast entered the camp standing upright on his rear legs. Four rifles fired, but the big balls seemed to have little or no effect on the animal. Charging suddenly, the bear jumped on Wild Bill and Coon could hear the man screaming. The other men backed away from the sharp claws and teeth.

Coon ran to the animal and aiming carefully, fired a shot that struck the bear in the right eye. Giving a horrible scream, the grizzly bear dropped Wild Bill from his mouth, stood and moved toward Coon. The old mountain man waited until the bear opened his mouth and then Coon fired between the animals teeth. The bear stopped, gave a mighty shudder, and collapsed right beside the red coals of the dying fire.

Shaking and spilling powder, Coon reloaded both of his guns, pulled his knife and then moved to the animal. When he touched the left eye with the tip of his knife, the bear gave no response, so he knew the brute was dead.

"Ya men come in here and drag Wild Bill near the fire. Clyde, ya get a fire started so I can see how to doctor 'em up, iffen he lives."

The bloodied man was soon by the flickering flames and Coon shook his head as he said, "Lawdy, he's tore up something fierce. Scalp about ripped off, claw marks on his chest and back, and at least two puncture wounds through his skull."

"What are ya goin' to do?" Jonas asked.

Pulling a small bottle from his medical supplies in his possibles bag, he said, "I'll give 'em a little laudanum, let him rest a minute and then try to put all the pieces back together again. Clyde?"

"Yep?"

"We're all shook up, so give each man a cup of whiskey. Then, bring me a jug so I can feed it to Wild Bill over night."

"Is he gonna live?" Cy asked.

"Hell, who knows, but I'll do what I can for 'em."

"Ya gonna cauterize those rips and tears on his body?"

"Yep, take yer blade," he said and handing his knife to Clyde, he continued, "put both of our blades in the fire. When they're red-hot, let me know."

"I've done 'er and had 'er done to me a few times. It hurts like a sumbitch, so expect him to pass out on ya. Most don't take a hot knife well."

"With the laudanum in 'em, he'll take it better than most men." Coon gulped most of his whiskey down, pulled out a spool of threat and needle, and dumped them in his cup.

"I think yer wasting yer time, because of the holes in his skull. Hell, even iffen he lives he ain't gonna be right in the head no more. He'll drool and slobber all the time."

"Ya just may be right, but some recover and we've got to try to keep 'em alive, because if it was one of us we'd want to be helped, right?"

"Well, I guess so, I've seen head injuries go either way. I knew this mountain man once that was kicked in his head and he was fine after a few days. Then, I saw a man take a glancing blow from a rifle ball and hardly even bled, but he was like a three year old child the rest of his life."

"Hand me a knife, they're ready."

"Here." Clyde handed him a glowing blade.

When he smeared the flesh on Wild Bill, the man gave a faint moan and that was it. Quickly rolling him over, he did the same on the other side. Then, placing the knives near the fire to cool, Coon said, "Now, I'll thread a needle and get this boys scalp back on 'em."

# CHAPTER 7

Nate and his men entered the sutler's store at Fort Atkinson and walked to the counter.  The clerk started to say something to the big black man, about colored folks not being allowed in the building, but remembered Nate and wisely kept his mouth shut.  Previously the clerk had had the frightening experience of Nate's big skinning knife tip on his throat, so he asked, "What can I do fer ya gentlemen?"

Nate said, "We're lookin' fer a man called Coon Turner. He's a big man with reddish hair and beard."

"I saw him about a week back.  He come in here and ordered a lot of supplies and about fifty gallons of traders whiskey.  He paid cash, so I had no complaints."

"Ya let the sumbitch have fifty gallons of whiskey?  Good God, yer about a dumb bastard, don't ya know what he'll do with it?" Cotton blurted out.

Wiping his counter down with a damp rag, the clerk said, "It ain't against the law to sell whiskey to any white man, in any quantity.  And, I really don't give a shit what he does with it, not really.  What he does ain't none of my business, but he said it was for John Butterfield."

Nate handed the clerk a list and said, "Fill this for us and add five gallons of whiskey to the order, if a black man can buy from ya."

Lowering his eyes, the clerk replied, "I didn't mean it the way it came out.  I just cain't sell whiskey to Injuns. I'll have yer order in about an hour and I'll add a little hard candy to the whole shebang because this is a good size purchase. Ya payin' cash?"

"I only do business with cash on the barrel head."  Nate replied.

'Possum laughed and said, "Ya know as well as I do, Mister Store Clerk, that Coon is gonna trade that whiskey to the Injuns. But, ya cain't sell Injuns none?  What's wrong with yer thinkin', son?"

The clerk gave a faint smile and replied, "I don't really know what he's gonna do with the whiskey and fer all I know, he mighten just have a big thirst."

Nate met the eyes of his men and nodded toward the door. "I'll be back in a bit to pay and pick up the supplies."  As a group, they turned and left the building.

Once outside, 'Possum said, "There's a saloon just outside the gate."

"Bit early fer drinkin'," John said but then added, "but I could use a double rye about now."

Cotton laughed and then said, "We can do some talkin' there.  I have a feelin' our Coon Turner is about to blow up a mess of trouble before too long."

After entering the saloon tent, the men moved to a table at the rear, so they could keep an eye on the entrance.  Nate noticed each man, including himself, checked their pistols before they sat.

A grossly overweight bartender asked from the bar, "What'll y'all have?"

"Bring us a good bottle of rye and four glasses.  Now, don't try to slip us some of that rotgut ya got, because we'll know the difference right off." Nate replied.

After the bottle was on the table, 'Possum poured the strong amber drink and said, "Coon is out to start a damned war.  Ain't much that scares me, but drunk Injuns with new guns does the job.  And if the Comanche get guns and whiskey, I'm movin' east."

The men knocked the first drink back, Nate refilled the glasses, and then said, "Fellers, Coon doesn't care about any-thing, but the money he'll make from Injuns.  See, a Hawken ri-fle will fetch him a lot of furs and with the number of guns he's got, he'll be a rich man.  Then, add the whiskey, why, he'll have money to burn.  I once saw a Shoshone Chief, who loved his whiskey, trade twenty horses for a gallon of panther piss.  Now, whiskey prices vary a great deal by the gallon, but a dollar or two investment in rotgut is cheap, when ya consider the horses were worth about ten to fifteen dollars a head."

Cotton blinked his eyes and then said, "Hell, twenty horses at ten dollars a head, that's, well, almost two hundred dollars, ain't it?"

Nate laughed and replied, "It is exactly that amount, Cotton. The man with the whiskey made a huge profit on the deal. But Injuns that drink often will trade anything to get a bottle or jug."

John smiled and said, "I once traded a quart of rye to a warrior to sleep with his oldest daughter for the night. At the time I was roostered and didn't give it much thought, but after I sobered up, I wasn't real happy with myself."

"I've seen the same thing," Cotton said, "and once had a chief offer me his wife for the night for a bottle of booze. I was shocked then and still am that he'd do that."

Nate chuckled and replied, "Ain't no white man that can think like an Injun. Now, I like most Injuns, even those out to lift my hair, because they're good people overall. The only reason most attack us is to move up the peckin' order of the tribe. The more scalps and coups a warrior has the more respect he's given by the tribe. But, I think whiskey and the diseases of the white man will be the end to the red race one day."

Possum asked, "How's that?"

"Everyone knows if whiskey gets to be a habit, it'll kill a man over time. The injuns livin' around forts, like this one, live here so they can get whiskey when they want it. Now, iffen they trade their daughters or wives favors for a bottle, it's just a matter of time before the woman gets the French pox, don't ya see? And, other illnesses that don't bother us much, like measles or mumps will kill an Injun. I don't know why but it—" Nate stopped talking and was looking at the bar.

"What's the matter, Nate, ya just stopped talkin'." Cotton asked.

"Coon Turner just walked in and he's at the bar. Now, don't ya'll look at the same time, but I'm pretty sure it's him. I've met 'em before and I'm positive it's him. John, take ya good look."

John glanced at the bar, gulped his drink down, and then said, "It's Coon, and I'd bet my life on it. The question is, what do we do about it?"

Nate gave the question some thought and then said, "He wronged ya first, 'Possum, so why don't ya and John brace 'em at the bar. After all, he killed friends of both of ya. Now, do the job one at a time when ya confront him, because we want this to be fair. John, if 'Possum takes a ball, then the man is yours. Try to get him to come in for a trial, but if that doesn't work, kill 'em."

"What iffen we both take a ball?" John asked.

"Then he'll have to deal with me and Cotton."

The two mountain men stood and made their way to the bar, where John ordered whiskeys for both of them. The big man was sipping a double rye when 'Possum said, "Coon, ya need to go back to Butterfield's place fer a trial. Ya killed some good men."

The man turned, looked at 'Possum and said, "My name ain't Coon, it's Floyd. And, who in the hell are you?"

"Who am I? Hell, ya lived with me for almost a year and ya claim ya don't know me? My name is 'Possum." 'Possum knocked back his whiskey, placed the glass on the bar and added, "Now, are ya comin' or do I have to get mean?"

"Partner, I ain't never laid eyes on you in my life. Now, be a good boy and leave me the hell alone, so I can have my drink in peace."

"We cain't do that," John said, "'cause ya killed some good men."

The big man laughed and replied, "What kind of talk is all of this? Ya both seem to think I'm somebody named Coon and you're a 'Possum, so this must be a joke, right?"

'Possum said, "It's no joke, Coon, it's serious business. Now, which will it be, ya comin' with us or do we have to kill ya where ya stand?"

Kramer's hand pulled a pistol and the shot was loud in the small tent. 'Possum was struck hard, fell to his knees, but brought his pistol up, fired and struck the big man in the left shoulder. The shot mountain man gave a sigh and fell to his left side. Knocked back to the bar by the impact of the big ball from 'Possum's pistol, Kramer frantically reached for his second pistol.

John, holding his gun straight out, fired, and smiled as his shot took the big man in the middle of his chest, only it didn't seem to have much of an affect on the Kramer, because he fired the second pistol. John screamed as the bullet took him low and in the belly.

Kramer, still standing, looked down at his bleeding chest, reached up and touched bright crimson blood and said, "Sumbitch, I've been kilt." He reached for his glass of whiskey, gulped it down and then moved to a chair where he sat down.

Nate and Cotton moved forward and as they neared the table with Kramer, the big man's head dropped suddenly to his chest. "Ya check our men, while I keep Coon covered," Nate ordered.

The bartender yelled out, as he went out the door, "I'll fetch a doc!"

"A doc won't do John any good, he's gutshot and unconscious right now." He then moved to 'Possum and said, "'Possum's gone under." Cotton made his way to the bar, grabbed two dirty towels and returned to John's side. Quickly bandaging the entrance and exit holes, he then lowered the man gently to the floor.

"Now, check Coon and be careful, because he's rattlesnake mean."

Grasping the man's greasy hair, Cotton felt the side of Kramer's neck, raised his eyelids and saw nothing but white. "Coon's as dead as hell."

Sergeant Major Armitage and a group of his men entered the saloon with guns drawn. He glanced at the two men on the floor and then Kramer before he asked, "Nate, what in the hell happened here?"

"Well, sergeant, pull out a chair and have a seat. I have a story of a renegade trapper to tell ya."

When Nate finished speaking, Armitage went to the bar, poured himself a double bourbon and returned to his seat, thinking about the words he'd heard from Nate. Finally, the sergeant took a sip of his drink, rose from his chair, and moved to Kramer. Once beside the dead man he pulled his knife. Cutting the back of the man's shirt from collar to tail, he pulled the material away, so the back was clearly seen.

Turning to Nate, he said, "This man's name is Floyd Kramer, not Coon Turner. Y'all killed the wrong man, but don't fret over it, because the law back east has been looking for him, as well as your Coon."

"Sergeant, that's Coon Turner. Hell, I personally know the man." Nate said.

The Sergeant Major moved back to his chair, sat and said, "Now it's my turn to tell you a story."

"I'm listening."

"Coon and Floyd are identical twins and they were separated shortly after birth. Their mother was a soiled dove that died during childbirth. Well, the whorehouse didn't want kids, so they turned 'em over to the sheriff. Now, the lawdog was finally able to give the kids to some folks movin' west, but to different families. It's likely neither man is aware of the other. I know this ain't your Coon, because he's got two twelve inch knife scars on his back and a bullet scar eight inches above his left nipple."

"I'll be damned, but how do ya know all of this?"

"We get wanted dodgers on folks the law is lookin' for. They're currently lookin' for both Coon Turner and this man. Kramer here has a pretty good reward too, five thousand dollars, and it looks like it'll go to ya and Cotton."

"Why is the law after Coon, I mean, he did his killin' out here."

"Not all of it, because it seems he killed a mountain man named James Blake in Missouri, and stole a big chunk of change from the telegraph office by claimin' he was another man. Ain't a lot of information on the theft of the money, but the killin' alone earned him a two thousand dollar reward."

Nate pushed his hat back on his head and said, "Sumbitch. O'Brien must have said something to the coppers, because he's the only man in town who knew of the killin'. I'll bet they dug the grave up and found some identification on James."

Armitage shrugged and said, "Who knows, but I'll contact the Federal Government and see the reward money for Kramer is sent here. I'll keep the letter of authorization of payment for ya, so ya can pick it up the next time yer around. Hell, it'll be six months before I hear anything too. Now, let me go through this man's pockets and see what we find. We need a lawman here, because it's a rough place, but the army doesn't think one is needed."

Nate noticed the barkeeper and doc enter.

The young military surgeon looked at Cotton and said, "This one's dead."

He moved to Kramer and said, "Dead."

Finally, he squatted, looked John over, and said, "This one's alive, but not for much longer. Sergeant Major, have some of your men take this feller to my cabin. I'll doctor him there and stay with 'em until he dies." He then pulled a small bottle of Laudanum from his coat pocket and gave a little to John.

"Hanks, Jones, and Taylor, help pack this injured man to the surgeons cabin and be quick about it, boys." Armitage ordered as he walked to the bar, picked up the bottle of bourbon and returned to the table. He began to go through Kramer's pockets.

Ten minutes later, the three men were sipping on bourbon as Nate said, "Sure ain't a hell of a lot to show fer a man's whole life, huh? Some money, letters, pocketknife, and a deck of cards."

Armitage counted the money, took out a twenty and as he handed it to Nate, he said, "Here, I'm not allowed to keep it. I took the twenty to see he's buried right with a marker, but the rest is yours. I count just a little over four hundred dollars."

Nate took the money, pulled out a twenty and handed it to the sergeant, "Give this to your surgeon. Now, I know the army doesn't take payment for doctorin', only give this to 'em and tell him thanks for helping John to the other side."

Nate divided the remaining money in half and handed a portion to Cotton. Cotton pulled a twenty and handed it to Armitage as he said, "See John is planted real good, Sergeant. He's a good man and deserves a good send off."

Armitage stood, place the folded money in his shirt pocket and said, "Pete, my boys will be over to get the dead men in a bit."

The bartender nodded.

Shaking hands with Nate and Cotton, Sergeant Major Armitage said, "I've work to do, but the next time yer around I'll have some information on the reward and maybe we can share a bottle of ole be joyful." He turned and walked from the saloon.

"A twin, now who in he hell would have ever considered that?" Cotton asked.

"Well, for sure not us, but we're lucky Kramer was a wanted man or we'd end up stretchin' some hemp rope. I was willin' to bet my life he was Coon."

Cotton finished his drink, stood and said, "We're wasting time, let's ride."

The morning was nice, but during the afternoon the temperature climbed and Nate could feel the sweat run down his back and face. He glanced at Cotton and he was in the same shape. Looking at the sky, not a cloud could be seen, so Nate said, "Here in another hour we'll call it a day. Too damned hot to be ridin' in this."

"I ain't gonna argue with ya none. Now I know how a baked biscuit feels. Lawdy, you'd think it was summer with the heat like it is."

Nate laughed and said, "Yep, the weather out here is funny, because we mighten have snow in the mornin'."

"I've seen snow in the mountains in August and sweatin' temperatures on the plains in February. Queersome, the weather out here is, and that's why I'm always prepared for the worst."

"I got movement in front of us. Looks to be Injuns, but I ain't sure."

"How many of 'em did ya see?"

"A couple, but it's the ones I can't see that worry me."

Cotton asked, "How do ya want to do this?"

"Keep ridin' and iffen things turn ugly, we'll deal with it then."

The men moved together, side by side, and less than a mile later a lone warrior was seen sitting on a horse in their path.

"Sioux." Cotton said.

"Yep, look to be a Southern group, but they might know old Hump.  Hell, he's about a million years old and everything wearing a loin cloth should know the man."

They stopped their horses about six feet from the warrior and Nate saw scars from the sun dance and he counted fifteen feathers in the man's hair.  This is one tough man, he thought.  He waited for the warrior to speak.

*"Why are you on Sioux land?" the brave asked.*

*"We are traveling to the lands to the north to visit my Sioux father, Buffalo Hump.  You may know him."*

*"I know of Buffalo Hump, but he is not my chief.  I am a member of the Southern tribe and follow Sharp Knife."*

*"I am Known as Big Raven Man among the Sioux and the man riding with me is called Snow on His Head."*

*"Waugh, you are not true warriors."*

*"You are wrong, my brother.  We fight when we must."*

*"It is a good day to die."*

*"I may die this day, but if I die, there will be much mourn-ing in the lodges of those who kill me."*

*"We shall see!"* The warrior raised a Hawken rifle in his left hand and twenty warriors stood from the buffalo grasses.  They completely surrounded the two mountain men.

# CHAPTER 8

Wild Bill had a rough night and moaned and groaned most of the time. At first, Coon fed the man a mixture of water and whiskey, but when his groans grew louder, he began to feed the man the strong alcohol straight. About two hours before first light, Coon fell asleep and didn't awake until well after sunrise. He checked on his patient and noticed he now labored for each breath. His heart was pounding and his face was covered with sweat. The mountain man knew Wild Bill would go under.

Jonas neared the fire, poured coffee into his cup and asked, "How's he doin' this mornin'?"

"Not good, and I think at some point today he'll die."

"Hell," said Cy, "he's torn to hell and back. I think he might have lived iffen not fer the holes in his skull. Cain't tell what those long teeth did to his brain."

"Well, if ya have gear to repair or things to do, get 'em done now. If he dies today, we'll leave as soon as we bury him."

Cy said, "Come on, Jonas and Thomas, we have a grave to dig. I 'spect we'll need it before this day is finished."

It was near noon, when Wild Bill gave a bloodcurdling scream and began to thrash around violently. He yelled at someone he saw in his mind, gave a loud sigh and a rattling was heard from deep in his chest. Instantly he fell back to the blanket—dead.

A week later, the group rode over a slight incline and entered a long wide valley.  The plains were not a place Coon liked, because it was too open, but yet had streams and gullies that were hard to spot at ground level.  Those same streams and gullies, often held Indians.  The long stemmed buffalo grasses were a bluish-gray and it was a known fact Indians often hid in the grasses.  *I just need to get to a village, then unload the guns, get furs and leave with my scalp still attached.  If I pull this off, just this once, I'll be a very wealthy man.*

"Shit," said Clyde, "look at all the damn Injuns.  I make 'em out to be Sioux, how about you, Coon?"  He pointed to the north.

"Yep, they're Sioux.  Now, none of ya fools put a hand near yer guns or all of us will die.  Let me and Clyde ride forward and talk with 'em."

Thomas said, "Ya best pray they want to talk, because they have this whole damned valley ringed with warriors."

Glancing around, just the shear number of braves scared Coon.  *Be brave,* he thought, *and ya might get out of this alive.* "Clyde, let's ride out a ways and see if they'll send someone to talk."

They rode about half way up the valley and then stopped.  A few minutes later, three warriors broke from the group on the hill and made toward the white men.  The Sioux looked huge, but Coon realized it was because they were riding small ponies and not horses.  The braves, however, looked solemn and grim as they neared.

They stopped about ten feet from the white men and the youngest of the warriors asked in heavily accented English, "Why are you riding on Sioux land?"

*"We look for the Sioux people,"* Coon replied in Sioux.

*"Why do you look for us?"* An older warrior on the right asked.

*"We have things to trade with the Sioux.  Guns and whiskey."*

*"Guns?"* The older man asked.

Clyde, who'd followed the conversation tossed his Hawken to the warrior and said, *"Here is my gift to a brave warrior of The People."* He then turned to Coon and winked.

*"Do you have the dirt that burns and soft rock that shoots from the gun?"*

*"Yes, for trade. I have many more guns, if your people want to trade."* Coon said and grinned inside, because by giving the warrior a free rifle, Clyde would now have all the warriors wanting one.

*"I can kill you and take your guns."*

*Easy here*, Coon thought, but replied, *"Yes, you can do that, but we will fight. If we fight, we will not die alone. Once we are dead, where will you get more guns, the dirt and soft rock? You will have many guns, but they will be useless to you."*

The old warrior nodded and replied, *"You speak with one tongue. What name are you called?"*

"Big Man is my Sioux name."

*"Bring your men, guns, and supplies. We will go to the village."*

*"We will go."* Coon replied, smiled to Clyde and thought, *if they wanted us dead, they'd not be takin' us to a village.*

The trip to the village took about an hour and of the white men, only Clyde and Coon were relaxed. Jonas, Thomas and Cy looked terrified. Coon dropped back by the men and whispered, "Loosen up, we're safe. If they wanted to kill us, they'd have done it on the plains. Relax, watch, and learn, but no matter what happens, don't let them know yer frightened. These people only respect brave men."

When they entered the village, everyone turned to watch them enter, but no one waved or shouted out a greeting. They rode to the biggest lodge, one of the warriors dismounted gracefully and scratched on the entrance flap. He then coughed.

A minute or so later, a small man with graying hair walked into the sunlight. He wore the scars of the sun dance, had numerous other scars and Coon spotted a couple of places where the old man had been shot. The warrior explained Coon and his men to the chief.

Finally, the warrior said, *"He speaks our tongue."*

*"Come, white men, and we will talk."* The chief turned and entered his lodge.

Once inside, Coon noticed the light was dim and a small fire burned. The chief motioned for Coon to sit on his right and the others next to the mountain man.  When Coon glanced at his men, they'd lined up in order of experience.

"*Running Antelope tells me you have guns to trade.  Is this true?*"

"*Yes, I have guns, the dirt that burns and the soft rock.  I also have whiskey.*"

"*The firewater we do not want. It makes a brave go crazy and then leaves him with a hurting head with a new sun.  Water of fire is not good for The People.*"

"*As you wish, father, I will keep the firewater.  Are you interested in the guns and other things?*"

"*Other things?  Let me see some of the things you have for trade.*"

Turning, Coon said, "Clyde, get some foofaraw and bring me a Hawken.  Also, bring a small bag of balls and powder horn for the chief.  The rest of y'all stay seated."

"*My friend will bring some of the things I have to trade.*"

The chief nodded and the lodge grew quiet.

Clyde entered a few minutes later, spread out a colorful blanket, and placed a new Hawken rifle down.  He then place a powder horn and bag of balls beside the gun.  Next, he made a big show of placing needles, vermillion, a hand mirror, a trade knife, and an awl on the blanket.  The chief's face remained as if chiseled from stone.

Clyde said, "*Please take these gifts as your own.  We want to be friends with The People.*" After he spoke, he waved his right hand over the blanket, to show all was for the chief.

Silence again.

Finally, after many long minutes, the chief said, "*I am called Buffalo Hump, or Hump, and I am the war chief of this tribe.  I will take your gifts.*"

Coon nodded, but did not speak.

Hump broke the silence and asked, "*Do you have more of the guns?*"

"*Father, we have many, but the guns must be traded for furs.  One gun will cost many furs, but the gun kills from a long distance.*"

Picking the gun up, Hump ran his hands down the smooth steel and hardwood stock. He picked it up and aimed it, then lowered it back to the blanket. He gave a slight grin, so slight all of the white men except Clyde and Coon missed it completely.

Coon thought, *yes, he loves the gun.*

*"You may trade the guns and things you have here, in the village. If any warriors want the firewater, you can do the trade after you leave here. I do not want it traded for in the village."*

*"I hear you and my mind understands. I will not trade the firewater in the village."*

Hump turned and said to his wife, *"Find Snow Bird and prepare a lodge for our visitors. She is to cook for them and see to their needs."* Two warriors sitting by the fire whispered to each other. Coon didn't hear the words.

The woman left and Hump asked, *"Two of you are dressed like the men who take the one who swims."*

*"We are men of the mountains."*

*"Then you know the ways of the Sioux. What of the men with you? Are they proven warriors?"*

*"No, we are teaching them the ways of being a man and warrior. None have taken a scalp of an enemy yet."*

*"It is a good thing you do, teaching the young braves."*

Coon shrugged and said, *"It is difficult and takes much patience."*

Hump chuckled and replied, *"It is the same for all young men. They want to lay with a woman all the time, hunt, sleep, or eat. To be a true warrior a boy must learn many things and some are not easy. But, once a man learns how to be a real man, it is never forgotten."*

A beautiful Sioux woman entered the lodge and said, *"Father, I have a lodge ready. I am sure the men have hunger."*

*"Go with my daughter, Snow Bird, and she will take you to your lodge. You are my guest and the lodge is yours until you leave. My daughter will see to your needs while you live with us."*

Coon simply nodded, because he knew the conversation was finished for the time being.

As they walked to the lodge, Coon realized other than Clyde, none of the other men had any idea what was happening. He said, "Once in the lodge, I'll tell y'all what's goin' on. I will say we're as safe as it gets and personal guests of Hump, the war chief."

Once in the lodge, the men looked around at the backrests, buffalo robes, and other items as Snow Bird prepared a meal. After the meat and vegetables were cut and placed in the pot, she left.

"Okay, the overall outcome of the talk with Chief Hump was we can trade with 'em."

Jonas asked, "Ya mean that skinny old man was chief?"

Clyde laughed and replied, "That skinny old man is one mean sumbitch and could kill ya with one hand tied behind his back."

Jonas laughed and said, "I don't think so.  A good wind would blow him away."

Gazing into the younger man's eyes, Coon asked, "Did ya see those two long scars on the man's chest?"

"Yep, so what?"

"He's done a sun dance.  A sun dance is where a shaman pierces a man's chest muscles, runs a rawhide rope under the muscle and the warrior dances until he pulls the muscle loose or it tears.  It's a religious ceremony from what I understand, and some of those men dance for days.  Often they'll attach a sacred buffalo skull to the secured muscle.  It has to hurt like a bitch and they dance around, lean back to tear the muscle and pray.  Any time you see those scars, you treat the man with re-spect, because he's a real badass."

"Sounds stupid to me." Cy said.

"It's their way, not ours, but learn to respect it if ya want to stay alive while we're here.  And, don't be messin' with the women either, because it might just get your throat cut."

The men made small talk about the tribe for an hour and then Snow Bird returned and dished out the stew.  The men were hungry and more than one of them had three bowls of food.  Finally, when the men were finished, Snow Bird collected the wooden bowl and left for the night.

Coon asked, "What'd y'all think of supper?"

Thomas said, "I love it and try as I can, I couldn't tell ya the meat in the stew.  I know it wasn't beef."

"The meat was buffalo, ya dumb ass." Jonas said and then laughed.

"Wrong," said Clyde, "it was puppy."

Cy's eyes grew large and he asked, "Puppy, like a dog?"

Coon said, "It's typical for the Sioux when respected guests arrive to kill a young puppy for their meal. It's considered a special dish reserved for visitors."

Cy started gagging and few seconds later, Thomas joined him. Soon they both made a run for the door and were gone.

Jonas laughed and then asked, "What was it, really?"

Coon didn't crack a smile as he said, "Dog, son. It was a puppy."

Jonas stood and made his way to the flap, but at the doorway he stopped and said, "Iffen I find out later this is a joke, I'll kill ya."

"Son, iffen it's a lie, I won't even fight ya. What I said to ya is the truth."

After Jonas left, Clyde said, "They've some growin' up to do out here. Hell, they'll eat worse than dog by the time we return to the states, most likely."

Coon stood and said, "I'm turnin' in. Yep, they need to grow up a few notches and iffen they live long enough, it'll toughen 'em up a mite. Come first light, we start the trading."

Dawn was cool, but not cold, as the men gathered by their trade goods. The trading supplies were laid out on colorful blankets brought along just for that purpose, to catch the eye. Within minutes the trading started and Coon established the trading rate for a rifle was forty beaver plew or ten buffalo skins.

"This man only has thirty plew, but wants a rifle." Cy said.

"Those rifles cost me forty dollars each, so the number of skins is firm. Let me see if he has anything else to trade."

"Sure, because I don't understand a damned word he's sayin'."

Turning to the short brave, Coon asked, *"Is that all you have to trade? Have you no other skins or other things a white man would want?"*

*"I have no other skins, but what does a white man want?  I do not understand the head of a white man, so I cannot say if I have anything of value."*

*"White men want skins, the yellow rock, or clothing made of skins."*

The brave thought for a few minutes, gave a slight grin, and said, *"I have the yellow rock, but my children play with it.  It is soft and of no use to The People."*

*"Do you have much of the yellow rock?"*

*"Let me go and return with all the yellow rock I have and then you can see."*

*"Yes, go and return.  I will keep a rifle for you, if you return quickly."*

The warrior walked from the blankets of trade goods.

Cy asked, "What was that all about?"

"That warrior has some gold, but I ain't sure how much.  He's gone to fetch it."

"Gold, out here?"

"Most likely from in the mountains.  The Sioux call it yellow rock and they have no use for it."

"Well," said Clyde, "we sure as hell have a use fer it."

The warrior returned holding a big leather bag with both hands.  When he handed it to Coon, it was so heavy, he almost dropped it.  Pulling the bag open, the mountain man's jaw dropped and his eyes grew large.

"Gold, huh?" Clyde asked.

Coon nodded and said, "Yep and a big-assed chunk too, close to twenty pounds."

Clyde smiled and said, "It'll fetch a pretty penny.  The last I heard, gold is goin' fer almost twenty dollars an ounce.  That rock is worth well over $5,000 dollars."

*Closer to $6,400 you damn fool,* Coon thought and then said, "Hell, he's brought enough gold to buy everything we have with us."

Jonas asked, "Well, what do I give 'em for it?"

"Give 'em two rifles, a pound of lead and a pound of powder."

Turning to the brave, Coon asked, *"Do you have more of the yellow rock?"*

*"No, I do not have more of the yellow rock. I know where the yellow rock is and can get more when I have need of it."*

*"How would you like to have ten of the rifles, ten pounds of powder and much of the soft rock that shoots?"*

The warrior smiled and asked, *"How can I get such things? I have no more of the yellow rock."*

*"Take me to the yellow rock and I will give you much of what I have."*

The warrior didn't speak for many long minutes, but finally he replied, *"Do you speak with one tongue? You will give much for the yellow rock?"*

*"I speak with one tongue and will give you the rifles, powder, soft rock, blankets, the glass that looks back, two hands and two fingers of skinning knives, and five horses."*

Like men the world over, greed came into play instantly with the brave. With all the white man will give, I will make my wife happy and others will want what I will have, he thought and smiled. A few minutes later he asked, *"I want vermillion, two awls, and all of the white man's red skins you have."*

Coon knew the red skins were the red cloth material he had and he quickly agreed. Then he asked, *"What are you called?"*

*"I am called Blood Face."*

*"Is the yellow rock many suns riding from this village?"*

*"Two suns to the rock."*

Coon smiled and asked, *"When do we leave?"*

*"Let me get my weapons of war and we can leave now."*

*"Good, get your weapons."*

Clyde, who'd heard the whole conversation said, "Who's goin' with ya?"

"I'll go it with one man, because I need ya here to speak the language and the others to do the trading. I'll bring a little back with me and then we'll finish here and go get more gold. We'll all share in the gold I find." Coon said, only he thought differently, *if there is a lot of gold, I ain't never comin' back here and the man that rides with me will die.*

"Well, now, the sharing part I like. Only, let me make one thing clear to ya, iffen ya don't come back, I'll come lookin' fer ya. When I find ya, I'll skin yer ass alive."

"Clyde, I'll be back, hell, look at the money this trade is bringin' us."

With narrow eyes, Clyde replied, "I meant what I just said."

Who's goin' with ya?" Thomas asked.

*I need a useless one with me and the dumber the better.* Coon smiled and said, "I'm gonna take Cy with me on the trip. Now, once we get this gold to Saint Louis, we'll split it evenly five ways, fair?"

"Yep, sounds good!" Jonas replied.

"Uh-huh," said Cy, suspecting it wouldn't happen once in the big city.

Thomas grinned and said, "Hell, I ain't never had more than a hundred dollars in my life.  Me rich, imagine that."

Clyde glared and thought, *iffen there is a lot of gold, we ain't never gonna see ya in this village again.  But, I can keep the twenty pounds of gold and the furs from the trade.  Then, iffen ya don't come back, I'll come lookin' fer ya.* "The gold this warrior traded stays with me."

"Sure, not a problem.  Just keep it safe until I get back, Clyde.  Cy, get yer gear, because we're leaving in a bit."

"Yee-haw!" Cy yelled as he ran for the lodge to get his gear.

# CHAPTER 9

Nate met the eyes of the warrior and then asked, *"As I said before, it is a good day to die, is it not?"* The rifle, laying across the black man's legs, slowly moved toward the brave.

Seeing the movement of the rifle, the warrior said, *"The Sioux do not scare you, white man?"*

*"I am scared, but if we fight, you will be the first Sioux to die, my brother. All things will die one day, so this may be your day to sing your death song. You can start now, if you wish."*

Silence followed.

Finally, when Nate's nerves were at the highest, the warrior said, *"I can see why Buffalo Hump calls you son, Big Raven Man. You are worthy of being a Sioux warrior."*

Nate nodded.

*"I, Kills Silently, will let you cross our lands in peace."* Then turning to a warrior standing in the grass he said, *"Come, Runs Fast, we will return to the village."*

After the warriors moved out of hearing distance, Cotton said, "I almost shit my pants. I thought we had a fight comin' fer sure."

"I did too, but we'd have gone under. There must have been a hundred braves on the hills around us."

Cotton pulled a bottle of whiskey from a saddlebag, pulled the cork, and said, "I need a shot of liquid courage after that scare. In all my years on the plains, that was the closest to dead I've ever been." He took a long pull of the strong drink and then handed the bottle to Nate.

Nate took a sip and said, "Let's ride, daylights a-wastin'"

After about a mile, Cotton said, "While the Sioux let us ride away, ya know it's likely some of the young bucks will make a play for the horses tonight."

"Yep, I've given that some thought. We'll make camp off to the right there and have a good supper."

Camp was quickly established and supper put on to cook. Cotton had killed a young deer earlier in the day, so the meal was beans with deer meat. As the main meal cooked, both men used sharpened sticks to skewer some smaller cuts of deer, so they could snack a bit before they got serious about eating.

A few minutes later, as his mouth worked around some cooked meat, Cotton asked, "What shifts for the guard?"

"I'll take the first half of the night and then you. Keep yer eyes open, because I seriously expect the Sioux to try fer our horses. If nothing else, some of the young braves might try to do the job."

As the beans cooked, Cotton asked, "Do ya think you'll ever take a woman and settle down someplace?"

Nate laugh loudly and once back under control he said, "Cotton, that ain't likely to happen, unless I take a squaw for a wife. How many black women do ya know out here?"

"Wait a few years, then move back east."

"Son, I'd be a slave again within a year. See, some slavers even gather up freemen and take 'em down South. It does the black no good to complain, because who're the lawdogs and courts gonna believe? The white man will win every single time."

"I hadn't thought of that at all. Well, times are changin' and it won't be long there will be American's out here in big numbers, too."

"I don't need a wife, and the kind of life we live ain't fer a white or black woman anyway. Hell, most couldn't survive out here and none would be comfortable."

Cotton grinned and then replied, "Bear and Ty both have or had good women, but they're Injuns. Bear's was a Shoshone, only I ain't sure about Ty. They're happy men, so a feller can be a mountain man and yet have a wife. The only problem is, folks back east consider them both squaw men."

"Who out here gives a shit what folks back east think or do? Even iffen I were a white man, I'd stay right where I'm at, because this is my home. We walk where eagles fly and see the results of God's hand every single day. No, suh, black, white or green, I'd stay here.  See, folks back east have an easy life and ain't none of 'em appreciate it, either."

"How so?  I mean when I lived back east in Missouri we had a bunch of hard times with no food or our place torn to hell and back by twister or storm."

Nate thought for a second and then replied, "Most of the time, iffen ya think back, ya had shelter, food, fire, and water.  And, I wasn't thinkin' about Missouri, but way back east mayhap in Ohio, Mississippi, or New York.  Now I ain't never been to Ohio or New York and I'll admit that, only I've read about the places.  Thousands upon thousands live in New York City alone."

"Damn me, I couldn't live like that.  Every single time ya'd break wind, someone would know about it.  I'm sure there is a mess of killin', robbin', rapes, and other crimes in them big places."

"Think about a disease like small pox or the plague, hell, there'd be no way to stop it until it ran it's course.  I heard tell thousands die in New York City every time a serious illness strikes.  I talked with Jeb[2] once, he rode with Hawk and Bear, about a year before he was killed.  He was once a doctor back in, oh, I think Boston or someplace like that.  Did ya ever know the man?"

Cotton grinned and said, "Hell, everybody knew Jeb.  I almost fell over when I heard he'd been killed in a saloon near Fort Atkinson.  He had bark, Jeb did."

"Anyway, Jeb told me that when he was a doctor, small pox broke out and thousands of people died.  He said it got so bad a wagon would drive down the streets each mornin' to collect the bodies of those who'd died overnight.  They'd take the bodies out to a big pit in the middle of a field and then burn 'em all."

"I'd imagine some whole families died, too.  It's a rough life for most folks and a person is lucky to reach the age of 45 or so these days.  Iffen one disease or another don't kill ya off, it's either an accident or yer murdered."

"I've seen a few old men reach 70, but by God, they are few and far between."

---

2 *See "War Paint", by W.R. Benton, copyright 2008*

"Lot of folks dyin' from fevers, but all they need is some willow bark crushed up and boiled and ya could save a bunch of 'em."

"Yep, fevers put a bunch down every year.  I think festerin' is something we need a cure for.  Once a feller or gal gets to festerin', all ya can do it clean 'em with alcohol and hope they live."

"The beans are done, so hand me yer plate." Cotton said as he pulled the cast iron pot from the flames.

They ate in silence, then Cotton stood and said, "I'm headin' to my robes.  If ya need me, just tap my ankle."

Nate nodded and then scooped the last of his beans into his mouth.  He then picked up his rifle and moved near the horses.  He'd just sat down, when he glanced up and saw millions of stars twinkling and flashing overhead in the clear sky.  He prayed, "Lord, it's me, Nate.  I want to thank ya for the life I live and the friends I have.  No, I don't need nothin' right now, just feelin' rich tonight and I know yer behind it all.  I believe strongly in ya, God.  I know that everything that happens on this earth is your will and none of this takes place by accident.  I do ask ya to keep us safe as we travel over this rough country, Lord.  And, while I'm a sinner, I do try to be the best man I can and live by the Bible.  This I ask in the name of Jesus, amen."

Most of Nate's shift was quiet and he did a lot of thinking about the big city of Saint Louis and the man they were searching for.  While the west appeared to be so large it'd be easy to hide, it just wasn't so, unless a man became a hermit in the mountains.  Most folks had contact with other people in one way or the other, ran into Injuns, or used a trading post for supplies.  Sooner or later, Coon's name would be spoken.  While living out west, he'd developed patience, which most American's lacked, so he'd wait and move once he heard of the man.  He'd not waste his time meandering all over the place searching, like Bear did for his revenge.

*What's that movin'? It was a good ways out, but something moved,* He thought. *No wind either, so I need to wake Cotton.* The night sounds suddenly stopped and it was quiet.

Nate crawled to Cotton and tapped him on the ankle.  When the man opened his eyes, Nate cupped a hand behind his ear.  Cotton nodded in understanding and taking his rifle moved into the darkness. Nate made his way back to the horses.

Almost an hour passed before Nate saw two dark forms moving toward him. He lined the sights of his rifle up on the bigger of the two and squeezed the trigger. A scream filled the night air and the man dropped to the ground and began thrashing around. Pulling his pistol, Nate looked for the other man, but he'd gone to ground. Two shots came from the other side of camp, followed by screams. The shots were close together, so Nate hoped Cotton could get reloaded in time.

Suddenly, a man rushed Nate just slightly off his right side and he was running hard. The mountain man lined up his pistol, fired, and the man fell in an unnatural way. He quickly reloaded both guns and pulled his second pistol, placing it on the ground near his foot. Hearing a noise behind him, he turned his head to see a man rushing toward him. He snapped a shot off with his rifle, missed and was in the process of aiming his pistol when the man struck him.

Both fell to the ground, as he tried to grab the others hands. Finally, Nate got a good grip and when they rolled over, the moonlight showed his attacker was none other than the Sioux, Kills Silently.

*"Have you sung your death song?"* The warrior asked.

*"I have no need this night, but you will. Wait for me on the other side and we can fight once more."*

The warrior broke free, Nate heard another shot across camp, and when he glanced at Kills Silently the man was smiling. The warriors hand, as fast as a striking snake, reached for Nate and he felt the knife tip enter his left arm, up high. He waited and when the warrior attempted to hit him again, Nate's foot kicked the knife into the darkness. He moved quickly to the Sioux.

Taking Kills Silently in a bear hug, Nate began to squeeze. The braves head shook from side to side as he attempted to get a hand free and he began to chant his death song. Applying all his strength, Nate squeezed again and then heard something snap in the brave's body, and he immediately grew limp. Throwing the body away from him, he quickly reloaded his guns and moved toward Cotton.

When he neared where he thought the shots had come from, he saw Cotton squatted beside a young boy of about fifteen.  In the bright moonlight, Nate could see the boys chest was covered in blood and only a handle of a Green River knife was visible in the center of the blood.

"Is it clear on this side?" Nate asked.

"It is now, I think."

"Ya hurt?"

"A little; took a ball to my foot, of all things."

"It happens.  I took a knife to my arm.  Come on and let's get back to the fire."

As they moved toward the long dead campfire, Cotton said, "It was the Sioux, just like we figured it'd be.  They were after the horses."

"Yep, over by the horses you'll find Kills Silently's body."

Using a scorched piece of cloth and his flint and steel, Cotton soon had a fire burning.  As he worked, Nate saw a bullet hole in the man's moccasin.  He pulled off his shirt and then said, "Clean me first, then I'll take a look at yer foot."

Cotton looked the injury over closely and said, "The blade went in about a fourth of an inch.  Hell, it ain't much, but she's bleedin' pretty good."

"Pour some whiskey on it and wrap it up, then."  He knew there was an almost empty whiskey bottle one the ground near the flames of the campfire.

Nate gave a light gasp as the alcohol hit the wound, but didn't cry out.  As he was wrapped in cotton material, he thought, *keep 'er clean and I'll be in good shape within a week.*

A few minutes later, Cotton said, "There, as good as new.  Now, look my foot over, she's startin'  to smart a bit."

Nate had Cotton sit in the dirt as he pulled the moccasin from his foot.  Shaking his head, he said, "Damn, son, ya lost one toe already and I need to remove the other, it's just hangin' by a thread."

"Which toes?"

"The two beside yer big toe.  At least takin' 'em off won't hurt yer walkin' none."  Nate placed his knife blade in the fire.  Once it was red-hot, he pulled it from the flames and waved it in the air until it cooled to the touch.

"Do ya need any panther piss before I do the job?"

"Not now, I don't.  Save the drink for when ya cauterize the stubs."

"Ready?"

"Yep, have at 'er."

With one quick sweep of the razor-sharp blade, the remains of the toe fell to the dirt. Cotton gave a loud groan and then said through clenched teeth, "Rough pain, but a smooth job. Now, get me the corn juice."

Nate chuckled, more with relief than humor, and placed his blade back into the flickering flames. He then moved to the supplies and pulled a jug of traders whiskey and two cups. Then, returning to the fire, he filled both cups and handed one to Cotton.

Cotton swallowed his drink in two quick gulps and said, "One more cup and then we can finish this job."

Nate took a sip of his drink, then refilled Cotton's cup, and handed it back to him. Then, glancing at his knife blade, he said, "Get that down and we'll start the dance."

Raising his whiskey with trembling hands, Cotton replied, "Do the job right the first time, so I don't need to go under another hot knife. Once is enough." He then raised the whiskey to his mouth and emptied his cup. Placing the cup in the dirt beside him, he laid back and said, "Let's get this over with."

Nate removed the glimmering blade and was glad the toes were side by side, because he'd only need to use the knife once. The wide blade would cauterize both toes at the same time. He touched the toes with the blade and heard Cotton muffle a scream in his hands. Suddenly, the man's arms dropped and he was unconscious. Removing the knife, Nate leaned the blade on a rock as he poured whiskey on the injury and then wrapped it to keep it clean.

*Now, I need to check those Injuns and make sure all are dead. Hell, I should have done that before we did the doctorin', but didn't. It was a pilgrim thing to do, nonetheless,* he thought as he picked up his rifle and knife.

The brave with the knife buried in his chest was dead as hell, as were two others on Cotton's side of camp. When he neared the horses, Kills Silently was still where he fell. Nate, squatted and removed his scalp, adding it to the others he'd collected.

When he neared the man he'd shot when the fight started, he discovered the warrior still alive and singing his death song.

Nate squatted by the man and then pulled his knife.  The brave met his eyes just a few seconds before the big knife entered under the man's rib cage and was pulled to the side.  As Nate pulled the knife, he twisted the blade, knowing the brave would die quickly.  The warrior screamed, then moaned once, and died.  The blade was cleaned on the dead man's pant leg.

He scalped the man and then returned to the fire.  Sitting next to Cotton, he picked up his cup of whiskey and took a sip. He knew he'd spend the night keeping watch, because his part- ner was in no shape to travel.  The remainder of the night was quiet, except for an occasional moan from Cotton.  Every few minutes, Nate would feed the injured man straight whiskey, knowing the toes could hurt as badly as any other injury.

At daylight, he move from camp and looked for the horse belonging to the Sioux.  He moved slowly, knowing he'd most likely find a horse guard, and when he finally saw the mounts, a young boy of about ten was sitting on a huge rock.  *Damn me, he thought, maybe I can take this boy out without killin' 'em.*

Nate could see the young man was sleepy, so he hoped to move behind him and knock him out with the barrel of his pis- tol.  He moved forward slowly, as he approached the boy from behind.  He was about twenty feet from the lad, when he turned, saw Nate, and pulled his pistol.  He pointed at the big man, but Nate's pistol spat fire and the boy was knocked from the rock.  Reloading, Nate neared the Sioux and saw he was dead, struck almost between the eyes.  "Damn it, I didn't want to hurt his boy!"

He rounded up the ponies and took them back to camp. When he arrived, Cotton was sitting up, but his eyes were out of focus.  "By God, we'd better move this day, even iffen I'm hurt and drunk.  The Sioux will be comin'."

# Chapter 10

The trail to the gold was easy riding, so far, and Coon was excited. He had big dreams of beautiful women, good booze, excellent food, and money to burn. It was then, Blood Face said, *"We will now move into the mountains. We are entering the land of the Blackfoot. They do not let others live that move over their lands. It is a good day to die."*

*"Go and I will go with you."* Coon said and then thought, *but I don't plan on dying with all that gold waitin' to be picked up.*

*"From this point on, we must see when we look. We must hear when we listen. If the Blackfoot find us, there will be a big battle."*

"What's he sayin'?" Cy asked.

"We're about to enter Blackfoot country."

"So. What's a Blackfoot?"

"It's a tribe of Injuns and iffen they catch us, there will be a fight and no maybe about it. They're about as friendly as a grizzly bear with a toothache. Iffen they get on our asses, they'll never quit until we reach the Sioux village again or some place of safety—unless they kill us. Hard warriors they are."

"A . . . are ya sure they're around?"

"Well, they ain't around here right now."

"How do ya know that?"

"Because you'd be up to yer ass in pissed off Injuns or dead. Now, button your lip and keep it that way."

The trail was a winding one, that led up the side of a short mountain. At times they had to dismount and move logs or rock, so they could continue. Speaking in sign language, Blood Face said, *"This is good. If we must clear the trail, others have not been on our path for some time."*

*"Yes, but we must keep our eyes and ears open."* Coon signed in return.

*"A Sioux warrior is always ready for battle and we move like ghosts."*

*"Your words are spoken with one tongue."*

They traveled slowly and once at the top of mountain, the going down the other side was just as slow. Rains and melting snow had eroded the soil above the trail and mini-mud slides had occurred, leaving the trail covered in rock and dirt. Boulders were also discovered on the trail as well as fallen trees, so each obstacle had to be removed or ridden around, and that took time.

An hour before dark, Blood Face said, *"We must prepare a camp for the night. We can have no fire and must remain quiet."*

*"How will the guard be made? Which man on first?"* Coon asked.

The Sioux smiled and said, *"Only you and I will guard camp. The untested man will not guard us, because I do not trust my life to a man with no scalps. Only proven warriors will guard when we travel over the land of the Blackfoot."*

Coon nodded, then turned to Cy and said, "You'll not pull guard with us on this trip."

"Hell," Cy said with a smile, "that's fine with me, 'cause it gives me more sleepin' time."

Supper was a hard strip of buffalo jerky washed down with river water. As soon as they'd eaten, Coon moved off a ways to stand guard; he'd wake Blood Face when he grew tired or at midnight. The camp was quiet as the men wrapped up in their robes to sleep.

Most of the shift passed quietly with the sound of small animals scurrying around Coon as they played or searched for food. An owl was heard, as well as the lonely call of a wolf way off in the distance. The wolf was answered, perhaps by a mate, a few seconds later. *I wonder if that really was a wolf or Injuns talking with each other? Well, as long as I can hear the normal sounds, we're safe enough.*

Just before he was to awaken Blood Face, the sounds stopped and it grew quiet. Coon moved to Blood Face and Cy, waking both. The moon was full, so he used sign for the Sioux as he spoke to Cy, *"Night sounds are gone. Something big is out there or about to come down the trail. Move near the trail, but don't fire unless I do first."*

After they were in position, Coon spotted a lone Blackfoot warrior mounted on a big bay moving down the trail. He knew if it had been daylight, the brave would have spotted their tracks. Cy slipped and fell forward and the warrior stopped immediately at the noise. Dismounting, he moved to the side of the trail, his bow ready for use.

Coon glared at Cy and shook his head.

Suddenly a rabbit broke from the brush lining the trail and crossed the trail. The Blackfoot laughed as he moved toward his horse. The man mounted, shook his head, and while still wearing a grin, tapped his horse lightly in the ribs. He moved down the trail at a slow walk.

Five minutes after the warrior rode by, a group of about twenty warriors neared and at one point a brave asked what may have been a question. A few seconds later, a man answered, but he seemed to be angry. When the first man replied in an angry tone, the voice of a third man silenced them.

Once the warriors passed, Cy started to stand, but Coon pushed him back down and whispered, "Not yet."

A few minutes later a man riding drag rode by, scanning the woods as he moved. Coon and company remained in position for a good thirty minutes before returning to camp.

*"Blackfoot war party."* Blood Face stated with a flat voice.

*"It is good darkness surrounds us, or they would have seen our tracks."*

Blood Face nodded and then said, *"If they do not leave the trail before daylight, our tracks will be seen."*

*"Do you think they will return for us?"*

*"I cannot speak for the Blackfoot. If they are on a horse raid, the horses will be on their minds and not three riders. I would not return to follow three men, if I could count coup on my enemies or steal horses. They will know two of us are white men, by the iron shoes your horses wear and the maize you feed them."*

Coon nodded, but remind silent.

Cy asked, "What's goin' on?"

The mountain man explained and then Cy asked, "How in the hell will the Blackfoot know we're feeding our mounts corn?'

Shaking his head, Coon said, "You've a lot to learn, young pup. As a horse moves, it shits on the trail right?"

"Sure, and all the time."

"All a warrior has to do is dismount, pick up a horse apple and break it in two pieces. He'll be able to see the corn."

"But, how does that tell the man a white jasper was on the horse?" Cy asked, and he sounded confused.

"Injuns don't feed their horses grains at all. They turn 'em loose in a field and let 'em graze. Also, Injuns don't shoe a horse, so most ain't wearings horseshoes."

"So, all tracks in the dirt showing horseshoes are made by white men, right?"

"Wrong, youngster, because Injuns steal horses from white men, right?"

"Of course they do."

"Well, ain't no Injun gonna pull the shoes off a horse they steal. Now, when ya see horse tracks out here, remember two things. If the tracks ain't got shoes, look to see if the horse is carryin' weight and if so, it'll be Injuns. If the tracks are horses with shoes, then the riders could be white or red men."

"What iffen the horses ain't shod and not carryin' any weight?" Cy asked.

"Then they're wild stuff or something that got away from a camp."

Coons eyes narrowed as he said, "Next time we see Injuns and ya make noise like ya did tonight, I'll kill ya."

"My foot slipped and I fell forward."

"Out here, keep yer head out of yer ass all the time or you'll end up a dead man. When ya made that noise I almost shit my pants. *Don't ever* do something that stupid again, understand?"

"It was an accident."

"Iffen that damned rabbit hadn't crossed the road and that warrior thought it made the noise, you'd be explainin' yer accident to Devil right now. Blackfoot are a serious threat, young pup, and ya best be rememberin' it, too."

*"We move. I have bad feelings about our camp. I think the Blackfoot will return."* Blood Face suddenly stated and met Coon's eyes.

*"I agree. I do not trust the Blackfoot."*

*"Neither do I and that is why we are old warriors. We are wise men. Young men who do not use their minds are dead men before too many seasons pass."*

"Start gatherin' up gear, we're movin'." Coon said.

"I figured we would."

Two days later, with no sign the Blackfoot were following them, they were deep in the mountains near a narrow stream that couldn't have been more than three feet wide. The stream ran up a steep side of the mountain. Blood Face stopped his horse and said, *"We are at the yellow rock."*

*"Is it near or must be walk to it?"* Coon asked.

*"No walking. The yellow rock is found near the trail, to the right of the rushing waters."*

"Dismount, Cy, because the gold is near the trail on the right side of the stream. Pull the shovel from the packhorse, too."

Coon unforked his horse and moved to the water. Looking on the right side, he immediately spotted a huge chunk of gold. He filled with greed instantly as he moved toward the gold. *Sumbitch, that hunk alone is likely worth thousands of dollars and there's very little rotten quartz in it, too. Coon, yer a rich man!* Gold fever struck Coon, and it hit him hard.

Cy arrived with the shovel, glanced at the golden rock and said, "By God, we're rich! We're rich, Coon!"

*Ain't no we're rich gonna happen, because you'll die before we return to the village,* Coon thought and then said, "Hand me the shovel and I'll dig this thing out."

By the end of the day well over five hundred pounds of gold had been removed and placed in buckskin bags. The bags were stored under a canvas shelter Coon had erected. Both of the white men were tired, but Blood Face was bored. He'd spent the day watching the two crazy white men dig for rocks and found the situation amusing. Only a white man would value a rock.

Over supper, a small deer Blood Face had taken with his bow as the white men dug for gold, the warrior asked, *"Why do the white men value a rock?"*

*"Because it is gold. Gold is used to make things for people to wear on their hands, hang from their ears, or to buy things."*

*"What does the word buy mean? I have not heard it before."*

*"It is like trading. I see something I want, I give the man the yellow rock and he gives me what I wanted. We trade."*

White men must be foolish to trade anything for a rock, Blood Face thought and then said, *"I understand, but why for a rock?"*

Coon thought for a minute and then said, *"With the Sioux a man's wealth is counted by the number of horses he has, right?"*

*"Of course, that is the way of my people."*

*"The white men use the yellow rock to decide how wealthy a man is or not. The more yellow rock he has, the more wealth. Do you understand my words?"*

*"But a rock has no value, because it is just a rock."*

*"With your people it is just a rock. The white man cherishes the rock because it is not easy to find, which makes it valuable to us."*

*"I think white men are crazy. You cannot make love to a rock, eat a rock, or ride a rock, but all white men want the yellow rock. What kind of people are you?"*

Coon laughed and said, *"With the yellow rock a white man can buy many women, get much to eat, and buy a big herd of horses. The ways of the white man are not the ways of the Sioux. We are different, but the Great Spirit made us the way we are, just as he made The People."*

Blood Face nodded and then said, *"I will take the first watch. We must leave with the coming of a new sun, because I feel the Blackfoot on our trail."*

As Coon wrapped in his robe, he thought, just the gold we dug up today is worth well over a hundred thousand dollars. He smiled then pulled a bottle of rye he kept in his robe. He slowly removed the cork, so as to not awaken Cy, but he suspected Blood Face heard the noise. The swallowed a good hefty drink and then replaced the cork. Yep, no more nasty assed soiled doves mayhap with the French disease and cheap whiskey, Coon, yer in the big money now, old son. A few minutes later the whiskey kicked in and he was asleep.

Near daylight, as Coon stood guard, he thought he saw something moving. He turned his head and allowed his peripheral vision to catch the movement. For many minutes nothing moved, but finally he saw a spot of brown move slowly over the trail. Coon moved to where Blood Face and Cy were loading the horses.

"I saw movement on the trail," he said in English, then in Sioux.

Both men nodded and then Blood Face said, *"We will mount and ride down the trail quickly. They have been watching us for hours, I think. If a man falls as we ride, leave him, because to stop is to die."*

They mounted and when Coon looked at Cy, his eyes were huge and his fear obvious. The Sioux warrior said, *"When I give a war cry, ride like the wind. Have a loaded gun in your hands and be ready to kill."*

Coon translated the words to Cy and saw the man nod. The mountain man held the reins to three horses, loaded down with gold and knew there was no way he'd leave it behind.

Blood Face gave a piercing cry and kicked his horse in the ribs hard. He shot from camp moving at a full run down the trail. A Blackfoot warrior standing in the middle of the path was struck hard by the Sioux's horse. Shots were fired, but the three continued moving.

Suddenly, Cy screamed and when Coon glanced at the man he had three arrows in his back, he rode another hundred feet and fell from his horse. Coon thought in fear, *please God, save me and the gold so I can finally have something in my life. I never had much and You know that. Please!*

After about a mile, they slowed to a fast walk and Blood Face said, *"We are short one man."*

*"Yes, he was struck by arrows and fell from his horse. Are you without injury as I am?"*

*"No, I have taken a soft rock to my back. But, we cannot stop now. I will tell you when it is safe. We must travel far and fast to move from the Blackfoot."*

*"If you feel weak, let me know. You can be treated quickly."*

*"My mind knows this, only this is not the place."*

The whole day they kept moving until near dusk, Blood Face fell from his horse. Coon looked behind him, saw no one, and then dismounted. Moving to the warrior, he squatted and cut the front of his shirt open with a skinning knife. Lawdy, this jasper has lost a bunch of blood. Looks like the bullet hit him in the back and then exited the front.

Quickly applying bandages to the entrance and exit holes, he tied them in place and then placed the warrior on his horse belly down. He tied the man in place, mounted, and then continued to move. He glanced overhead and saw rainclouds moving toward him and he prayed for rain, because the water would wash away his tracks.

Coon rode until late and it had started raining hours ago. He'd heard nothing from Blood Face and when he checked on the man, he was dead. The mountain man cut the ropes and let the body fall into the mud. Pulling up under a large pine tree, he ate some jerky and curled up in his robe. Three hours later, he was up and moving again. Only now he had two horses, so he could ride the other when one grew tired. The pack horses were tired and he knew it, so he turned toward the Sioux village for safety. He rode through the night.

Late afternoon, the next day, as he rode, he noticed movement on his left and when he glanced in that direction he spotted a Sioux dog soldier watching him. Coon raised his hand and waved at the warrior, but continued riding for the village. He felt great relief, just knowing the warrior would spot the Blackfoot if they were still on his tail.

Just as he started feeling cocky and thinking he'd gotten away clean, a small group of four Blackfoot warriors broke from a stream bed on his left, and rode for him. He raised his rifle, fired and one warrior fell from his horse, screaming. Pulling a pistol, he aimed, fired, but missed. Pulling his last pistol, he waited for the other three Blackfoot to grow nearer.

Suddenly two shots rang out and two of the Blackfoot dropped to the grasses, but the last was determined to kill Coon. On the warrior came and within ten feet of the white man, the brave raised his arm and Coon saw a club made from the jaw bone of a buffalo. Using his rifle to block the strike by the warrior, he hardly felt a knife blade enter his right shoulder. The Blackfoot quickly turned his horse and came at the mountain man once more. When the warrior neared, Coon swung his rifle like a club and felt the heavy weapon strike the man on his neck. The brave fell to the ground and before he could move, the mountain man jumped from his horse and cut the braves throat.

As the dying Blackfoot's feet kicked madly at the grasses, Coon felt dizzy and dropped to the ground. He looked at his wound, saw blood flowing down his whole arm, and reached for his possibles bag. Removing a long piece of cotton material, he wrapped it up tightly. Then, he reloaded his guns.

Hearing a noise behind him, he swung his rifle around, but saw four Sioux warriors watching him. Finally, the one in the middle said, *"You have scalps to take, if you can do so with your injury."*

Knowing the Sioux expected him to take hair, Coon stood and moved toward the man he'd shot. He scalped the man and then moved to the second one. Running his knife around the warriors head, he suddenly felt faint, but after a few seconds the hair was in his hands. Unlike the Sioux warriors, who raised the hair to the heavens and gave a war cry, the mountain man simply mounted and moved toward the village. When he entered the small community, he spotted Clyde by the trade blankets.

Approaching the man, Coon suddenly grew lightheaded and fell from his horse. He was out before he struck the ground. Clyde, seeing the horses, smiled and thought, *iffen the sumbitch dies, all that gold will be mine. I wonder where Cy and that warrior is that went with 'em?*

# Chapter 11

"Nate sat by the fire and fed alcohol to the feverish Cotton most of the night. The injured man had spent a full day in the saddle, but he wasn't sitting straight doing the job. He'd tied a full whiskey bottle to his pommel and at times Nate had seen him taking a nip or two. Nate knew Cotton had sand in his craw, because he was as tough as they come. Most men back east would have been in bed calling for their wives every few minutes to get them something. No, Cotton was a mountain man and a tough one.

Nate pulled the rag down that covered the knife wound to his arm, sniffed the injury and grinned, because it was healing nicely. He picked up a cup of raw traders whiskey, poured a little on the injury, and gritted his teeth against the pain. He then wrapped the arm in a new bandage and burned the soiled one in the fire. He poured another cup of whiskey, but for his pain, and thought, *we're both injured but we keep movin' which is much more than most flatlanders could do. We need to get to Butterfield's Tradin' Post so we can both rest a mite. With a little luck, we should be there at some point in the mornin'.*

About three hours before daylight, he ate a long hard piece of jerky, let the fire die down and then rolled up in his robe. *I need some rest, if we're travelin' tomorrow. I just hope I don't come down with a fever or there'll be hell to pay. One of us has to stay alert or we'll have problems.* Seconds later, he drifted off to sleep.

Right at daylight, Nate opened his eyes, sat up, and glanced at the sky. Not a cloud was seen, so he made his way to Cotton and discovered his fever broken and he was awake.

"How ya feelin' this mornin'?" Nate asked.

"Like a team of horses ran over my ass.  I hurt in places I didn't even know I had.  Nonetheless, I'll ride today."

"Yer fever is gone.  Do ya feel like eatin'?  Ya didn't have any supper, so ya should at least have some broth."

Picking up the whiskey bottle, Cotton took a long swallow, grinned at his partner and replied, "Yep, I'll get the broth down, but nothin' heavy yet.  We should be at Butterfield's place be- fore noon and I'll eat some of his cookin'.  Yer a good man, but ya cain't cook worth a shit."

Nate chuckled and then moved to the long dead fire.  He soon found a live coal under the gray ash and before long had flames crackling as they ate at the dry kindling.  He kept his fire small, about the size of a dinner plate, and as soon as it was burning good, he placed the broth and coffee on the flames.

Over the simple breakfast they made small talk.  Cotton wanted to talk about Coon, but Nate said, "Iffen he's out here, we'll hear about 'em sooner or later.  However, iffen he isn't here, we'll start to look, because he owes us his life, and I in- tend to collect the payment.  The subject is a dead horse as fer as I'm concerned."

"Well, let me have a couple of good snorts of this whiskey and we can ride.  How's the arm wound?"

"Clean and healing good.  Sore as hell, so when ya finish your drink, I'm needin' a couple belts myself."

After Nate's drinks, they mounted and headed toward But- terfield's, both looking forward to a little rest and a good meal or two.  The old trader was a good cook, but folks often teased him about his food, which he took in good humor.  While on the outside Butterfield appeared rough and mean, inside he was as gentle as a lamb.  His kindness came out when someone was injured or sick, then he'd do what it took to care for the person.

As they rode, Cotton said, "Ya know, you'd figure havin' two toes shot off wouldn't hurt as much as it does.  Damn, they're healing fast too, but I'm sore as all get out."

"I think any body part that's removed hurts, or at least any I've lost hurt when the job was done.  I remember a couple of years back when we removed a leg from Bill Thomas, and it only hurt him for a day."

"What?  Ya mean ya removed a man's leg and it only both-ered him for a day?  Now, I ain't callin' ya a liar, but that's hard to believe."

"Actually," Nate said as he gazed into the other man's eyes, "since he died on us, the pain didn't last as long as it usually does."

"Ya can slide, old son."

Two days later, they stopped on a slight hill and gazed at But-terfield's Trading Post in the valley before them.  The weather was cool, but not cold and both men wore copotes against a light wind from the north.

Cotton said, "Ya know, the tradin' post ain't much, not really, when ya look at 'er, but she'll do fine when ya hurt like a sumbitch."

"Yep, I'm hurtin' a mite as well.  Let's go down, order a bottle of panther piss and relax a little.  I feel like death warmed over, and suspect I have a slight fever."

They rode to the hitching post and as they were tying the horses, Butterfield came out holding a big double-barrel Greener shotgun.  When he recognized the two men, he low-ered and then placed the gun against the wall of the structure. Smiling he said, "Well, now, iffen it ain't ugly and uglier, and in the flesh, but ya both look a bit rough around the edges."

"We're both injured.  Cotton lost two toes and I took a knife to my right upper arm.  It's not that big a deal, but we were headed this direction when the Injuns attacked.  Ya got any food cooked?"

"Yep, beans and deer meat with biscuits, unless ya want me to fry ya a steak."

"No, it'll do and bring us a bottle of good whiskey, too." Cotton replied.

"Well, come on in and take a table, before ya both fall over. Nate, I suspect ya have a fever by lookin' at yer face and you've one as well, Cotton." Butterfield picked up his shotgun and entered the log structure.

The trader filled two plates and added three biscuits to each and took them to the table. Then, returning to the counter, he pulled out two bottles of good Kentucky whiskey, and brought three tin cups. Placing the drink on the table, he filled the cups and slid one in front of each man, keeping the last one for himself. He then pulled out a chair and sat.

"Anything goin' on we need to know about?" Nate asked around a big bite of deer meat.

"Yep, seems Coon is, or was back, and livin' with the Sioux. I had a young warrior by the name of Running Pony come in here, oh, 'bout a week back and he told me about Coon. I don't think the man will stick around."

Cotton had a spoon of beans almost to his mouth, but hesitated and asked, "Oh, and why not?"

"Running Pony said the man traded Hawken rifles and some other foofaraw to the Sioux and then went into the mountains. It seems once he was in the hills, he found a hell of a lot of gold. Now, ya both know the Sioux don't measure weight, so when I asked how much yellow rock the man had, the brave told me, 'many horses.'"

Nate thought for a moment and then asked, "Was Coon still in the village?"

"Running Pony said he was, but I suspect he's gone by now. He told the Sioux he'd bring them many more guns the next visit, but iffen he's got all that gold, why would he return?"

"Greed. He ain't satisfied with the money from the plew he took, and the gold won't be enough either."

"Yep," Cotton said, "and we all know Coon is greedy. Hell, that's why he killed 'Possum's and John's trappin' buddies to start with, for the furs. I hate men like that, ya know, the kind that think they can get something fer free. Hell, life ain't never gave me nothin' free, but a hard time."

Nate took a sip of his whiskey and then asked, "Butterfield, where is the closest place for him to have that gold assayed and to sell it?"

"Fort Atkinson, but he'll not get top dollar fer it. Iffen he's smart and as greedy as ya claim, he'll take 'er to Saint Louie, where he'll get some good money. He'll get top dollar fer it there."

"Did Running Pony say how many men were with Coon? I know the sumbitch didn't come out here alone, because he ain't got the balls."

"I ain't rightly sure, but I seem to remember his sayin' Coon had three fingers of men with him. He did say Coon had an injury to his shoulder and as soon as it healed, he would leave."

Cotton gazed into Nate's eyes and asked, "We've been ridin' together fer years, so what's on yer mind?"

"Well, I don't think Coon will be that hard to find in Saint Louis, not iffen he's got all that gold with 'em. See, he'll have to sell it to a bank, establish an account, and with all that money he'll get a hankerin' to spend some of it."

"By God, so would any man."

"And," Nate said and then took a bite of beans, "I'll bet ya dollar against a horseshoe, he'll enter the town alone. I suspect he'll kill the men ridin' with 'em, but not until he's close to the city. Coon's a smart man, or he has been up to this point."

Cotton grinned and asked, "So, when do we leave for the city?"

"In a week. We need time to heal and the time will be well spent. Coon will relax, figure he's safe, and then start to spend some money. Once the word gets out about the man, we'll find 'em, so there ain't a rush."

Butterfield said, "That's smart thinkin', Nate."

"Momma Grisham didn't raise no fools, but ain't none of us considered handsome." Nate said and then laughed.

"Now, I'm gonna heat up some water and I need both of ya to get a bath. Once yer clean, we'll doctor up yer wounds and ya can drink some willow bark to cut yer fevers."

"Boil the bark first and by the time it cools down, I'll have my bath done. I'll add it to my whiskey." Cotton said.

Nate said, "I agree with Cotton, iffen ya want us to drink anything, it'll go in our whiskey. I hurt all over, so let's get this job done."

"I need one of y'all to get some more firewood that's stacked by the side of this place and the other to run to the river and fill a few buckets of water. Since Cotton has the foot injury, Nate, why don't ya fetch the water."

Gulping the remainder of their whiskey, the two men started on the chores.

An hour later, as Cotton soaked in the tub, Butterfield was working on Nate's arm. The old trader picked up a jug of alcohol he used to treat hurts and said, "This will sting a mite, but it's startin' to fester on ya, so that's why ya had the pain."

When the rough traders alcohol hit his wound, Nate gave a loud sigh. His eyes watered and he asked, "Ya don't have to cauterize it, do ya?"

"No, no, it's not that serious. The injury is not deep and for sure not serious, but it'd turned that way in a week or so. How often did ya change the bandage?"

"That's the second one."

"We'll change it everyday and use alcohol on it, too."

Cotton entered the room wearing clean buckskins, just like Nate, and sat on a chair. He waited until Butterfield completed wrapping up his partner before he said, "The ends of my toes are red, but no streaks or sign of festerin' that I can see."

"Well, prop that foot up here, twixt my legs and let me take a gander." Cotton propped the foot up, Butterfield smelled the injury and looked it over closely before he added, "Yers is actually healin' better than Nate's. I'd suspect in another three or four days yer pain will be gone."

"Wounds are queersome, iffen ya ask me. I've seen fellers with gunshot wounds heal faster than a hangnail and I cain't fer the life of me figure it out. Hell, ole One Eye Johnson died from a finger he cut skinnin' a buffalo."

Butterfield chuckled, wiped his hands off with a clean towel, and then said, "Ain't nobody that knows what causes it. Some doctors say it's the air, dirt, or water, that cause an injury to go bad. I've learned iffen ya keep the injury clean, pour whiskey on it everyday, it'll likely not go bad. Now, I never burn a man with a hot knife without pouring whiskey on it when I'm done, either."

"Speakin' of whiskey," Nate joked, "let's get down to some serious drinkin'."

"Well, just make sure ya add some willow bark tea to the drink and you'll be fine." Butterfield said with a grin.

Four days later, the two men rode from Butterfield's and headed east. It was fall now, and the weather would likely turn bad before they reached the big city by the muddy river. They had a packhorse loaded down with supplies and some canned foods they'd purchased from the old trader.

Cotton looked up and said, "Either rain or snow comin' and today, fer sure."

Nate shrugged and replied, "It doesn't matter much to me, because I've traveled in both."

"This damned Coon is turnin' hard to catch. Ya was right, though, he did turn up in the mountains and Butterfield had word. We should have stayed in Saint Louie when we were there the last time."

"Hell, ya and I both know, we'd gone crazy in that place if-fen we stayed more than three days. I can't stand to feel crowded and that city does the job."

Snowflakes began to fall and Nate asked, "Keep ridin' or hunt a hole?"

"Keep ridin', because I don't think this will amount to much."

Two hours later, the snow was flying horizontal and the wind had picked up.

Yelling to be heard over the weather conditions, Nate asked, "Ya ready to hunt a hole yet or do ya still think it won't amount to much?"

Cotton grinned and then shouted, "Hunt a hole!"

Since both men were seasoned mountain men, establishing a camp was easy and fast, with a fire dancing wildly from the wind. Pulling out a side of bacon, Cotton started frying three thick pieces for each of them and heated some beans Butter-field had placed in fruit jars. Pulling out two large chunks of cornbread, Nate placed them near the fire to warm.

"Every damned time I head toward Saint Louie, it either rains like a sumbitch or snows, never fails." Cotton said as he met Nate's eyes.

"It's because it's such a long trip, not because God wants the weather rough for us. Ya figure it'll take almost forty-five days to get there and that's a lot of time to travel."

"How about when we come back we ride a boat up the Missouri River, huh?  I ain't never been on a big boat and ya said it was faster."

"Oh, it's a lot faster.  Ya got the kind of money they'll want fer tickets?"

Cotton scratched his scraggly looking beard and replied, "No, I ain't."

"Well, it won't happen then, unless the money for killin' Kramer is waitin' fer us at Fort Atkinson.  Iffen the money is there, we'll take a boat upriver."

"It could be, because we've been gone a spell, ya know.  And, five thousand dollars is a lot of cash money, too."

"We'll share it, like we do everything, except it's likely we'll have to take the bank draft to Saint Louis to cash it.  Ain't no banks at Fort Atkinson."

"Hell, that ain't no problem, because we're goin' there any-way."

Fort Atkinson had changed little and folks were still running around like a hill of ants, in all directions.  Nate took a good look as they entered the only open gate and said, "Ya reckon most of these folks are always in a rush?  Every time we come here, folks seem to be in a hurry."

Cotton replied, "Most of the men are army troops and they're always in a hurry to get someplace, so they can wait. See, they rush to eat, but wait in line.  They rush to form up nice and pretty in the mornin's, then wait for some officer to come to talk with 'em.  Sergeant Major Armitage told me the unofficial motto of the army is, 'hurry up and wait.'"

"Speakin' of Armitage, let's ride to the orderly room and see iffen he's there.  We can find out about the reward money, too."

"Well, it's off on the left side there, so let's ride over and find out."

They'd just tied their horses to a hitching post when the door opened and out stepped Sergeant Major Armitage.  He gave a big smile and then said, "I've something for ya in the orderly room.  Come in with me and I'll give ya a letter of authorization from the Federal Government for payment of $5,000.00, which ought bring a smile to your faces."

"Lead the way," Cotton replied and then added, "Then we'll share a bottle with ya."

As they entered the log structure, Armitage replied, "Not this afternoon, because I've some serious work to do.  It seems the Sioux have been using some new rifles and raisin' hell with any whites they find on their lands.  Captain Carter is leadin' A company out to search for 'em and I'm to go along to keep the young man out of trouble.  Hell, Carter don't know a Sioux from a Crow."

Nate said, "Iffen that's the case, any Injuns the good Captain sees will be Sioux."

Armitage laughed, as he walked to his desk, opened the top drawer and pulled out an envelope. Handing it to Nate he said, "It's payable to Nate Grisham and Cotton Top Thomas, so either one of ya can cash 'er.  Nearest place to cash it would be Saint Louis, but hell, I've ridden that far before and for a lot less."

"Me too." Cotton said.

The Sergeant Major shook both of their hands as he said, "I need to get my horse ready to ride.  Best of luck with all of that money.  Oh, before I forget, did ya find Coon Turner?"

"No, not face-to-face, but we know where he's headed." Nate replied.

"Where would that be?"

Cotton laughed and said, "Same place we are—Saint Louis."

# Chapter 12

Coon was happy and yet angered at the same time. They'd done well with the Sioux trading and he knew they had thousands of dollars in horses, furs and gold. His anger came from the fact they'd taken some horses in trade while he'd been looking for gold with Bloody Face. He'd planned to kill three remaining men once they got closer to Saint Louis and while he could yet do that, the horses were worth around twenty dollars a head. If he kept the horses, then he'd be forced to share some of the fur and gold money and he didn't want to do that. Since he was three days out of Saint Louis, he was wondering when to kill the men riding with him.

*Hell, the whiskey alone brought me a couple of thousand dollars in furs*, he thought with a grin. He'd traded each gallon jug of traders whiskey, which cost him a dollar, for ten furs and while the quality of the furs varied, most were prime skins.

"Startin' to snow, Coon. Do ya want us to hunt a hole?" Clyde asked as he rode to the man.

"Naw, hold off a spell and let's see what the weather does. I'd hate to get a camp up and then see this shit stop."

"Iffen the wind picks up or this stuff starts to stick, we'll have to camp."

"What did I just tell ya?"

"Okay, yer the boss." Then turning to Thomas and Jonas, he yelled out, "Keep 'em movin' for a bit longer."

An hour later, with the wind now screaming, the men established camp. The temperature had dropped and snow was coming down hard. Starting a fire was a task, even for Clyde, but finally the flames were flickering and dancing as the wind blew.

"Take a couple of pieces of canvas and make a windbreak on the wind side of our fire or we'll freeze our asses off out here.  Hell, with the flames being blown like they are, we'll not even be able to cook." Coon ordered.

Clyde said, "Jonas, pull some canvas from our supplies and let's block this wind.  Thomas, ya cut some of that deer meat and put it in our big pot, along with some beans.  We'll need hot soup on a cold night like this one."

Minutes later, the wind now blocked from the fire, Thomas placed the pot on the flames.  Coon reached behind him and pulled a bottle of traders whiskey near.  He pulled the cork and said, "Get yer cups and each of us can have one cup of joy juice to fight off the chills."

"How much gold do ya think we have?" Jonas asked as he held his cup out.

"Well, with gold fetchin' twenty dollars an ounce, and I guess we have about five hundred pounds, the value will be around a hundred and sixty thousand dollars." Coon said.

Clyde smiled and then said, "That's roughly forty thousand each, if we live to spend it."

Coon cringed, suspecting Clyde knew they'd not live to reach the city alive, but he replied, "We'll make it, hell, why not?"

"That much money could turn an honest man bad and do the job quick like, too.  I don't trust a single one of ya sumbitches, but at least I'm honest about it. Just so ya all know, from now on, I sleep with one eye open."  Clyde said as he held his cup out for some of the drink.

"Look," Coon said, "we have to trust each other or we'll end up killin' each other.  We do that and we'll end up with nothin', but a grave."

Thomas took a drink of whiskey and said, "Well, I ain't greedy.  Whatever I end up with is more than I have right now.  Shit, I ain't never had over a hundred dollars in my life.  Iffen I get that kind of money I'll buy me a farm, a couple of good lookin' women, and stay drunk all the time."

Jonas laughed and said, "Hell, that's the only way ya could get a woman is buyin' one.  Yer so ugly I'll bet yer momma didn't even kiss ya goodnight when she put ya in bed as a kid."

His eyes narrow, Thomas said brusquely, "Ya leave my momma out of this. She's a good woman and I won't take no bad talk about my family."

"Relax, Thomas, I meant nothin' bad about yer momma. I was just teasing ya is all and don't take it as any more than that."

"Okay, but leave my family out of our talks in the future."

Coon finishing his drink said, "I'm still chilled, so one more and then I'll put the jug away."

As he poured the whiskey, he thought, *the first to die will be Clyde, he's the most dangerous of the three. Then, I can kill the two kids any time. I just have to figure out when and where. Then, I can just leave the horses and go on my way. Better yet, I need to think on this a while.*

After the drinks and simple meal, the men turned in early, and Coon was on the next to last guard shift. As he rolled up in his buffalo robe, he thought, tonight I'll kill Clyde and take care of the horses. Then, at some point in the next day or two, I can get rid of the other two, once we're closer to the city.

Jonas woke Coon a little after midnight, but not a word was spoken as they changed places. Once Coon heard Jonas snoring lightly, he pulled his sharp skinning knife. He made his way to Clyde slowly. Once in position, he wasted no time as he threw his hand over the mountain man's mouth and slit his throat. Clyde's eyes flew open and he stared Coon in the eyes as his blood spurted with each beat of his heart and his feet kicked madly in all directions. Coon thought the man was pleading, only it was too late for that, because within two minutes, Clyde was dead.

Moving to the Sioux horses, Coon cut the ropes and when the animals stood unmoving, he shot his pistol into the air. Horses ran wildly from camp, as the other mounts danced on the picket line.

"Injuns!" Coon screamed.

They all moved into the darkness for many long minutes, but after an hour, just as the sun was peeking over the trees, Coon called out, "Yell yer name and let me know iffen yer okay!"

"Jonas, I'm fine."

"Thomas and I'm okay, too."

"Jonas, get the fire built up and Thomas, meet me by the fire."

Once they were all at the dying fire, Jonas added wood as Coon asked, "Did either of ya see Clyde, because he didn't answer my call."

"No, I saw nothing or no one the whole time."  Jonas replied.

"Me either."

Coon said, "Thomas, go check where Clyde was sleepin' and iffen he's hurt give us a yell."

As Thomas moved toward Clyde's sleeping spot, Jonas asked, "Did we lose all the Sioux horses?"

"From what I could tell we did, but it's hard to tell in the dark.  I suspect that's what they were after from the start."

"Coon, ya need to come over here!"  Thomas called out.

Standing, then dusting his pants free of snow, he made his way to the young man. Stopping just outside the lean-to Clyde put up, he asked, "What's wrong?"

"Looks like the Injuns killed Clyde.  I don't know iffen he was stabbed or not, but his throat was cut."

"They caught 'em sleepin' then.  Has he been scalped?"

"No, he's still got his hair."

"Then when I shot at 'em I must have scared the brave off."

Thomas thought for a minute and then said, "Could be, but I don't know much about Injuns.  Those Sioux were the first I've ever seen and I didn't trust 'em at all, even iffen they did treat us pretty good."

"Let's move back to the fire, hell, the Injuns are gone and ain't no use fer us to freeze our balls off, especially when it won't help Clyde."

"What do we do now?"  Jonas asked.

"Load up and get ready to move.  We have no idea if those injuns went back for help or left for good. I know I hit one, but I couldn't tell iffen the shot was a killing one or not."

"We ain't gonna bury Clyde?"  Thomas asked.

"Ya can, iffen ya want, but I don't think we should stick around any longer than needed.  Next time those Injuns come back, they'll want our scalps."

Jonas said, "I agree."

Coon said, "Now, get it all loaded and let's move."

Most of the snow was still on the ground, but Coon suspected most of it would be gone by noon. If *so, he'd kill the two boys a little after midday. Maybe do the job at our nooning, because I'm close to the city now.*

While they rode, the two younger men joked about what they would do with their share of the money, which was larger now that Clyde was gone.

"I'm gonna buy me a whorehouse and saloon. Hell, there's always money to be made in women and whiskey." Thomas said.

"Not me. I'm gonna go live in New Orleans and get three women to live with me. But, first I'm goin' on a week-long drunk. How about you, Coon?" Jonas replied and then looked at the old mountain man.

"Not sure yet. I may keep it in the bank a while, but I'll likely get a woman and drink a spell."

The rambling went on all morning and when they stopped for a noon meal, Coon had Jonas start a fire and Thomas gather wood. He considered shooting them then, but decided to eat a bit first. He was in no hurry, because he knew at some point today both men would die.

Once a meal of warmed up beans and fried bacon was gone, they mounted and headed east. They were riding along side a narrow stream, in a short grass covered field, then Coon said, "You two go on ahead, I'm gonna drop back and check the knots on some of that gold."

As Jonas and Thomas moved forward, Coon picked up the rifle he had laying over his saddle and aimed at the man on the left. At the sound of the hammer cocking, both men turned to look at him and Coon squeezed the trigger. The shot took Thomas in the middle of his back and blood and bone blew out his chest as the bullet exited. He screamed and fell from his horse, where he began to thrash and jerk.

Jonas brought a pistol up, but before he could fire, Coon fired his pistol and the shot took the young man in the forehead. His skull exploded as the big fifty caliber bullet struck and he fell to the grasses   dead before he hit the ground.

Coon dismounted and pulled his skinning knife. He'd come too far to leave a witness alive. He walked to Thomas and squatted by the dying man.  Thomas met his eyes and asked, "W . . . why?"

The old mountain man gave a mighty laugh and replied, "Well, now I have all the gold to myself.  See, when I hired y'all, I intended to kill ya before we returned to Saint Louis anyway, only I never expected to be rich on the way back."

"Y . . . you . . . no good . . . *sumbitch.*"

Quick thrusting of his knife under the younger man's rib cage, Coon pulled the knife from side to side, jerking the blade as it moved.  Thomas gave a horrible scream, gazed into the mountain man's eyes, as if to ask why, and then gave a violent shudder.  One loud sigh followed—he was dead.

"Damn, son, but ya die hard." Coon said as he wiped his knife clean on the dead man's trouser legs.  Mounting his horse, taking the reins of the pack animals with the gold, he then began to sing:

"A woodpecker pecked on an outhouse door,
He pecked and pecked until his pecker got sore,
Then he flew away and didn't peck no more."

He then gave a loud insane laugh.

Riding to a fur trader, other than O'Briens, Coon walked in and said, "I've a bundle of plew outside.  Get a couple of men and unload them for me.  Count them and weigh them, and I'll be back for payment later.  Now, don't try to trick me, because I know exactly how many plew I have."

"I'm James E. Westman and I run an honest business here."

"That ya might do, Westman, but the last time I brought furs into this town I was robbed."

"Well, by God, it wasn't by me.  I pay a fair amount fer all plew. John, Mark, and Luke, unload the man's packhorses."

"I'll be back in an hour, because I have some trouble to report."

"I'll have ya a draft ready, but I need a name."

"Turner, Robert Turner." Coon replied.

Coon walked from the building right behind the three men and mounted.  Taking the reins of the horses carrying the gold, he move toward the first bank.  Glancing at the name, First Missouri National Bank, he tied his horse to the hitching post. Speaking to a young man walking by, he asked, "Do ya want to earn a dollar for fetchin' the manager of this bank fer me?"

"Why cain't ya do it?"

"I hurt my back and can't move as well as I once did.  Tell the man I have some very serious business to speak to him about.  I'll give this to ya when the manager comes out that door."  He pulled a silver dollar from his pocket.

"Sure, I'll do the job."  The man entered the bank.

Five or ten minutes later, the young man walked out with an older man and said, "This is Mister Franklin, he's the bank manager."

As Coon and Franklin shook hands, the mountain man said, "I'm Robert Turner."

"Is that all you need, mister?" The young man asked and the mountain man knew the boy wanted payment.

Coon tossed the young man a dollar and said, "Now, get lost, I've some business to discuss with this man. "

Once the young man was moving away from him, Coon said, "Do ya buy rough gold?"

"Yes, sir, we do. The going rate is twenty dollars an ounce, but does it have a great deal of quartz?"

"Hell, I don't know much about that quartz shit, but it's a big chunk."

"And, how much is a big chunk, roughly, sir?"

"Over five hundred pounds."

Turning, the man said, "Wait right here until I get someone to look the gold over and post some armed guards."

Coon walked to his saddlebags and said, "Ya get who ya need to get, but I'm gonna have me some whiskey while I wait."

Franklin entered the bank but was back out with three men sporting shotguns and another man that looked to at least seventy years old. Lifting the bottle to his lips, Coon took a long deep swig and then asked, "Which of ya wants to see the gold?"

"Why, Bill and I both have to see it. I will have it brought in and weighed, just as soon as Bill verifies it is in fact gold."

Coon unforked his horse.

Bill, the old man, moved with Coon to the first horse. The old mountain man pulled his knife, cut the canvas holding the gold and pulled out a chunk that must have weighed ten pounds. He handed it to Bill.

"This appears to be of excellent quality, Franklin, but I need to take it into the bank and run an acid test and look it over closer. I see very little rotten quartz."

Coon raised his bottle, took another long drink and said, "Do what ya have to do, peckerwood, but remember where that piece come from."

Bill met his eyes and replied, "Yes, yes, of course. Franklin, get some men to unload this gold, weigh it, and place it in the vault. By the time you're finished I'll have the results of my testing."

Coon stood by the horses as each piece of gold was unloaded, and before the trip he'd counted how many pieces he had brought east. Since the smallest chunk was the size of his fist, the numbering had been easy.

Thirty minutes later, he was in the vault counting the gold, just to make sure none had disappeared en-route. Finally, he said, "It's all there, once Bill adds his piece back."

Bill entered the vault and said, "Mister Turner, you have a fortune in gold here, well worth over $165,000.00 at the current rate. It's of the finest quality and passed all tests with flying colors."

Franklin said, "Add the tested gold to the rest and exactly how much gold was brought into the bank?"

"I show five hundred and ninety six pounds and one ounce. That comes to $195,740.00, even."

"Good God, that much?"

"Yep, but this is good quality, Franklin."

*It's worth more than that to these bastards, but that's more than enough for me to live a hundred lifetimes,* Coon thought and said, "Put most of it, for right now, into an account for me. I want a thousand dollars in cash today, so would that be a problem?  Now, before ya ask, I don't have a home yet, just got into town from the mountains."

Franklin gave a false smile and said, "Not a problem at all, because we at the bank fully understand.  If you'll come with me, I'll see, personally, that your account is opened and do the paperwork.  I want to thank you for choosing us as your bank."

"Sure, peckerwood, let's get the paperwork done and let me get the hell out of here."

At the fur traders,  James E. Westman smiled as Coon entered his small office.  He reached into the top drawer of his desk, pulled out a bottle of bourbon and asked, "Drink before business?"

"Sure and fill my glass.  I'm tired, dirty, hungry and need a woman."

Pouring the amber colored drink into water glasses, Westman handed the first one to Coon, smiled again, and said, "To future business together."

Downing about half of his drink, Coon asked, "So, what are the plew worth?"

"Right close to $10,000 but I cain't pay that much."

The old mountain man knew the game and played along, "How much can ya offer?"

"Six thousand."

Coon slammed his glass down on Westman's desk and said, "Load them damned plew back on my animals!  I have to have over eight thousand or I walk out the door.  My God, man, I had friends on this trip that were killed and I promised to send their share to their families."  He sprang from his chair.

"Whoa, sit back down and let's talk.  To be honest with ya, I can only go as high as exactly eight thousand and not a penny more.  I'm not a rich man, but I do well enough.  If that's not enough, then I can't buy yer furs."

"Write me out a bank draft right this minute.  I'll take yer offer, but I'll not be back."

Westman looked shocked as he asked, "Why not, I was honest with ya?"

Coon laughed and replied, "No, it's not because of ya at all.  See, on this trip the Blackfoot almost killed my ass.  I promised myself I'd never return to trappin'.""

"What will ya do now?"

"Send a big portion of this money to the families of my dead men and see iffen I'll have enough for a small farm way back in the hills."

Filling out a bank draft, Westman handed it to Coon and said, "You're a good man then, because most men wouldn't do what you're doin'."

Downing the rest of his drink, Coon took the draft, grinned and said, "Thank ya, Mister Westman, and it's been nice doin' business with you."

"May God bless you, Robert Turner." Westman said as they shook hands.

I surely hope so, Coon thought.

# Chapter 13

Cotton found Clyde's body when they stopped for the night. It'd been there for a week and the smell caught the old mountain man's attention.

"Nate, got a body over here and he's dressed in buckskins."

The big mountain man walked to Cotton, looked down at Clyde and said, "Be hard fer his own momma to know who he is, because the critters been feedin' on 'em."

Cotton squatted and picked up the possibles bag laying next to the dead man. Opening it he pulled out the usual stuff: flint and steel, bullets, jerky and then a stack of letters. He opened a letter and read silently. Finally he said, "This fellers name is Clyde Anderson, and he was a mountain man from Boston. Looks like this letter on top is from his momma, and she says she's worried about 'em and been prayin' for 'em."

"Keep the whole collection and we'll mail it to the woman once in the city. I'll write 'er a nice letter and tell 'er he died quickly and with no pain. Mayhap she'll get some comfort from my words."

"I hear ya. Nate, most of his clothes are ripped to hell, but I don't see no bullet holes in this jasper at all. Well, not that hit any bone, but with him opened like he is from the animals it's pretty hard to tell."

"Who knows what killed 'em, but where's his horse and supplies? I can't imagine his partners not buryin' 'em, unless they were all up to no good. There weren't any Injuns hard on their asses, because the tribes here are all friendly. Anyway, bring those letters and see if you can find anything else on or around him. I'll take our animals about a hundred yards up wind, so we don't have to sleep with the smell."

Later that evening after supper, as they sat around the small fire, Cotton was silently reading papers he'd recovered from the body. Nate, however, was looking over a clump of gold that'd been found in the dead man's pack. *Now, according to Butterfield, Coon was out with a Sioux warrior looking for the yellow rock, so mayhap this feller was one of the men with 'em,* he thought.

"Didn't Butterfield say that Coon was known to have found some gold?"

Looking at the gold in Nate's hands, he nodded and replied, "Yep, and a bunch, iffen ya want to believe the warriors that came to trade. And, I've never met a Injun that lies."

"Well, I think this yahoo was one of the men riding with 'em. If so, we'll find more bodies up the trail a mite. Any man who'll killed for plew will surely kill for gold, and he'll want it all for himself, too. Coon Turner ain't ever been known to share, not since he turned bad."

"Gold can bring out greed in the best of men. Hell, it's like a disease once the word gets out. Some folks can smell it, others feel when it nears, but all I've ever seen it do is cause problems. Hell, that's how Bear lost his wife a while back."

"I know Bear's story, so don't go kickin' a dead horse. Did you find anything important in those papers?"

"Clyde was the dead man's name and he's from Boston. He spent two years out west, as a mountain man, and seemed to think he was close to makin' some big money. His wife asked him to be careful and reminded him of the kids. Then the usual family stuff in the letters."

Shaking his head, Nate said, "Coon has to be stopped. I don't know how many people he's killed since he murdered his partners and stole their plew, but most likely a handful or so."

"We'll get 'em, but iffen he has gold, he'll be harder to find."

"No, I think he'll be easier, because he'll be a boar hog dressed in gold. He won't have the refined manners and speech most rich folks have."

"How much gold did ya find on the man?"

"Just this chunk and I'd imagine Coon knew nothing about it or he would have taken it, too. I guess this weights maybe two pounds."

"Any idea what it's worth?"

"I don't have any idea of the value, no, but we'll stop at the first bank we find and ask.  Then we'll send the money to Clyde's wife and kids."

Cotton nodded and said, "That'd be the proper thing to do and it's what God would want us to do.  It's blood money and I want nothing to do with it.  This way it can help his family out a bit."

"Ya take the first guard and I'll take the second.  Any problems will likely be either the Osage or Fox attempting to steal the horses."

"I'll move out there now.  When we wire that money to the widow in Boston, let's mail these papers back to her as well. Ya can write a nice letter tellin' her how he died and the fact he was buried."

Nate laughed and said, "I ain't got no idea how he died and neither do you.  As for the buryin', I don't think we'll take the time to do that.  I'm startin' to worry that Turner might leave Saint Louis on one of those big paddle boats and he can get anywhere on one of those."

Picking up his Hawken rifle, Cotton made his way near the horses to stand guard.

Nate reached into his pack and pulled out a book, because he liked to read each evening and it helped him sleep.  While not a strong reader, he was better than average for the time, and could read all but the hardest of books.  His writing, however, left a lot to be desired, mainly due to poor penmanship.

Three days later, Nate and Cotton entered Saint Louis.  The big man had given a lot of thought about where Coon might go in the big city and finally realized it would be the first place that bought plew and the first bank, most likely.  He knew the guns and whiskey were bought mainly by the Sioux with plew, because they had no concept of money.  Of course, he had gold, but Nate didn't have any idea how much the man found or traded for, not that it mattered.

They'd found the bodies of Jonas and Thomas, by circling buzzards and while they had no gold on them, Nate knew they'd been killed by Coon.  One was shot in the back and the other in the head, but it was the knife wounds that convinced Nate who the killer was.  Only a mountain man or trained killer cut the throats of his enemies, just to make sure they stayed dead, and both of the men had their throats cut.  I could never prove Coon did the killin's, but I know he did.

Pulling up in front of Westman's Furs, Plew and Skins, they saw a man near the door.

"Ya the big bug?"  Cotton asked.

Westman laughed and said, "I guess ya could call me that."

"I'm lookin' fer a good friend of mine, named Coon Turner, and he's a big man near my size.  He's a white man though, with red hair, and I wondered iffen you've seen 'em."  Nate gave the man a big smile.

"Uh-huh, I know the man.  He come in here a few days back with a huge damned load of plew and they were worth well over $10,000.00, which I didn't have. He took less, but that's business between him and me."

"Any idea where he went after he left here?"

"Nope, he didn't say and it ain't none of my business.  Do ya two have skins or plew to unload?"

"Not on this trip.  See, we're hunting a killer and we appreciate the information you've given us." Nate said.

"Killer?  Who, Turner?"

"Yep, and he's wanted by the law, too."

"Shit, I had no idea or I wouldn't have bought his furs.  Were the plew clean?"

"I ain't thought about the plew, but he got 'em trading foofaraw and whiskey to the Injuns, not to mention Hawkin rifles."

"Tradin' guns to Injuns will get a man tied to the short end of a long rope around this town."

"I think yer safe enough, Mister Westman, but if ya see 'em again, get the law.  Ya try to take 'em on yer own, he'll kill ya and never bat an eye." Cotton said.

"Take care." Nate said and then tapped his horse gently with his heels.

"There's a bank over there." Cotton said as he pointed.

"We'll try there first since it's the closest bank to Westman's business. A man with gold would want to get rid of it quickly."

Making their way to the bank, they dismounted, tied their horses to a hitching post and walked inside. Nate walked to the closest teller and asked, "Do y'all buy rough gold?"

The teller blinked rapidly and asked, "Rough gold? How much do ya have?"

"Now that all depends on yer answer to my question."

"It ain't none of yer damned business how much gold we have, so answer Nate's question." Cotton said with narrowed eyes.

"W. . . why, yes, we buy gold. If ya can wait a minute or two I'll get the bank manager. He's the only one here with the authority to buy gold." The teller was more than just a bit intimidated by the two men dressed in skins. The last man with gold had been dressed the same way and was just as crude, too.

Cotton said, "Get the manager, or the owner, or even the janitor, just as long as they can judge and pay fer raw gold."

"We'll wait." Nate said.

A few minutes later two men well over forty walked to the window and the youngest of the two said, "If you'll come into my office we can discuss your business."

Following the banker to his office, they were offered a seat and the youngest said, "I'm Franklin and I'm the bank manager. This is Bill and he does the assay of any raw gold brought to us for purchase." Then opening his desk drawer, Franklin asked, "Drink, gentlemen?"

"Sure." Cotton instantly replied.

"Just one, because it's a mite early for me." Nate replied.

Pouring the drinks, Franklin handed each a drink and then asked, "How much gold do you have?"

"I ain't real sure, but close to two pounds." Nate said.

"We ain't got as much as ole Coon Turner had, but he hit the motherlode." Cotton brought Coon up to see the response he'd get.

"Coon Turner, did you say?" Bill and Franklin's eyes met.

"Sure, Coon and us go way back, and he found a mountain of gold out west, only Injuns killed his buddies, so he had to run."

"Oh, we know Coon and he's one of our largest depositors. Now, if you'll be kind enough to let Bill take your gold, he can give us an estimate of it's value and an accurate weight. As of this morning the rate for gold is twenty-one dollars an ounce." Then placing the bottle on top of his desk, he added, "Help yourselves to the whiskey whenever you have the urge."

Nate placed the lump of gold on the desk and then said, "You'd better come back, Bill, or I'll go lookin' fer ya in a few minutes. How long does this testing take?"

Bill gave a loud gulp and then replied, "I'll return within twenty minutes. Gentlemen, your gold is safe with us. As you may have noticed when you entered, we have three armed guards."

Cotton knocked his drink back and as he refilled his glass he said, "Just remember what Nate said, because it's true. Iffen ya ain't back twenty minutes after ya leave, we'll both come for ya, and we're likely to be pissed, too."

"Gentlemen, please," Franklin said, "we have requirements and paperwork that must be done in order to buy the gold. Without testing, we have no idea of the quality of the gold or the weight. Patience, it won't take long."

Bill picked the nugget up and walked from the room.

Nate said, "We also have an authorization for payment from the U.S. army. Can ya help us with that, too?" Nate handed the letter to Franklin.

The man read the letter closely and said, "Yes, we can provide funds from this authorization. Have you thought of opening a bank account?"

Cotton looked at Nate and when he nodded, Cotton said, "We want it in both of our names, they're shown on that letter from the army. Leave us five hundred in spendin' money, but deposit the rest. But fer the gold we need a bank draft fer Myrtle Williams. Will that be a problem?"

"No, no, not at all. If you can provide me with an address, I'll have the money wired, which means the woman won't have to wait for the money. If we use a bank draft it'll take her longer to get paid is all, because they'll have to contact us, then we respond, and then she'll get paid only after we receive the check here. The whole process could take up to a month."

"Wire it, but take the cost of the sending the money out of our account, not the money from the gold." Nate said.

Bill walked in with the gold, placed it on Franklin's desk and said, "You've two and half pounds of excellent quality gold, gentlemen, and that comes to eight hundred and forty dollars. But, I do have a question."

"Yep?" Cotton asked.

"Did you find your gold close to where Coon found his? The gold looks as if it's from the same batch."

Nate laughed and replied, "It came from the same mountain, but that's all you'll get out of me. When ya have gold, folks always want to know where ya found it."

"Bill, make a wire transfer for purchase of the gold out to this woman." he handed Myrtles name and address from a letter Cotton had shown him. "I want this sent out immediately and make sure you get a confirmation from the other end."

"Now what?" Cotton asked.

"We'll open your account and fill out some forms." Franklin said with a big genuine smile. It was a good week so far and the profits from buying gold from both Coon and Nate had given him a nice fat commission.

Outside the bank, about thirty minutes later, Cotton asked, "What now? Do we look for Coon or get a hotel room and some food in us?"

"We'll try to get some food, but I might have a hard time findin' an eatin' place in a city like this."

"It won't be the first or the last time."

"There's a place across the street, so let's try there."

They no sooner entered than a big man wearing a filthy apron said, "We don't serve black folks in here, so you'll have to go someplace else to eat."

Cotton gave a mean look and said, "He's with me."

"Like I give a shit?  His kind ain't allowed in here, so be off with ya."

Cotton started to go for his gun, but Nate's hand on his stopped him.  When he looked at the big black man, Nate shook his head and said, "Let's go."

Outside, a rough looking white man dressed mostly in rags approached.  Cotton smiled and asked, "Do ya know where two fellers could eat around here iffen one of them is a black man?"

The man stopped, grinned and then replied, "Down by the docks.  They'll feed anyone with money and won't care about the man's color doin' the job either.  Up here is were all the ritzy folks live and shop."

"Thank ya, we appreciate yer help."

The man nodded and walked away.

Moving toward the docks, they both heard a loud clap of thunder and looking up, dark clouds were low overhead.

"Gonna rain in a few minutes." Cotton said.

"There's an eatin' place off the right there."

The building looked rough, with unpainted oak boards, but as long as the cook knew the business, they'd get no complaints from either of the mountain men.  They entered and a woman of middle-age waved them to her from across the large room.  Once by her side, she showed them a table and then asked, "What would ya like?"

"Do ya have a special?" Cotton asked.

"Ya have a choice, either beans and ham or pot roast and both will cost ya fifty cents."

"Give me pot roast, with coffee."

Nate grinned and said, "I'll have the same."

At that point, a loud *crack* filled the air and rain began beating on the window panes.

"What are we doin' after we eat?"

Nate replied, "Find us a cheap hotel for a few nights.  I have no idea if Coon is still in town, so this evening we'll visit a few saloons and see if he's having a party."

"He might just shack up with a whore in his hotel room, or have ya thought about that already?"

"Yep, I've given it a lot of thought, but we don't know iffen he's into women.  I do know iffen he's been a mountain man, he'll be lookin' for some good whiskey."

"Hell, we can't visit every hotel in town, it'd take us a year."

Nate chuckled and said, "When we visit the saloons, we'll talk with some soiled doves, they'll remember a big man like him."

The food was hot and tasty and both were full when the last of the gravy was sopped up with a biscuit.  Nate leaned close to Cotton and said, "We're bein' watched by three white men near the back.  They look like trouble to me, but iffen we pull guns in here people will die."

"Yep, too crowded."

"Shit, they're makin' their play now and here they come."

# Chapter 14

The feelings Coon had for the whore was mixed, and it was all the soiled doves fault. While she was a stunning woman, which was rare for a whore, she wanted too much for her services. However, the more he looked at her ravishing body, the more he wanted her. Joy was a very beautiful woman and she knew it, so she was expensive.

Finally he asked, "I have a business proposal for ya, but I need some answers in order to complete our transaction. But, the money will be good."

"Okay, I'm always interested in money, honey." She replied and then laughed.

Refilling her drink glass, Coon asked, "How much do ya make a month workin' in this saloon?"

"It depends on how many men buy my services. Some nights I make good money and on others not so good. It's like any other business."

Smiling, Coon asked, "Do ya make over two hundred a month?"

"Hell, I wish I made half that much. The saloon keeps sixty percent of my income, but they do provide free room and board."

"I'm lookin' for a full-time woman who'll make a hundred a month, free room and board, as well as free whiskey. Are ya interested?"

"For that kind of money, I'll do what ya want and when ya want it. But, there has to be a catch."

Coon laughed and said, "No, not really, except a couple of rules. What ya hear at my place is not to be discussed with anyone, what ya see is the same, and that's pretty much it. Except you're to play anytime I want and I don't want yer ass drunk all the time."

"Honey, for that kind of money you'll get special treatment everyday. When can I start this new job?"

"I'm looking at houses tomorrow and ya can start the day I move into the place. Payday will be the first of each month and you'll have that day, as well as the next day, free to do as you wish. However, let me warn ya, if I catch you plying your trade on the side, I'll kill ya, understand?"

"That won't be a problem with me, and I agree."

"Good, now get over here and let's see if you're worth a hundred dollars a month."

The next morning, Coon was in a buggy with Franklin as the banker showed him a series of homes and mansions. The mountain man was sipping good quality bourbon as they visited the homes.

Finally, Coon said, "I'm interested in seeing one outside the city, but close enough to ride to the city in minutes."

"Well, I have one, priced at $30,000.00, that is three miles away and the place comes with forty acres of land, a lot of cattle, and near a hundred horses. It's fairly grand for a country home, but not as lavish as the ones you've seen so far today."

"Let's take a gander at it, because I'm a simple man."

Coon liked the place right away, because it was surrounded by huge oak trees, had a narrow lane of cobble stone leading to the home, and the building was fairly new. Turning to Franklin, he asked, "Why are they selling this place?"

"The wife died and the husband is moving back east. I think if you allow me to haggle a bit with the man, I may be able to save you a few dollars," Franklin replied and then thought, *I'll not only get a good commission, I'll charge Turner more than what Wilson wants and pocket the difference. Hell, that could be thousands now that he needs to sell the place.*

"Ya do that, but I expect ya to be honest. Iffen I find out later ya stole from me, I'll kill ya."

"Y . . . yes, sir, I fully understand."

Seeing an old man working near some rose bushes, Franklin called out, "Tom! Tom Wilson, it's me, Franklin, and I need to know if your place is still up for sale."

Smiling, the man made his way to the buggy and said, "Sure it is, and I'll take a good bit lower than my askin' price, too. I need to move back east to be near my kids." He shook hands with the two men.

"Mister Turner here is interested in your place, so how about you show us around?"

A little over an hour later, as they walked to the buggy, Coon said, "I like it a lot and Mister Franklin will handle the hagglin' and final price with ya. If I buy it today, when is the quickest I can move in?"

"Is the day after tomorrow okay with you?"

"That's fine. Now, Franklin, how about you and I return to the city and do the paperwork? Then ya can come back and discuss money with Mister Wilson."

"Perfect and I was about to suggest just that."

Extending his hand, Coon shook with Wilson.

Two days later, Coon moved into the house with Joy and she was impressed with the place. There were three bedrooms and a huge kitchen. "Ya don't expect me to cook too, do ya?"

"It'd be nice iffen ya would."

"Ya say that now, but I ain't no cook, not really."

"Well, the first thing I need ya to do tomorrow is to find us a good cook. I'll also give ya some money, so ya can stop dressin' like a whore. I want you to look delicious, but not cheap, okay?"

"Cook will likely cost ya another fifteen to twenty dollars a month.'

Coon shrugged and replied, "Just get one and try to find a man to care for the animals, too.  I have no desire to clean shit out of stalls and feed the damned things."

"Both will cost ya about thirty a month, give or take ten bucks."

"Make it happen.  Right now, come with me and let's check the bedroom.  I want to make sure we have a good mattress on the bed."

Toward evening, Coon said, "I'm headin' into town to see about some business, and I'll be back directly."

"Ya might want to bring us back some decent food, since my supper almost killed us."

Coon laughed and then said, "I'll do that.  Ya know, yer the only woman around who can't fix bacon and eggs.  This mornin' I ate the first black eggs I've ever had."

The ride to town was short and Coon was happy with himself, because now he had money, a good lookin' woman and place of his own.  *I deserve all I have and no one will ever take this from me.  I'll deal with Franklin later.  I can't believe the man ripped me off for almost three thousand dollars.  I warned 'em, but I guess it didn't take.*

He pulled up in front of a saloon and entered the batwing doors.  Seeing food on the bar, he bellied up and ordered a rye with a beer chaser.  Glancing around the inside, he only saw a couple of men, who looked like dockworkers nursing their beers near the back wall.  He took a small plate and loaded it down with food, thinking, *Joy is great in bed, but she can't cook worth a damn.*

When his drink was placed on the bar, he asked, "Do ya know some men who'll do what they're told and keep their mouths shut?"

"I know three right off, why?"

"I just moved here and want some security at my home.  I live west of the city, two miles and then right.  I have a white fence that runs around my property.  Send them out there to-morrow to talk with me.  I want men good with guns and fists, so no lazy jaspers that sit on there asses lookin' for easy money."  Taking a double eagle coin from his trouser pocket, he placed it on the bar and added, "This is fer yer trouble."

"Hey, thanks, mister?"

"Turner, Coon Turner."

The doors swung inward and in walked a lawman. He walked to the bar and said, "Give me my usual, Hank." He then gave Coon a close looking over.

A beer was placed on the bar, money exchanged hands, and then the lawdog looked at Coon and asked, "What's yer name""

"Turner."

"Ya look a lot like a man named Kramer or are ya him?"

Coon laughed and said, "No, I'm not Kramer and I've been checked already. Kramer has two long knife scars on his back and a bullet scar above his left nipple. Iffen ya want, I'll even pull my shirt off."

"Yer right, so why don't ya pull the shirt open so I can see above yer left nipple. Iffen yer not Kramer, I'll buy ya a couple of drinks. I don't want to do this just to anger ya, but he's armed and considered dangerous."

Coon unbuttoned his shirt, pulled it open and said, "See, no scar and none on my back either, iffen ya want to look."

Tossing money on the bar, and the sheriff said, "Sorry about that, but ya sure look like 'em."

Finishing his drinks, Coon said, "Give me the same and this will go down easy, since it's free."

The lawman smiled and asked, "I'm glad yer a good sport about all of this. Some men wouldn't be at all."

"What else can I do? I mean, I could pull a gun every single time, but eventually I'd get my ass blowed away. Besides, yer the law and I respect yer position." Coon started buttoning his shirt.

Slapping Coon on the back, the man finished his beer, and said, "I'll put the word out that ya look like Kramer, so maybe my co-workers will leave ya alone."

"Ya do that."

As soon as the sheriff left the saloon, Hank said, "I'll send some men out to yer place in the mornin'."

Finishing his drink, Coon wiped his mouth off with the back of his hand and said, "Thanks fer the help, Hank."

Early the next morning, less than an hour after sunrise, four men rode into the barnyard of Coon's home. As they tied their horses to the hitching post, Coon stepped out holding a double-barrel shotgun in his hands.

"Hey, go easy with that damn scattergun, it ain't a toy." A man close to the mountain man's size said. He was heavy, looked fat, and his hair and beard were brown.

"W . . . we're the men Hank sent out." Said a thin man, obviously the oldest, due to his lined face. He looked to be a man who'd recently made his living in a saddle.

The other two were nothing special and actually, they almost looked like twins, except one had a look in his eyes that suggested he wasn't carryin' a full load.

"Come around to the back, because that's where you'll be stayin', if we can reach an agreement."

Behind the house was a long building and inside it was sectioned off like hotel rooms. Franklin said it was for the hired help. Coon had placed a little food and a couple of bottles of whiskey in one room, so they could discuss business privately.

Unlocking the door to the room, the mountain man entered and said, "Come on in boys and take a seat."

After each man was seated, Coon filled glasses with whiskey and said, "I'm lookin' for a few good men, who'll do what they're told, with no questions asked." He then passed the glasses around. Taking a sip of his whiskey, he met each man's eyes.

"Let me tell ya who we are first," the big man said and then continued, "I'm Moses, the ugly guy is William, but we call 'em Bill, then the twins. Mark and Luke are their names and Luke is a bit nuts when it comes to killin'. He loves his knife."

The small group broke out laughing and when it quieted down, Bill asked, "What's the pay?"

"Twenty a month, free room and board, bottle of whiskey a week, and one day off. At Christmas you'll get an extra months pay as a bonus."

"Hell, sounds fine to me." Bill replied.

"Me too." Moses said.

"I'm in." Mark commented and then looked at his brother.

"I want to know the rules and I know ya have some." Luke said.

"Six days a week you're to be here, not out gallivantin' around town. Ya can drink anytime, but the only time I expect to see ya drunk is yer day off. If ya drink so much ya can't get up one mornin', ya can consider yourself fired. Any other questions?"

Moses grinned and said, "What's our first job, because I suspect ya have one or you'd not have come lookin' for us."

Coon grinned and said, "Not so fast. There is one aspect of this job each of ya needs to understand, I am the only boss. Once ya say yer in, can't change yer mind later and just walk off. If ya have problems with booze and I cain't wake ya up, I'll kill ya. Iffen yer fired fer any reason—I'll kill ya. Now, with each robbery or killin' ya do fer me, you'll get a bonus, but the amount will depend on the job. I have some plans to make Saint Louis ours. Now who is in or out?"

To a man they all agreed to work for Coon and do his dirty work, without question. The mountain man knew he needed to hire some snitches and others to keep an eye open in the big city.

Coon said, "One of ya hire about ten kids, old enough to watch and listen, and keep their mouths shut. Pay 'em two bits a day fer any information they might have. If it's about money or a good robbery location, pay 'em a buck. I'll give ya yer money back. Iffen the kid or kids squeal on us or ya get a feelin' ya cain't trust 'em—kill 'em.

Moses thought for a second and then said, "That's it? Ya want us to run a bunch of pickpockets and kids?"

"No, you'll do some more serious stuff, I assure ya."

"Like what, boss?"

"I want the banker Franklin killed, but it has to look like a robbery gone bad. Do ya think y'all can do the job?"

"I hate bankers, so can we rob him after he's dead?" Luke asked.

Moses turned to the man and said, "Luke, use yer head for something besides holding yer hat off yer shoulders. We have to rob the man to make it look like a robbery, ya damned fool."

Luke exploded from his chair and out of nowhere a skinning knife appeared in his right hand, blade up. He said in a level tone, "Don't talk to me like that, or I'll gut ya like a fish, understood?"

Moses stood slowly, glared at Luke and then punched the smaller man in the middle of his face.  Luke fell like he'd ran into a clothesline.  Looking at Mark, the big man asked, "Do ya want to try for a piece of my ass, too?  If so, come on, but iffen not, keep yer mouth shut."

Coon, liking the way Moses handled the situation said, "Moses, you're the ramrod of these men and I'll come to ya iffen I have problems.  Yer pay is now thirty a month."

"Hot damn!" The big man said and then smiled.

Luke, groaning, sat up and asked, "What hit me?"

Moses said, "I did and the next time ya pull a knife on me, I'll stick it up yer ass.  I'm the ramrod around here and you'd better get your shit together, Luke."

Luke shot a glance at Coon, who nodded.

"When do ya want this job done?"  Mark asked.

Coon replied, "No hurry, but do the job right the first time. I think ya need to get a good look at the man, learn a bit about his comin' and goin', and see iffen he has any bad habits, too."

"Details like this will take time, boss."  Moses said.

"We're in no hurry, as long as he ends up dead, and I'm sure any one of ya could do the job.  Now, do any of ya need to return and get any clothing or gear?"

When no one did, Coon said, "I have a pleasant surprise fer y'all tonight.  Tonight will be a party night and none of ya will have to work tomorrow.  So, I have whiskey and loose women coming right after supper."

"Hot damn!" Moses said.

"However, iffen ya break anything in here, the cost will be deducted from yer monthly pay," Coon said as he pulled out a set of keys.  Then he added, "This is the largest room and it will belong to Moses, since he's the ramrod.  I want all of ya to come with me and we'll let each of ya pick a room.  I don't care how clean ya keep the room, but if smells start coming from the place, I'll be on yer ass. Fair?"

"There won't be any smells from any rooms." Moses said.

Luke said, "There might be from Mark's room, he's always passin' gas."

Everyone broke out laughing, but the laughter quickly died down.

Coon rolled his eyes, thought about the comment and realized the whole bunch were childish, and said, "Come with me and let's get everyone a room.  I'm sure you'll want one before the ladies get here."

# Chapter 15

Nate and Cotton didn't look up, even though the men were standing beside their table. The tallest of the three men asked, "Are ya lookin' fer trouble, boy? Yer kind ought not be allowed to eat with white folks."

Both mountain men kept eating, hoping the men would leave.

"By God, when I speak to a boy, I expect an answer!" The tall man said abrasively.

Nate glanced up and said, "I don't see no boys in here, but I do see three men who will be dead shortly iffen they don't leave my table and let me eat in peace."

Leaning over, his hands on the table and his face in Nate's, the tall man said, "Time fer ya to leave, boy, and I mean now."

There came a loud thud, followed by a piercing scream and when Cotton glanced at the table top, the tall man's right hand was pinned in place by a big Green River skinning knife. Blood was already pooling under the quivering palm. Moving swift, Cotton brought his knife up and opened the nearest man from crotch to brisket. While moving toward the last man, the tall man fell to the floor, his throat now a gaping hole spurting blood, and Cotton stopped. Nate, moving forward, stuck his knife to the hilt in the last man's belly. The wounded man screamed and fell to the floor.

"Mister, I seen it all!" A man at the next table said, "They had it coming and wouldn't leave ya alone."

A man stuck his head out of the kitchen and yelled, "Sandy, find us a copper and do the job now."

Removing guns from the injured men and a few pig stickers, the two mountain men returned to their table and continued eating.

Five minutes later, a portly sheriff entered the restaurant, moved to the dead men and asked, "Who did the killin'?  And, John, send fer an undertaker and a doctor.  One has a gut wound and is still breathin'."

John must have been the owner, because he gave shouted orders to a young lad of about fifteen and off the boy went.

"We did the killin', but were left little choice in the matter." Cotton replied.

"Oh, and why did ya decide to kill these fellers?"

"First, they started it and we tried to ignore 'em, but they wouldn't let go.  Second, it seems they were determined to die today."

"What's yer names?"  The sheriff took out a stub of a pencil and small pad of paper.

Nate replied, "I'm Nate Grisham and the other man is Cotton Thomas."

The lawman looked around the room and asked, "Did any of ya see this?"

The man at the table beside the to mountain men said, "Tom, I saw it all, and these two men tried to avoid fightin', but them dead men was determined to kill 'em.  When one of 'em went fer a gun, these two put a stop to 'er and quick too, by God."

Looking around Tom asked, "Anyone else see it that way?"

"It happened jus' like Tim said, Tom."  A fat man across the room said.

"I seed the whole shebang and iffen anyone deserved to be kilt, it was them three.  They acted like they were gonna kill these two fellers come hail or high water.  Only it didn't work out that a-way."

After writing down witness statements getting names and such, the lawman asked, "Anybody in town that would want the two of ya dead?"

"No, not that I can think of, and besides, all of my enemies would try to do the job face-to-face and not use hired guns." Nate replied.

Cotton added, "Our enemies would for sure brace us straight up and never hire a killer.  I suspect they just didn't like the idea of a colored man bein' in here."

"Since every witness agrees with what ya told me, you're free to go."

"I want to finish my meal first." Nate said.

Right then, the man with the belly wound screamed, so the sheriff squatted beside the man and asked, "What's yer name?"

"A . . . Aker . . . God, I hurt."  His fingers clawed at the hardwood floor.

"First name?"

"Jen . . . Jenson."

"And these other two?"

"James . . . Wood and . . . J.C. Henry."

A old doctor entered the building and taking a glance at the two dead, he moved to Aker and squatted beside the man. Pulling a small bottle of laudanum out, he pour a little into the man's mouth, stood and said, "I need a couple of you men to move this feller to my office.  He's got a gut wound and won't last long."

The sheriff had been going through the clothing the dead men wore and found little.  He placed a hundred dollars on the table top, some change, a pipe, and two letters.  Raising one letter, Tom opened it and read silently.  Finally he said, "The three of them are related and I can send their belongings and money to their families."

Nate finished eating and said, "If ya need us, we'll be stayin' at the Do Drop Inn.  We don't have rooms yet, but the clerk will know where to find us."

Writing it in on his pad, Tom said, "I don't think I need ya, but it's good to have in case I have questions later."

Cotton and Nate stood and made their way to the hotel. The walk was short, since the place was on the same side of town, but there was no way a hotel up on the hill would ever allow Nate to have a room.  Entering the hotel, Nate smiled at the clerk and said, "Good to see ya again, Oscar."

"You as well, Nate, Cotton."

"Where's Jonah, doesn't he usually cover the day shift?"

Oscar was a huge black man, closer to seven feet than six, over two-hundred and fifty pounds, and was as gentle as a lamb, unless angered.  He lowered his eyes and said, "Jonah was killed about two weeks back when a couple of men robbed this place. Now, what kind of stupid men would rob a run down hotel in the dock section of the city, when all the hotels with real money are up on the hill?"

"What happened?" Cotton asked.

"Well," Oscar wiped a tear from his eye, "we don't really know for sure what happened. One of our guests was leavin' to eat supper when two rough lookin' men walked in. When the same guest returned a little later, he saw Jonah's bloody arm sticking out from behind the counter. He'd been stabbed over twenty times and his throat cut. Of course, all the money was gone, but they couldn't have gotten much. I don't think there was three dollars in the money box."

"Have the police found anything?"

"No, and they won't either. See, around here the coppers won't look into the killin' of a freed man, just white folks. Now, what can I get the two of you?"

Cotton said, "Give us a single room for five days and send up a bottle of rye whiskey in a bit."

"That'll be two dollars and four bits for today, then two more dollars for the rest of the week. The whiskey is two dollars, but it's good stuff from Cain-tuck."

Flipping Oscar a golden eagle coin, Nate said, "Keep the balance on our tab in case we want food or more drink, okay?"

"Yep, I hear ya."

As they took a key and started to leave, Nate turned and asked, "Do ya have any protection, Oscar?"

"By God, I got this." He held up a shotgun that had both barrels and the stock shortened. To Nate, it almost looked like a shotgun turned pistol.

"That ought to do the job, huh?"

Oscar laughed and replied, "It'll do. Enjoy your stay."

The room was nothing special, and was typical for most western hotels, with the mirror cracked, the picture on the wall a cheap print, and a badly sagging mattress. Cotton sat on the edge of the bed and asked, "What now?"

"We'll snoop around a bit, but no hurry. I can feel Coon and he's here. Besides, that banker Franklin said the man was a big depositor, so he'll stay close to his money."

Cotton thought for a minute or two and then asked, "What causes a man to go bad like Coon did all of a sudden? When I met the man, he seemed okay to me."

Nate sat in an overstuffed chair, sighed and replied, "Some men get tired of wading waist-deep cold water fer plew, only to discover they break even at the end of the year. Mayhap he expected to get rich after a couple of seasons and when it didn't happen, he turned mean. Hell, I really ain't got a good answer fer ya, except some men lack patience or expect life to be different than what it really is for most of us."

"What now?"

There was a knock at the door and when Nate asked, "Who is at my door?"

A male voice replied, "It's me, Roscoe, and I work for Oscar. I have a bottle of whiskey one of you ordered."

Nate moved to the door, pulled his pistol and hammer clicked as it locked back. Opening the door just a crack, he looked into a black face. Opening the door wider, he said, "Sorry about the gun, but these are dangerous times."

Roscoe chuckled and said, "Don't tell me about how rough things are. Jonah, our day clerk was killed just a little while back, but we know who did the killin'."

Nate met Cotton's eyes. The big man asked, "Who would kill a man like Jonah and take the money from the money box?"

"Nate, it looked like a robbery, only it wasn't. I shouldn't say nothin', 'cause it could cost me my job, but it was a show of force. See, Oscar had a white man, shady lookin' feller, come in with two other men 'bout a month ago. They wanted the hotel to pay for protection, meanin' nothin' bad would happen here as long as they got paid every week. Oscar told 'em to go to hell, because he's owned this place for over four years and never needed any protection. Well, shortly after, Jonah was killed and the till box emptied."

Cotton said, "When I lived in Boston for a spell, organized crime, mostly Italians, had the same racket goin'. As long as ya paid, they protected ya against them, or if somebody else robbed ya, the Italians would kill 'em. But, once ya quit payin' bad things started happenin'."

Nate asked, "What kinds of bad things?"

Cotton chuckled and said, "Well, they'd start out with something small, like a broken window, door kicked in, and iffen ya didn't take the hint, they might set your place on fire or injure a worker.  Usually, by that point, the owner would pay the protection fees.  If not, then someone would die."

"Couldn't the coppers control it?" Nate asked.

"They couldn't do the job well in a big city.  Every man they arrested had witnesses of bein' someplace else when the crime was committed.  Usually, they'd be out of jail within a day or two."

Roscoe said, "Oscar is expectin' the man to visit him tonight at six and personally, I think he'll agree to start paying for protection.  The death of Jonah hurt 'em and I know Oscar thinks it was his fault.  Most of us that work here are good friends or family."

Nate said, "I wonder why Oscar didn't say anything to us?  I think when the man comes tonight he might just meet me and Cotton.  But, first I'll have to speak with Oscar."

"Lawdy, I wish you wouldn't do that, because he'll know you got the information from my big mouth and I shouldn't have said anything.  No, sir, please don't talk to Oscar about this.  I have a wife and five kids at home and jobs for a black man are hard to find in the city.  I used to work the docks, until my back started giving me trouble and I had to quit.  Please don't say nothin'."

"We'll keep our mouth's shut, but we will be in or near the lobby when the man arrives tonight.  I think we can find out who's behind this and put a stop to it."

Moving to the door, Roscoe opened it and said, "I don't know nothing about all of this and I've not said a thing to either of you.  I will warn ya though, the men I saw were some mean lookin' owlhoots and killers for sure."

"Thanks for bringin' us the drink," Cotton said as he pulled the cork from the bottle with a loud *pop*.

"You're welcome, sir, and enjoy your stay with us."  The door closed.

Filling two clean glasses, Cotton asked, "How do we handle this?"

"We'll play it by ear.  But, remember, we need to catch one of 'em alive, so we can find out who's the brains behind the operation."  Nate picked up his glass and took a sip.

A little before six, Nate and Cotton were seated just outside the doors to their room.  They each had pistols in their belts, knives, and were ready to step in when the men downstairs turned loud.

Right at six, the front door opened and small brass bell jingled. Footsteps were heard approaching the desk. A muffled conversation was heard, then Oscar said, "I don't make that kind of money. If I had it, I'd pay it, but I don't."

"Listen, you'll pay up each week or more folks will start to die."

Nate gazed into Cotton's eyes and nodded. They walked down the steps. They could see three men near the counter and the biggest of the men had Oscar by his arms.

"What's all the damned noise about? Other than I know who killed Jonah now." Cotton asked.

One of the men pulled a knife and said, "Iffen yer smart, you'll leave and not remember ever seein' us."

The big man released Oscar and said, "It's nothin', just a little business chat. So get out of here before I get mad and start bustin' heads. And, take yer boy with ya."

Nate smiled and said, "Ya callin' me a boy? Hell, I ain't been a boy in twenty years. Besides that, I think ya need to leave before I decide to hurt someone. Only before ya leave, you'll apologize to me, because I don't like bein' called names." He took a couple of more steps down the stairs.

Big man laughed, pulled a long bladed skinning knife, and said, "Looks like these two want to dance for a song or two, boys."

Now at the foot of the stairs, about six feet from the counter, Nate said, "Mister, ya better think twice about what yer fixin' to do, because we'll tear y'all a new ass."

"Take 'em boys!"

The first pug-ugly moved to Nate and made a mad slash with his knife blade for the big man's head. As his arm went over him, Nate stuck the man low and in the belly. He screamed, dropped his knife and fell to the floor. Nate glanced and saw Cotton was handling his own against the other, but the remaining crook moved toward him, and it was the big man. The room suddenly filled with the loud blast from a shotgun and the big man fell to the floor, almost blown in two pieces. Pulling his pistol and letting his knife fall, Nate pointed it at the last man as he ordered, "Drop the knife."

"W...what are ya goin' to do to me?"

"Shut up until I tell ya to speak.  Cotton, check this idiot and the other two for guns and such." Nate said and then lookin' at Oscar he said, "Thanks for the shotgun backup, because it does the job and well, too."

Throwing knives, guns, straight razors and even a pair or brass knuckles toward Nate, Cotton said, "They're clean."

"Pull some rope from your possibles bag and tie this last man's hands behind his back.  We'll take 'em to our room fer a little talk."

"What do I tell the lawmem?"  Oscar asked.

Nate walked to the counter, placed the pistol he'd fired on top and said, "Tell 'em these two tried to rob ya.  One is dead and the other one will be shortly.  Cotton's knife cut his lights. Since ya were robbed once before, they'll have no reason not to believe ya."

"Come with me son, because the Injuns taught me how to torture a man.  I'll soon see how much sand ya have in your gizzard."  Cotton said as he tied another rope around the man's neck. Once the rope was in place, they moved up the stairs.

"Oscar, we'll end this mess before we leave town."

"Lord, I hope so, or I'm a dead man."

Hearing steps at the front door, Nate ran up the stairs. When he got to the room,  Cotton already had the man tied to a chair.

"Well," Nate said as he entered the room, "I see you have our new friend all ready to play with us, huh?"

"Yep, but I don't think he'll like the way we play."

Nate pulled his big Green River knife and neared the man. Squatting in front of him, he said, "Son, we can do this the easy way or the hard way.  Now, it doesn't matter much to us, not really."

"Ya cut me and Coon will kill ya!"  The man spat out in anger.

"Coon Turner?" Cotton asked, surprised.

"Yep, so ya know the boss, huh?  Good, because it's likely he'll kill ya both anyway now.  See, Moses and William were his favorite men."

Nate gave an evil grin and replied, "Where does Coon live?"

"Ya ain't gettin' shit out of me, you damned Nig—"

"Hold his mouth shut, Cotton."

Cotton held the man's head still with one hand and covered his mouth with the other. Nate's big knife slashed twice and both of the man's ears fell to the floor. His feet kicked madly and his body thrashed, but Cotton kept his hand over the man's mouth. Minutes later, the man grew still, but tears ran down his cheeks.

Placing the tip of his knife between the man's legs, Nate said, "Now, I'm going to have my buddy take his hand from yer mouth, but iffen ya cry out, I'll remove yer tallywhacker, under-stood? Nod if ya agree to be quiet."

The man nodded.

"Release him."

"Don't hurt me no more. I'll tell ya what ya want to know."

"Wrap his ears up with part of a pillowcase." Nate ordered, then turned to the man and asked, "What is yer name?"

"Mark."

"Now I know ya work fer Coon Turner, so give me the man's address and tell all about his place."

Mark started talking and an hour later was still talking, when there came a light tap at the door. Pulling their guns, Cotton asked, "Who's there?"

"It's me, Oscar."

"Are ya alone?"

"Yes."

# CHAPTER 16

Luke looked at the grandfather clock and said, "It's almost 10 and they should have been back by now.  Hell, how long does it take to intimidate an old colored man and collect a few bucks?  I'm tellin' ya, something has gone wrong."

Sitting behind a massive solid oak desk, Coon said, "Bullshit. More than likely those fools stopped in some damned saloon and are drunk right now."

"I don't know, boss, not with Moses with 'em.  That big man keeps 'em straight most of the time and it ain't like 'em to do that sort of thing."

"Well, go lookin' fer 'em iffen ya think ya can find 'em."

Joy entered the room and said, "Mark is in the living room and looks like shit.  He's had both ears cut off."

Coon took a long drink of his whiskey and said, "Funny woman. Now, we're talkin' business and I don't like jokes."

"No joke, Coon."  Turning Joy called out, "Get in here, Mark, and show the boss yer ears."

Mark entered the room with pillowcase from Nate's room still on his head.  He lowered his eyes when Coon stood in shock.

"Where are the other two?"  Coon asked.

"Moses is dead and iffen William ain't, he soon will be.  I need to collect my wages and leave.  A big black jasper by the name of Nate Grisham said fer me to tell ya, 'he's comin' fer ya.' Now, iffen you'll pay me, I'm headin' east as fast as my ass will take me."

"First," Coon ordered, "tell me what happened and then all you can about Nate Grisham."

When Mark was finished, Luke said, "I'm leavin' too. I didn't sign up with this outfit to end up in jail. Ya never told us about any killin's you've done before."

Coon broke out laughing and said, "Oh, and ya told me of every bad thing you've ever done before? But, if ya two want out, let me pay ya what's owed and then I want ya off my property."

He moved to his desk, opened the top drawer and pulled out a large tin box. Placing it in the middle of his desktop, he said, "I'll give ya both a little extra, just to show there are no hard feelin's.'

He opened the box, but instead of removing money, he pulled out two pistols and pointed them at the two men. "Remember what I said when I first hired ya? There is no quittin' on me and I meant it then and still do." The pistol in his left hand fired, the shot loud in the small room, and Mark's head exploded, splattering blood, brains, and gore on the walls.

Luke pulled his pistol, fired and had the satisfaction of seeing his shot hit Coon, but the mountain man fired a split second later and Luke collapsed screaming. Luke's world slowly faded from gray to black, and then he died.

Coon staggered from the impact of the heavy lead ball, but grinned when he saw his ball take Luke in the center of his chest. Glancing down, he saw he'd been shot in the shoulder.

The door swung open and in ran Joy and seeing the bodies, she screamed.

"Shut the hell up and get something to bandage my wound."

A few minutes later, the job complete, Coon said, "It's a good thing yer good in bed, 'cause ya ain't worth a shit as a cook and yer lost when it comes to doctorin' a man. I want ya out and right now. Pack all yer shit and leave." He quickly reloaded his pistols, expecting Nate and Cotton any second.

"Where am I to go?"

"You can go to hell, for all I care. Now leave."

Joy slapped him in the face hard and Coon backhanded her to the floor.

"That's enough, Coon! I'll not have ya beatin' on a woman!" Nate yelled from the doorway.

Coon stood straight and said, "Well, now, iffen it ain't Nate Grisham.  Care fer a little panther piss?  I've got a full bottle of good Cain-tuck bourbon."

"We're takin' ya back to the mountains." Cotton said as he entered the room to stand beside Nate.

Coon pulled his pistol, fired and saw Nate fall.  He then grabbed Joy by the hair, pulled her to her feet, putting her between him and Cotton, and said, "Move, and I'll kill this bitch." He now held his second pistol in his right hand.

"Coon, this has gone on long enough.  Iffen ya go back with me, I'll guaran-damn-tee you'll have a fair trial."

The older mountain man laughed and replied, "And, then you'll hang me, right?"

"It's likely."

"Get out of my way.  I'm goin' out the front door, but iffen ya get in my way, I'll kill this woman and her blood will be on yer hands."

Cotton knew he was treed.  There was no way he'd make an attempt to stop Coon, not if the man had a woman.  He said, "Go on, Coon, and get.  But, remember, old son, we're on yer ass and we'll catch ya sooner or later."

The man was frightened, but not overly so, and as he moved he kept his pistol firmly against Joy's head.  He moved to the stables, saddled a horse and then said, "I hate to do this, Joy, but ya know too much."  Coon shoved her to the hay covered floor.

"Coon, don't do this.  I'll come with ya and keep ya happy when ya feel the need for a—"

The shot was loud and the bullet took Joy right between her beautiful breasts.  She screamed once, quivered a few times and then died, her blood staining the straw behind her.

Coon mounted and rode for town, knowing he'd move east a mite, then swing South.  He was scared, but he didn't panic as the horse moved quickly over the cobblestone streets.  I have a few hundred dollars on me, so I'll wire for more money once I get to another town.  Right now, the most important thing for me is to get some distance between me and Saint Louis."

Nate awoke on the floor, with Cotton tending to his bullet hole. "Coon get away?"

"Yep, he took the woman hostage and I let 'em go, but he killed her anyway."

"She knew too much, most likely. How's my wound?"

"Just a hair higher than your collar bone, which makes ya a lucky man."

"I reckon, but I don't feel lucky."

Cotton stood and walked to Coons desk. Filling two glasses with whiskey he said, "Here, I figured since the sumbitch shot ya, he can supply the whiskey to kill the pain. I took all the money he had in that box too, close to two thousand dollars. I figure we'll use it as travel money fer when we go after him."

"Help me to the divan in the parlor and bring the whiskey with us. Once I'm comfortable, you need to ride into town and fetch the law. I'm sure they'll have a million questions and it's likely I'll be too drunk to answer 'em."

"I'd go, but only iffen ya think you'll be okay alone."

"Ain't no danger here and with this fancy decanter filled with booze, I'll be just fine."

An hour later, Cotton was back with a doctor, undertaker and three lawmen. When they entered the parlor, Nate was as drunk as a dog and sleeping. "Take a look at my buddy," Cotton said to the doctor and then turning to the undertaker he said, "I'd imagine once the law takes a look at the bodies, ya can remove them for burial."

The doctor still hadn't moved, so Cotton asked, "Doctor, didn't ya hear me about caring for my friend?"

The middle-aged man said, "Oh, I heard ya, but I don't work on colored folks."

Angered, the mountain man pulled his pistol, jerked the hammer back and said, "By God, you'll work on one tonight, or I'll kill ya where ya stand."

"Whoa," one of the coppers said, "ya shoot him and I'll take ya in and throw ya in jail."

Cotton's eyes narrowed and said, "Bullshit. Ya might try to take me in, but ya ain't man enough to do the job. Now, I ain't lookin' fer trouble, but my friend *will* be treated, he's been shot."

The copper said, "Treat 'em."

The doctors eyes grew huge and he replied, "I'll do it, but the job will cost ya more."

"Fix 'em up and do the job now."

The lawdogs looked the place over and one of them asked, "Who killed the men in the den?"

"Likely it was Coon, because they were dead when we got here. The only other person in the house was his whore and he killed her in the barn."

The doctor approached and said, "He'll live, and change the bandages each day. Now, my fee is ten dollars."

Cotton reached into his pocket, pulled out a dollar coin and flipped it to the man as he said, "No, your fee tonight was a special price and it's all you'll get from me. Take it or pull a gun, it doesn't matter to me. See, yer about a worthless sumbitch in my mind and shootin' yer ass would make my day turn out fine."

Muttering the doctor left and the lawmen were right behind him. One sheriff stayed behind and said, "We have an arrest warrant for Coon out, for the killing of a trapper in Missouri. The reward is a thousand dollars, but it's sure to go up now that he's killed three other people here and this protection racket he had goin' on."

"We're goin after 'em, but he'll not be brought here. He killed some trappers out west and he'll have his day in court there, not in Saint Louis."

"Son," the old lawman said, "Don't take the law into your own hands or you're just as bad a man as he is."

"Bullshit, now, are we free to go?"

"Yes, but remember my words."

Cocking his head to the side, Cotton asked, "What words?  It seems I cain't remember much these days.  I don't remember well at all when I get pissed over killin's."

When the copper left, Cotton moved to Nate, pulled up a chair and poured a tall glass of whiskey.  He gave thought to Coon.  *He'll likely move east and then either north or south. He'll need a bank so he can have some funds sent to him, but that depends on how much money he has on him right now. Iffen he moves east, he'll have to find a way across the river, eventually.*

Coon decided to see a doctor about the bullet hole in his shoulder and then move south, along the river.  Entering the town, he saw a doctors office and moved his horse in that direction. Dismounting in front of the place, he tied his horse to the hitching post and knocked on the door.

A few minutes passed before a young man opened the door and asked, "Yes?"

"I've been shot in the shoulder, but it ain't a killin' wound.  I wondered if ya would take a look at it and bandage it up better.'

"Yes, of course, so come in."

After looking him over and cleaning the wound, the doctor said, "You need a couple of weeks of bed rest and something for the pain.  I have laudanum or whiskey."

"Give me a big bottle of both."

"Did the law catch whoever shot you?"  The doctor pulled two large bottles from his desk drawers.

"Uh-huh, they got 'em."

"Well, the whiskey is what I suggest most of the time, but if the pain gets severe, use a little laudanum.  Use the medicine sparingly, because you'll soon develop a desire for it."

"I've used it before, so it's nothing new.  How much do I owe ya?"

"Two bits for the visit and three dollars for the whiskey and medicine."

Coon paid the man and left.

Once outside he pulled the cork from both bottles, took a swing of whiskey, followed by a small swig of laudanum. *I've got to be able to move, come whatever,* he thought as he put the drinks in his saddlebags. He then mounted and move south by west.

Just outside of town, a sharp crack of thunder filled the night air, and Coon cursed, because he had no supplies, no food and only two pistols. At that point he almost turned back, but his concern of being discovered by Cotton kept him moving. An hour later, it began to rain. While the temperature was not cold, it added to his discomfort by chilling him.

Near dawn, just after the rain stopped, he spotted a crude looking log cabin and made his way toward the structure. Smoke was coming from the chimney, so someone was home. Coon dismounted and made his way to the door. Just as he was about to knock, a man spoke behind him, "Turn around slowly and let me get a look-see at ya."

Coon noticed the man was small, perhaps a couple of inches over five feet tall, blond hair and beard, with deep blue eyes. He was dressed in a homespun shirt, wearing bib-overalls, and a felt hat of gray. In his hands he held a double-barrel shotgun.

Giving his warmest fake smile, Coon said, "I'm Coon Thomas and wondered if ya had a little food I could buy. I need to warm up a bit and I've not eaten since yesterday."

"I see two pistols on ya, so drop 'em both on the porch."

Pulling his pistols, Coon dropped them and then said, "Yer not very trustin'."

"No, I ain't. I've been robbed too many times, shot at and missed, shit at and hit. I take no chances, now open the door, walk in and then move to the table."

Coon entered, moved to the table and then asked, "What now?"

"Sit down at the head of the table, where I can keep on eye on ya. Ruth, we have a visitor and he's a hungry man. Come dish 'em out some beans." The farmer then moved to an empty rocking chair.

"Do ya have a name?" Coon asked.

"Yep, I do."

Ruth, who Coon suspected was the man's wife entered the room and asked, "Who's our guest, Joseph?"

Ruth was a fine looking woman on the low side of her twenties, with an hourglass figure and head of blond hair. Her complexion was smooth and her green eyes bright. She wore a smile.

"Coon. Dish 'em up some beans, let 'em eat, and then he can get his ass out of here."

Coon raised both hands, palms open and replied, "Sir, I mean ya no harm." Then looking at Ruth he thought, *yer a mighty fine lookin' woman to be a farmers wife. I'd enjoy a couple of nights with ya.*

Ruth neared the stove, with a ladle in her hand and said, "We were robbed about six months back and lost both our horses, what money we had, and they even took some silver that'd been in the family for over two hundred years. We're just being safe, Coon."

"I understand," Coon said and added, "but could ya point that shotgun away from me as I eat?"

"It won't go off unless I pull the trigger and if I do that, yer a dead man."

Slowly reaching into his coat pocket, Coon pulled out a straight razor and held it by his thigh. He'd not pushed his chair in, so his lap was exposed. When Ruth brought the simple meal, Coon grabbed her and forced her onto his lap. He then placed the sharp straight razor blade against her throat.

Joseph shot from his chair, and said, "Lower the blade or I'll kill ya where ya sit."

"Ya shoot at me and you'll kill this woman, too. Now put the gun down."

"Mister, iffen ya kill Ruth, you'd be doin' me one big favor. All she does is bitch, complain, and argue over shit that don't mean a blame thing. So, if ya want to kill 'er, have at the job, 'cause you'll save me the trouble of doin' it myself. She's been talkin' of runnin' off anyway."

Poking her with his free hand, Coon asked, "Is he right?"

"Pretty much and I was plannin' to run away just as soon as I got my hands on some money. Why?"

"I said drop the damned razor or I'll blow ya and her a whole bunch of new assholes."

Coon pulled the blade from Ruth's throat, let it fall to the floor, and then asked, "What now?"

"Ruth, run into the bedroom and pack ya some clothes and a couple of blankets."

"What's goin' on?" Coon asked.

Ruth got up from Coons lap and ran into the bedroom, returning a few minutes later. Coon saw she was smiling as she stood by the table.

"Place your stuff on the table and go saddle ole Elijah. I'm gonna let ya leave just like ya been plannin', Ruth."

Ruth ran from the cabin.

In less than ten minutes she returned, still smiling, and Joesph ordered, "Coon and Ruth, walk out the door and mount. Now, in case yer wonderin' about yer guns, Coon, they'll stay with me. Seems we just traded two very fine pistols fer one loud-mouth useless woman and an old mule. While she looks good, you'll soon discover she ain't much in bed."

As soon as they mounted, Joseph added, "Now both of ya get and iffen I see either one of ya again, I'll shoot to kill."

Pulling their mounts around, they started down the narrow wagon road that led from the farm.

They'd not traveled far, when Ruth said, "He's a mean sumbitch and worthless as a man. We never had much and what little he's got now will be gone in a year. He's a hard worker, but doesn't know a damned thing about farmin'."

They rode in silence for a couple of miles and then Coon asked, "Is what he said true about you in bed?"

"No, it ain't true, but a woman wants a little passion before things get serious. All he cared about was himself."

Coon grinned, gave her a wink and said, "Mayhap tonight we'll find out, huh?"

"Ya wouldn't take a woman against her will, would ya?"

"Nope, I never have, but I don't think you'd be unwillin'. How far is the closest town to yer old place?"

"Eight miles due southwest and iffen we stay on this wagon road, we'll be there in a couple of hours. Why?"

"Well stop, get ya some nice lookin' clothes, get ya cleaned up, and then I'll buy ya supper in a restaurant. How does that sound?"

"I ain't never ate in a restaurant before.  Now, I ain't no soiled dove, so get that thought out of yer mind.  Only, iffen ya do all of that fer me, I should at least show ya how much I ap- preciate it, don't ya think?"

"Yep, I do my dear, but I'll do that for ya and maybe much more, depending on how well ya treat me," Coon replied and then thought, *like I've always said, all women are whores, some just charge a man up front.*

# Chapter 17

Nate was on his feet, but a week had passed and he still had some pain when he turned over while sleeping. The pain had dropped and the deep throbbing he'd experienced the first few days was gone. He was standing beside his horse as Cotton came out of the saloon with a keg of traders whiskey.

"Ya sure Coon headed south when he left here?"

"Pretty sure. One of my black friends, Sanders Mooney, that runs a cleanin' service here in town said he heard Franklin complaining that he'd been forced to send Coon fifty thousand dollars. The best Sanders could recollect it was the First National Bank of Ironwood, which is about forty miles from here."

"Well, by God, he's long gone by now."

"Sure he is, but we'll find something on the man."

Nate mounted, gave a light groan and said, "Let's ride, because we need to end this mess."

Night found them in a grove of oak trees with a small fire burning. Both were relaxed, because they considered Missouri much safer than in the mountains. Their biggest danger was snakes and robbers, but both they'd kill in a minute.

The night was uneventful and shortly before noon, they rode into the small town. The first place they stopped at was the livery stable and once they unforked their horses, they made their way inside.

A big man was pounding on a red-white hot horseshoe as they neared him. He placed the shoe back in his forge, turned and asked, "What can I do fer y'all?"

"We're lookin' fer a man. This man is about the size of me, red hair and beard."

"Got a woman with 'em?" The smithy asked.

"He didn't the last time I saw 'em," Cotton said and then added, "but anything is possible."

"I had a man come in here, oh, about a week ago. He boarded his animals for six days and from what I could see, he had the money. He paid me in cash, up front, then gave me a two dollar tip when he left."

"What do ya mean by he had the money?" Nate asked.

"Well, the woman with 'em was dressed in homespun when they got here, but that changed pretty damned quick. I saw 'em a few days later, coming out the Golden Spoon restaurant, it's a fancy eatin' place, and she was dressed to kill. Now, I don't mean she looked cheap, but good. All her clothing looked new to me."

"Any idea which way they moved after they left here?" Cotton asked.

"They moved due west, right into the Ozark Mountains, but there ain't shit there but a couple of small towns."

Cotton flipped the smithy two bits and said, "Thank ya kindly fer the information."

Catching the coin, the big man asked, "Are ya two the law?"

"Ya could say that." Nate replied and then laughed. He then tapped Cotton on the arm and they left the building.

"Where in the hell did he pick up a woman out here?"

"Likely she's some soiled dove he brought with 'em from Saint Louis." Nate said.

"I really don't see how he expects to run with a woman along."

"I don't think the man is running. I believe he thinks he got away from us clean."

"But why in the hell would a man with money move toward the Ozarks? There ain't nothin' there. I cain't even think of a town big enough to have a hotel there yet, unless it's Springfield and that's all the way across the state."

"He's up to something, but I ain't sure yet. Look, let's get a room and nose around a few places."

"I'll swear, I've spend more time in hotel rooms this last month than in my whole life combined."

There was only one hotel in town, so when they entered, Nate expected a problem. The clerk looked up from his newspaper and asked, "May I help you?"

Cotton asked, "How much are yer rooms a night?"

"Fifty cents."

"We'll take one, and how about sending up a bottle of rye in a few minutes?"

Reaching under the counter, the clerk pulled a bottle out and handed it to Cotton. He then said, "The total cost, including the drink is three dollars."

Cotton paid the man, and they signed the ledger.

"Ya seen a big man in here with reddish hair and about my size?" Nate asked.

"Sure, he spent five or six days with us, why?"

Cotton said, "He's my cousin and we're lookin' fer 'em. His momma has had some trouble at home and needs him to re-turn. There was a death in the family."

"I can't help ya there. Once they leave, well, I have no idea where they go. I do remember he was with a beautiful woman, but she for sure wasn't a whore. They acted like they were newlyweds, if ya know what I mean. Sorry, boys, that's all I can tell ya."

Nate grinned and replied, "Thank ya for tellin' us what ya did."

"Let's get to the room, I'm beat." Cotton said and they en-tered the hallway with key in hand. About half way down the hall, Nate pointed to a door on the right said, "That's our room."

Cotton was surprised by the room and said as much. The bed and mattress looked new, as well as most of the furniture. The mirror over the dresser was clean and not cracked, so they knew they'd found a hotel that took pride in their place.

"This stuff all looks new." Cotton said as he sat on the cor-ner of the bed.

"I don't think it is, see, this place most likely doesn't get a hell of a lot of business, and that's one of the reasons the clerk didn't raise a stink over my color. They need the money. I mean, this place is miles from the nearest railroad or busy road, and there ain't much here to bring visitors."

"Ya want a shot of red eye?"

"Sure, pour me about three fingers worth. I've a lot of trail dust to wash down my gizzard."

As Cotton pour the whiskey into two glass tumblers, he asked, "Who do we talk with now?  I mean we know where he's headed, so why did we get a room?"

"We need to visit the store to find out what kind and how much supplies Coon purchased.  The bank won't tell us anything about the man, so no use in visiting them.  We'll check the saloon too, but I doubt he spent much time there, since he had a woman along."

"He still has me confused.  I mean, why would a man with money not go east and get lost in the big cities?  Hell, we'd never find 'em in a large place.  And, why a woman?"

"I can't say why he's moving west, but the woman might be someone he loves or cares for a great deal.  He has no idea we're on his ass, so why not?  It might be he's one of those fellers that needs a female around all the time."

Cotton shrugged his shoulders and then handed a glass of whiskey to his partner.

An hour later, the drinks finished, Nate said, "It's still early, so let's go talk with the storekeeper and the bartender.  I plan on riding out of here come sunup."

"It doesn't matter to me, only I don't think we'll learn much from either of 'em."

The saloon wasn't very large and when they entered the place was empty.  They walked to the bar and Cotton said, "Two beers."

Placing the drinks on the bar, the man said, "That'll be a dime."

Nate noticed the bartender was typical of most and usually they had a head full of information, just from listening to conversations of their customers.  Cotton paid the man, and then Nate took a drink.

After a minute or two Cotton asked, "Have ya seen a big man, close to the size of my partner here, with red hair and beard, in lately?"

"Yep, and his name is Coon or that's what he told me anyway."

Nate asked, "Would ya call the man a big drinker?"

The bartender laughed and said, "He loves his rye or bourbon and that's for sure.  Except he held it well and I never had any problems with the big man.  He was the quiet type that never sat with his back to the door.  I had the feelin' he expected someone."

"He is expecting someone." Cotton said.

Nate said, "I heard he was with a woman."

"Hell, now that I don't know, but he didn't act like he had a woman.  He took Sally, my only soiled dove, for a couple of rides and according to her, he paid well."

"Yep, that sounds like Coon." Cotton said and then laughed.

The bartender suddenly asked, "Are you two the men he's expecting?"

Nate grinned and replied, "Nope, see, he's my brother and momma has turned sick.  I've come to fetch 'em home."

The bartender blinked rapidly for a few seconds, then broke out laughing.  Once he sobered he said, "Brother?  Well, it ain't no business of mine, but there ain't nothin' more I can tell ya.  He'd come in every night, have a few drinks, poke Sally and then leave. Like I said, he was a quiet man."

Gulping down his beer, Nate said, "Thank ya fer the information.  Come on, Cotton, let's go."

Outside, Nate asked, "Now why in the world is he travelin' with a woman and usin' a soiled dove too?  That's a might queersome to me."

"Who knows, so let's go talk with the storekeeper."

The storekeeper was a tall thin man wearing silver wire-rimmed glasses low on his large hawk-like nose.  He pulled out a sheet of paper and said, "He bought a lot of gear, along with twenty rifles and a hundred weight of powder and lead.  When I asked him about the rifles, he told me, well, what he said was he's was going to trap beaver and needed the guns for his men."

"He might be at that, but twenty rifles isn't really very many." Cotton replied.

"He bought thirty top quality blankets, all the tomahawks I had in the store, which was fifteen, and two dozen lookin' glasses.  He also bought yards of material, awls, needles by the case, and a whole bunch of other stuff.  It's almost as if he planned to trade with the Injuns, instead of trapping.  But, hell, I don't get many cash paying customers, so I gave 'em what he asked for and gladly, too."

"With all that stuff, where did he get the horses to pack it all?"

"He didn't use horses. I do know he bought a dozen mules from James Trout and his animals don't come cheap. He even hired a man to herd the mules into the Ozarks."

"Let's go, Cotton, and thank ya fer the information." Nate said.

Once back in the room, Cotton said, "I'm more confused now than I was before we spoke to those men."

Nate laughed and said, "It's simple, really, Coon is headed back to the Sioux to trade."

"Why? Hell, he's got enough money to live four lifetimes as it is, or is he greedy?"

"It doesn't matter. See I have an idea and I'm pretty sure it'll work."

"Oh, now that scares me." Cotton said and then laughed.

"We're finished trailin' after Coon."

"Huh? Why are we stoppin'?"

"Because I suspect he'll return to Buffalo Humps band of the Sioux and when he gets there, we'll be waiting for 'em."

"What iffen he goes someplace else?"

"Ya know how Injuns work. Hell, no matter what tribe the man goes to trade with, the word will get out quickly."

"Can we go back by boat this time? I'd like to ride at least to Fort Atkinson, because it'd save us a lot of travelin'."

Picking up the bottle of whiskey, Nate poured a couple of fingers of alcohol in each glass and said, "Yep, we can go by boat, but we need to go back to Saint Louis to do the job."

"We need some supplies anyway and that's likely the cheapest place to buy 'em, right?"

"Yep, we'll get 'em there. We'll leave in the mornin' two hours before first light."

Cotton was all eyes as he watched the shore pass by as he stood near the railing of the big paddle boat. He was like a kid at a circus, with his eyes huge and his mouth open, taking it all in and enjoying every second of the travel.

"By God," Cotton said, "this beats ridin' a horse any day. I mean, look how fast we're movin', we have a room with a bed, good grub, and iffen it rain's we'll stay dry."

Glancing up at the gray clouds, Nate replied, "It looks to me like we'll get a chance to see how dry our room is shortly."

"Let 'er rain, we'll be as snug as a bug in a rug on this thing. We'll just retire to our room and sip whiskey until the storm passes."

There sounded a loud *crack* of thunder overhead. Nate decided to pull Cotton's chain a little, "What if lightning strikes this thing? I mean it must happen at times, right?"

Looking up at the low gray clouds, Cotton said, "Life is full of danger and just bein' alive is dangerous. I'll place my life in the hands of God and pray for the best."

"Let's go to the cabin, because it'll be rainin' in a minute and it looks like some rough weather comin'."

"Sure, we still have that bottle of rye, right?"

"Yep, we do, so let's go share a bit."

Once in the room the boat began to move roughly on the waters. Nate poured the drinks, handed a cup to his partner and asked, "Do ya get seasick?"

"Hell, I reckon not, since I don't know what it is and I ain't never been on a sea."

"It's the rocking and movement of a boat."

"Waugh! I'm Cotton Top the mountain man!"

*We'll see in a few minutes, my friend, because the wind is pickin' up a mite,* Nate thought and threw back his drink. He poured another one, climbed into his bunk and opened a book.

Cotton sat on the lower bunk and started reading a newspaper. All went well for about thirty minutes, when the man suddenly said, "I'm feelin' weak and dizzy."

"Ya'd better get the washbasin and put it on the bed beside ya."

"I think I'm gonna thro—" Cotton puked on the floor and then made a mad dash for the washbasin. Nate heard the man emptying his stomach.

Looking out the small window near his bunk, the big mountain man saw trees on the far shore bending from the winds. Water was slapping the vessel hard and with each slap the boat rolled to one side. Nate didn't have a problem with seasickness, but the smell from Cottons vomit was getting to him. He jumped from his bunk, grabbed a towel and cleaned up the mess on the floor. He opened the cabin door and dropped the towel in the hallway. Then, he climbed back in his bed.

Cotton finally quit puking, but continued with the dry heaves for many long minutes. Finally he made his way to his bunk, sprawled out and with teary eyes said, "I'm sick as a dog."

"You'll eventually get use to the movement and it won't make ya sick after that, but it might take a day or two."

"A day or two! Damn me, I'm almost dead now."

Nate leaned over the side of his bunk and looked at his buddy. Cotton's face was white, eyes watered, and he did look bad. He had his left arm wrapped around the washbasin, hold-ing it tightly. "I think you'll survive."

"I ain't sure, but iffen I go under, ya can have my Hawken."

Nate laughed and said, "Waugh! I'm Cotton Top the moun-tain man!"

"Nate, ya can just go to hell. I'm sick I tell ya."

"Try to sleep, it'll help ya feel better."

Hours later, Cotton was still sleeping, and Nate tired of reading. *I'll go eat something and walk around the deck a little. Sounds like most of the wind has stopped.*

Cotton cracked his eyes open and asked, "Where ya goin'?"

"Eat. Are ya hungry?"

"Oh, Lord, I can't eat right now. I might not ever eat again." He closed his eyes.

Nate chuckled, placed his hat on his head and left the room.

While the wind was less, it was not a gentle breeze and the boat rocked and rolled in the water. Entering the ships dining area, he saw it was almost empty, so he knew most of the pas-sengers were ill. He was seated by a young man who also handed him a menu. Nate expected high prices, but one quick glance shocked him. *They want two dollars for a steak. A beer is two bits and a slice of apple pie is a dollar. Well, since Cot-ton won't eat, I guess I can spend for the two of us.*

When the waiter returned the big man ordered a steak, medium rare, baked potato, beans, and a glass of milk. When he asked for milk, the waiter snickered.

"Son, do ya have something against milk?"

"Oh, no, sir, except with you dressed in buckskins and likely a mountain man, I just found it odd."

"Milk is good fer ya and it'll help keep ya strong. Now, I happen to like milk, when I can get it, and suggest ya leave my choice of drink to me."

"Yes, sir, I understand."

"Ya tell the cook to burn the outside and I want to find blood on the inside when I cut that meat."

"I'll tell 'em."

Later, his meal spread out in front of him, Nate had just picked up his fork, when he heard a voice say, "Nate Grisham, I've been lookin' fer your ass!"

# Chapter 18

Coon looked across the fire at Ruth and thought, she's a real tiger in bed at times and other times she's like a corpse. I'll keep 'er a spell and maybe trade 'er to the Sioux. I'll bet they'd love get their hands on her and for no other reason than she's different. They don't see many blond women out that way, so she'll be valuable. Hard to say how many furs they'd trade for her.

"What are ya thinkin' on over there?" Ruth asked.

Coon grinned and said, "How many furs the Sioux would trade me for a prime piece of woman flesh like ya."

She laughed loudly and then said, "Ya are too funny. Where are we to meet those men of yours?"

"Up near Independence. It's a bit of a ride from here."

"I hope this trip of yours is a good one. Do ya think we might make enough to retire some place nice?"

"I'm thinkin' of goin' to New Orleans."

"I heard of it, but don't know nothin' about the place."

*Ya don't know nothin' about anything, but ya ain't goin' with me anyway,* Coon thought and then said, "We'll get the men and some more rifles in Independence. We'll buy all we can get our hands on and then take 'em to trade with the Injuns. See, a Hawken costs a bunch of money, but a warrior will trade forty or more furs to get a rifle. We more than double our money, easily."

"Yer a smart man, Coon."

*Sometimes I wonder, especially when it comes to women,* Coon said, "Thank you, my dear, now go get our bed ready for the night."

Coon poured a cup of coffee, leaned back against a log and sipped the strong brew. The overhead sky was clear, with stars sparkling and shining brightly. He thought of his childhood. He'd grown up dirt poor, his father a drunk and his step momma selling herself to feed her laudanum habit. She said it, "Settles my nerves." Coon knew anything a person craved everyday couldn't be good for them. One day his momma drank too much of the medicine and when she fell asleep, he'd poured more into her mouth. When his pa came home, she was dead. That same day his pa threw him out and at the ripe age of thirteen, Coon Turner was on his own. The next day, he returned home, found his pa passed out from whiskey and blew him to hell with a shotgun. He found his step momma's body still in the bed, so he'd shot her as well.

He'd walked to Saint Louis, well over a hundred miles. He then turned to petty theft and was soon a better than an average pickpocket, except he was arrested by the law off and on. Because of his tender age and graceful lies, he was always released. Finally, the boys he had working for him started being murdered. He'd taken his money and what little he'd owned, mounted a stolen horse, rode west, and never looked back. The problem was, Coon had never stopped running.

"Ya comin' to sleep?" Ruth asked from the darkness.

"I'll be there in a bit, I'm thinkin' on some stuff." *Damn her, she's startin' to sound like a full time wife, and I won't put up with that shit long.*

Independence was thriving with men and women moving in all directions, when the two finally rode into town near dusk. Wagon wheels creaked and groaned as they moved from the town carrying heavy loads to some unknown destination. Pulling up in front of the Great Western Hotel, they dismounted, tied their horses to the hitching post and entered.

An obese bald man stood from his chair and waddled to the counter. Giving a fake smile, he asked, "How may I help you fine folks this evening?"

"How much are your rooms?"

"A dollar a night for the room, ten cents for a bath, and we have the best food in town."

"Do ya eat here?" Coon asked.

"Of course, sir, the cook is my wife. I rarely miss a meal and must say it's excellent."

"By God, by lookin' at yer lard ass, I'd say ya ain't never missed a meal in yer life." Coon placed a dollar and twenty cents on the counter. "Now, get me a key."

Pissed, but knowing the man in front of him was dangerous, just by his crazy eyes, the clerk said nothing. He turned and pulled a key from the wall. Handing it to Coon he said, "Sign the register and I'll give you the key."

Coon quickly signed the register, pulled out two dollars and said, "I want a good bottle of rye or bourbon sent to my room in a few minutes."

The key exchanged hands and Coon made his way to the room. They'd only been in the room a few minutes when a young boy brought the whiskey. Pouring two fingers of the amber colored drink into two water glasses, he handed one to Ruth and said, "Well, we have a bed to sleep in tonight and that'll be a welcome change."

Ruth took a sip of her drink and asked, "When are ya to meet the men?"

"Tomorrow morning at a saloon called the Dirty Dog. Now, there will be twenty or thirty of 'em and each will be a rough man."

"You'll handle 'em and I have no doubts."

"Finish your drink and let's find a place to eat."

Ruth chugged her whiskey, wiped her mouth off with the back of her hand and asked, "Why not eat here, at the hotel?" She placed the empty glass beside the bottle.

"I don't want to eat in the hotel, because they'll charge us an arm and a leg for anything they serve. Come on, let's go find a place to eat." Coon put his hat on, checked both of his pistols, and made his way to the door. At the door, he knocked back his drink and sat the empty glass on the dresser.

A little more than a block from their hotel, they found a placed called the Golden Spoon and the prices were very reasonable. Over a meal of beef steaks, potatoes, and corn, they made small talk about the coming adventure and the dangers involved with trading rifles and whiskey to Indians.  They'd just finished their meal when a man holding a shotgun at the ready approached their table.  *What in the hell is this?*  Coon thought, as he pulled a pistol and placed his thumb on the hammer.

"Kramer, I cain't believe you'd come in here after all the damn killin' ya did the last time ya was here.  By God, I warned ya the last time I saw ya I'd kill ya on sight."  The man was middle-age, white hair, and thin.  His teeth were brown and broken, and he wore wire-rimmed glasses.  He was clean shaven.

"I'm not Kramer and I have papers to prove it.  If you'll let me pull the papers from my inside coat pocket, it'll clear this up."

"Not Kramer, my ass.  Look, I know ya and in case ya forgot, ya killed my son in here, ya no good sumbitch.  But, pull yer paper out and iffen yer hand comes out with anything other than paper, this scatter gun will send ya to hell pretty damned quick."

Nervous, because a man with a cocked shotgun was serious business, Coon pulled the paper slowly and handed it to the old man.

Reading the wanted poster, he handed it back to the mountain man and said, "Pull the front of yer shirt open.  I want to see the left nipple on yer chest."

Coon stood, removed his coat and then unbuttoned his shirt.  Pulling his shirt open wide, he said, "See, I don't have a scar one on my chest and I ain't Kramer, though I've been confused with the man more than just a few times."

"I . . . I'll be damned.  I would have sworn ya were the man.  Hell, yer voice even sounds the same to me."

"Sit down, old timer, and let me buy ya a drink.  I don't know yer name, but I'm Coon Turner and this it my wife, Ruth."

The old man said, "I'm Andrew Roddy, and I'm sorry about all of this.  When Kramer killed my son, Lewis, I almost lost my mind.  See, earlier in the same year I lost my wife to fever and a daughter died durin' childbirth.  I was suddenly a man alone and it's hard on me.  Hell, it takes all I have to even want to live anymore.  I've been drinkin' too much and to tell ya the truth, I just don't give a shit about nothin' no more."

Flagging down a waitress, Coon had a bottle of whiskey brought to the table and then said, "Andrew, we all make mistakes, but thank God ya didn't walk in here and just start shootin'. Ya might have killed the wrong man or I'd have killed ya."

Lowering his head, Andrew said, "I wouldn't have done that, because I wanted Kramer to know who did the killin', don't ya see?  I want revenge, but I need for the sumbitch to know why he's dyin', or it's a wasted bullet."

Pouring three drinks into the shot glasses on the table, Coon handed one to Andrew and the other to Ruth, he said, "To better days."

When they finished their drinks, Coon asked, "What do ya do fer a livin', Andrew?"

"Hell, I used to own this place, but sold 'er after the death of my family.  And, call me Andy, not many call me by my given name."

*I'll need a cook on the trip to keep the men happy, but he might not like us tradin' guns to Injuns, so I'll have work around that part during the trip,* Coon thought and then asked, "Are ya a good cook?"

Andy laughed and replied, "Likely the best cook in town, so why the question?"

"I'm leading a large group of men into the plains and hope to trade with the Sioux.  They'll trade well for a looking glass, skinnin' knife, a bolt of material, or even needles.  I don't have a cook and it'd be a good way to keep my men happy."

"What's the pay?"

"Three dollars a day and that's a dollar more than the men. A good cook is hard to find.  Now, I have to warn ya, the job could be dangerous as all hell.  Also, no drinkin' unless I give it to ya."

Andy thought for a minute or two and then said, "I don't need the money, not after what I made off this place, but I need to get away from here a spell and a little danger won't scare me off.  I fought in the War of 1812, so I know how to fight, need be. Then again, iffen I get killed, it don't matter much anyway."

"Good, experienced men are what I'm lookin' fer.  Ya be in front of the Dirty Dog Saloon three days from now and we'll ride.  Make sure ya have what ya need when we go, or you'll do without it.  I'll furnish the supplies and cooking utensils, so don't worry about that at all.  Make sure ya have ten pounds of power and the same in lead.  We're ridin' into some rough country."

"Any rules I need to know about?"

"Just three, but they're needed.  One, I am the boss and what I say goes.  Two, no drinkin' at all, like I said, unless I give ya the drink.  Three, no messin' with the other men."

"I don't think I understand the last one."

"If you're a man who wants a male lover, I honestly don't care, but not on this trip.  If ya want to do that sort of thing, wait until we return."

"Good God, have ya had problems with that sort of thing in the past?"

"Once."

"What'd ya do, run the feller off?"

"Nope, I killed both of 'em.  Like I said, I don't care what ya do once we finish the job, but on the job it's all business, agreed?"  Coon extended his hand.

"Agreed, but I'm not like that.  I like women too much."  Andy took the offered hand and shook.  He then gave Ruth a wink.

Morning dawned with rain, and thunder boomed as Coon crawled from bed and started dressing.  He glanced at Ruth and thought, *she was wild in bed last night, but why?  Was it because I took her out to eat or the thought of our coming trip?  Maybe her passion comes from bein' dined, adventure, or maybe the few glasses of whiskey she had to drink.  Regardless, we'll eat out again tonight and I'll give her a few drinks, so I'll see.  I can't figure women out at all.*

"Where ya goin'?" Ruth asked from bed.

"Did ya forget I have to meet the men this mornin' at the saloon?"

"Oh, now I remember." She said, then turned over and continued, "I'll sleep a bit more and maybe when ya return I'll be ready fer another round. How does that sound?"

"Sounds good, but business first, my dear." Placing his hat on his head he left the room, enjoying the feeling of his big pistols in his sash.

A different man at the front desk gave Coon directions to the Dirty Dog Saloon and the walk was short, just a couple of blocks. The thunder was still *booming and cracking*, only a very light rain fell during his walk. He pulled his hat down lower and in a matter of a few short minutes he was there.

Walking through the batwing doors, he stopped and glanced around. The place was empty and looking at an old clock hanging under a mounted deer head, it was a little after eight in the morning. He took a seat at the rear of the bar, with his back against the wall, and with him facing the door.

He pulled a chair close, removed a pistol, cocked it, and placed on the chair for easy access. He wanted to be ready if a man turned mean on him or someone bent on revenge turned ugly. He'd learned years ago, you never know who you'll meet when looking for men to ride for you.

The bartender, a stout man holding a gray rag that may have once been white, neared and asked, "What'll ya have?"

"Quart of rye and a dozen glasses. I'm conductin' interviews for a job today and there will be a lot of men comin' in."

"Sure, not a problem. About how many men will show, or do ya have a notion?"

"I'm lookin' for between forty and fifty to ride for me, so at least that many, why?"

"I'm just wonderin'. Iffen they hang around I might make a few bucks."

Coon laughed and replied, "You'll make more than just a few bucks, because I'm givin' all the men I hire half a months pay up front. I suspect most, if not all, will buy a drink or four."

Returning with the bottle, the bartender said, "Listen, iffen that many men come through those doors, this whole bottle is on the house. Hell, I'll make fifty times what this bottle cost."

"Agreed. While I wait, bring me a double bourbon and a beer chaser."

"Be with ya in the minute."

At that moment a big man entered and by his blond hair, Coon recognized him as one of his childhood friends, "Culp Cobble, I'll be damned, ya did show up. Get yer ugly ass over to my table and let's have a drink."

Cobble moved stiffly to the table, pulled out a chair and sat. Coon passed him a drink, which he downed and then held his glass out once more. As the mountain man filled it, Cobble said, "I'm a lucky man. I was out west with some boys making meat for one of the eatin' places in town, when we ran into the Oto. When we left town there were twenty of us, three of us returned alive and every single one of us has an injury. I took an arrow though my calf and it still hurts like a bitch."

Coon stood and said, "Bartender, bring my table another bottle of rye."

Cobble tilted his head, blinked his eyes a few times and then asked, "Coon, are ya okay? I mean ya just ordered a bottle and ya got almost of full one in front of ya."

"This one is for ya to kill yer pain. Ya got a room around here?"

"I had one, but since we didn't get any meat, I'll have to leave the hotel today. I still owe 'em for two nights and I'm flat busted. Hell, I don't know what I'm gonna do now. Seems like life was just lookin' good and then the Oto come along, and ended it all. I was makin' three dollars a day sellin' meat."

"How'd ya like to go back to makin' three dollars a day and have a ration of whiskey everyday as well? I can't have ya drunk, but food is included in the deal."

"Doin' what and for who? I don't need no trouble in my life right now."

"Look, I'll do better than three dollars a day and pay ya ten, how's that? What I've got in mind will make us both a pile of money." *I can promise the world, because I don't have to deliver a damned thing in the end.*

Looking over his shot glass at Coon, Cobble said, "You didn't answer my question. Doin' what?"

"Tradin' guns and whiskey to the Sioux."

Cobble coughed and then choked as the whiskey shot out of his nose. After a few minutes he got his coughing under control and said, "Coon, if the army catches ya, you'll stretch hemp. But, ten dollars a day is temptin'."

"I'm hirin' a bunch of riders. We'll go to the Sioux, trade and then move toward Saint Louis, where we'll sell the plew. We'll be in and out in less than a month. Three hundred dollars would last ya a long time, Culp. I want ya to ramrod the men."

"Can ya go as high as fifteen a day?"

"Hell, yea, for an old buddy like ya, I can." Coon said and thought, *yer greed will get ya killed when we near Saint Louis, my old friend.*

"I thought so; iffen yer gonna make a mountain of money from this tradin', I'd like a bit too."

Pulling out a wad of bills, Coon counted out forty dollars and said, "Here's an advance. Go now and take that bottle of whiskey for yer pain. Two days from now be ready to go at sunup and be in front of this place ready to ride. Understand?"

"Sure, Coon, I'll be here."

# Chapter 19

Nate turned toward the voice, and saw Deacon and Bear grinning at him. The two were old mountain man friends from way back and Cotton knew them, too. Releasing the hammer on his pistol and glancing at his Hawken rifle, he knew he was with friends, so neither weapon would be needed.

"Where's that butt ugly, Cotton?" Deacon asked.

"Sick as a dog in our room right now. He started puking just when the water turned rough and ain't stopped yet. It was his idea to come on the Washington, not mine. I ain't got any love for big ass boats."

Bear said, "Some stomachs can't handle it when a boat starts to dance a mite."

"By God, Cotton is one of 'em."

"We're heading for the deck to smoke a bit, want to join us?" Deacon asked.

Nate stood, place the money for his meal and a tip on the table, and grinning he said, "Sure, because I'm in no hurry to return to the room and smell puke."

The day was cool, but not cold and once on deck, Nate checked the clouds as a matter of habit. The winds had died down a great deal, but the sky was gray. *Rain or snow comin' before dawn tomorrow*, the big man thought as he pulled his pipe from his shirt pocket. Pulling a small leather bag from his larger possibles bag, he began to stuff the bowl of his pipe.

He pulled a piece of pine, actually just a long sliver about four inches long from his possibles bag, and made his way to one of the constantly burning lanterns on the side of the boat. Lifting the globe, he placed the tip of his sliver of pine into the flames. When it caught fire, he removed it and lighted his pipe. He then handed the still burning pine to Deacon, who in turn gave it to Bear.  Once Bear's pipe was burning, he tossed the pine over the rail into the water.

The three men were talking in low voices, when the first arrow struck the rail, about six inches from where Nate stood.

A lookout on the top of the Washington, screamed, "Injuns on the port side!"

When everyone moved to the side of the boat the three men were on, all holding guns, the captain yelled, "About half of ya fools move to the other side of the ship!  Often they'll attack the side with less defense.  They have canoes, ya know!  Now move!"

Men began to hustle to the other side, when Nate raised his Hawken and fired at a Oto brave on shore.  The man screamed and fell unnaturally to the grasses.  Three other shots rang from the other side of the boat, and then someone yelled, "Canoes, they're trying to get on the boat!"

Four braves on shore ran to the waters edge and pulled back their bows.  The three mountain men brought their rifles up, aimed, and fired so close together it sound like one shot.  Three warriors fell, with two screaming and one dead before he struck the mud.  The remaining brave let his arrow fly and Nate heard a grunt.  Looking to his left, a small man stood with the arrow in his throat, and his pleading eyes met the black man's.  About half of the arrow shaft was protruding from the back of his neck and blood began to spurt onto the front of his shirt with each beat of his heart.  He suddenly collapsed to his knees for a few seconds, then fell to his left side.  His body quivered violently a couple of times and then the man lay still.  Nate noticed the index finger on the right hand kept twitching for a few seconds.  Then, the man was dead.

Two pistol shots sounded and the brave fell to the mud unmoving.

"Look at all the damned canoes on the river!  They're floating down stream toward us!"  The captain yelled.

Cotton appeared at Nate's side, looking pea green, but held his rifle is his hands.

"Let's move to the front of the boat and start shootin' or we'll lose our ride up river."  Nate said as he ran to the bow.

"I need five men on the stern!"  The captain ordered.

"We have the bow, Captain!"  Deacon called out.

Once at the bow, Bear said, "Deacon, ya and Nate shoot, while me and Cotton load. Take yer time and try for a killin' shot each time."

Leaning two loaded rifles against the rail, the loaders waited. Nate fired first and a huge warrior toward the rear of the canoes was knocked into the water, but he didn't surface. Deacon shot and the canoe furthest away had a man down. On and on the firing went. With almost every shot fired, a Oto fell wounded or dead. Finally, with a loud shout from one of the canoes, the warriors paddled for the far side.

Before the Oto reached the shore, Nate and Deacon had added six more injured braves to the growing list.

"Every available hand to the stern! The Injuns are board-ing!" Someone squalled and Nate and his group moved to the rear of the big boat.

"Move the boat to the center of the river and do the job now!" The captain ordered.

Nate saw the Injuns were on the boat and hand-to-hand fighting was taking place. He estimated a good two dozen war-riors were fighting about half that many white men. The new men, including Nate's group, didn't hesitate and waded right into the fight. A huge warrior rushed toward Nate, with a tom-ahawk held high in his hand, so the mountain man raised his ri-fle to block the blow. The impact was so hard, it stung Nate's hands. As the warrior brought his tomahawk back once more, the mountain man slammed the butt of his rifle against the Oto's head as hard as he could. He felt something break when his stock hit the Indian, so he cast his rifle aside and pulled his tomahawk and Green River knife.

Feeling the prick of a knife tip to his back, he turned to see a warrior fighting with Cotton and somehow a knife blade had struck the big man. With one hard sweep of Nate's tomahawk, the warriors head split almost in half and he collapsed to the deck of the boat. Giving Cotton a quick wink, Nate turned and engaged a brave that held two knives, edges up.

Dropping his knife, Nate pulled his pistol, lined it up with the Oto's chest and squeezed the trigger. The Indian was blown off his feet by impact of the heavy fifty caliber lead ball, which took him high, about an inch below where his neck met his shoulders. Nate dropped the now empty pistol and pulled his last one. The Indians were leaving the boat now, many simply jumping over the railing and into the water. As one climbed the railing and made ready to jump, Nate's pistol spat lead and the warrior's chest exploded with bone, blood and gore spraying in all directions.

"Cease fire! Cease fire, ya bloody fools! They're leavin' ship!" Someone shouted from above them.

Nate glanced around the boat deck and saw white men and Indians scattered all around. Moving to his knife, he picked it up and joined the other mountain men in cutting the throats of all Oto they could lay their hands on. The nasty job completed, they threw twenty red bodies into the slow moving river. Nate noticed Cotton looked fine, without any obvious injury, but Deacon had a long gash on his left cheek. Finally spotting Bear leaning against the railing, his chest leaking blood, the big man moved to his side.

"How badly are ya hurt?" Nate asked.

"Took a knife slash to the chest and lost part of my little finger. I'll live, but I need to get them cared for because I'm losing blood."

"Hang tight and I'll see how the injured are goin' to be treated." Then, reaching into his possibles bag, Nate removed some white cotton material and said, "Rip this in half and have Cotton doctor ya some. I'm goin' to see somebody about the doctorin'."

Seeing the boat captain near the railing on the port side, Nate made his way to the man, avoiding the injured as they cried, screamed, and prayed.

"Sir, what of our injured?" Nate asked.

"Leave the most seriously injured where they be for right now, but take the others to the dining area. I have men in there who are trained to treat injuries. We'll try to treat those most seriously injured where they lay." The Captain replied to Nate and then yelled, "Cromwell!"

"Sir!"

"Get me an accurate body count and number of injured." Then he turned to Nate and asked, "would you assist Cromwell in determining the condition of the most seriously injured? I can tell by your dress, you're an experienced man."

"Sure, I'll help in any way I can, sir."

"Cromwell, take this big man with you to look the injured over. He'll determine who is to remain on deck and who is to go for immediate treatment."

Cromwell was a small man; if anyone had said he was five feet tall, they might have been stretching it a couple of inches. He walked to Nate, extended his hand and said, "Let's get the dirty job done. Ya give me yer views on the man's condition and I'll do what's needed with 'em. We have over a dozen on the deck, so blood will make walking slippery, and that doesn't even count the walking wounded."

Nate yelled, "All of ya that can walk, make yer way to the dinin' room. Once there, line up fer treatment. Cotton, ya stay with me."

As soon as the men moved away, toward the front of the boat, Cromwell asked, "What about this one?"

Nate looked the man over, noticed he was unconscious, breathing, but had a number of deep stab wounds to his chest and blood was running from his open mouth. As the man breathed, bloody bubbles formed on his chest injuries. "Lung injury, so he'll not make it. Cotton, drag this man off to the right."

The next four men were dead, beyond any doubt, with vicious injuries to all parts of their bodies. Nate listened for a heart beat, but there was none. "Cotton, drag these fellers to the left side."

Of the remaining seven, five would survive if given treatment, and the other two would die. Cromwell looked at one of the seriously wounded and said, "I don't see much except his eye is bleeding."

"He was stabbed in the eye and the blade entered his brain. If ya listen to his heartbeat, you'll hear it's weak, not regular, and the beats are slowing down. I suspect this man will be dead in just a few minutes. This other one, has been gutted like a deer, and while he'll live a while, there ain't no way in hell we can save him. Gut injuries can take days to kill a man."

"Aye, I've seen 'em before. I served for over twenty years in the navy, retired and then took this job."

"So, ya know."

Cromwell nodded, stood and called a name, "Wright! Fetch the medical supplies and don't forget the big bottle of laudanum.  Hurry now, son, and don't take all day.  We have some seriously wounded we must attend to right now."

A few minutes later, Wright handed the bag of medical supplies to Cromwell.  Glancing at Nate, the old navy man said, "These two we'll feed some laudanum and kill 'em.  I'd want it done fer me and I suspect ya would as well."

Nate, who'd been working with the man stabbed in the eye, turned and said over his shoulder, "Ya can forget about this man, he's dead.  But, uh-huh, I'd want it done fer me iffen I had no chance to survive.  It'll surely cut down the pain fer a man.  Ain't no reason in hell fer a man to suffer, not iffen we can't heal 'em, for days on end."

Cromwell poured about a half a cup of laudanum into the gut injured man's mouth and then said, "Forgive me Lord, because I have murdered this man.  I'm not killin' this man out of anger, God, but compassion."  He then crossed himself and added, "I've killed this man just as sure as iffen I'd used a gun."

"Well, I ain't Catholic, so I have no idea what that means in your religion, but in mine, I'd simply ask the Lord for forgiveness and I'd have it.  God knows our hearts."

Cromwell gave a weak smile and replied, "Yes, I suspect he does know our hearts.  What's yer name, sir, and what are ya doin' on me boat?"

"I'm Nate Grisham and I'm a mountain man.  I'm ridin' yer boat as far as she goes, so I have less distance to ride to my shining mountains."

"Yer about the biggest black feller I ever did see.  Are ya a runaway?"

"That, Mister Cromwell, is none of yer damned business."

Cromwell broke out laughing and finally said, "Nate, I'm just curious.  I have no problems with black folks, but actually know very few.  We had a few in the navy, but they were cooks, servants, or powder monkeys."

"Well, by damn, I ain't nobodies monkey!"

"No, you misunderstand the name, sir.  A powder monkey is a job on a ship, not a name for one single man or group of men.  Anyone, regardless of their color, that fetches powder on board a ship is called a powder monkey.  So relax a mite, my friend."

*He said, my friend, so at least he considers me a friend and his equal,* Nate thought and then said, "Being black ain't always easy."

"Hell, bein' white ain't always easy either. Anyway ya cut it, life is hard, but I suspect it's harder on those that ain't born white. Ya be a good man and we'll get along, no matter yer color, deal?" He extended his hand.

As Nate took it in his powerful hand he replied, "Deal."

Standing, Cromwell said, "Wright, go through each dead man's clothing and try to find any kind identification, room key, or anything that might hint at who they are. Most will have a cabin and the room key should be on them."

"Hows a room key gonna help?" Wright asked.

"Young Mister Wright, we can check the room number on the key against our ships listing of passengers and arrive at a name. It may be all we have for some of these men. Hurry now, lad, the Captain is wanting a total count on our dead and injured."

Cotton asked, "What about these injured men?"

"I'll have some men take them to the cargo area and we'll treat them there. I'm sure once the cook is finished treating the walking wounded, he'll come there. Most seriously injured are kept in the hold, so the healthy men cannot be reminded of pain and death." Cromwell then turned and yelled, "Henson!"

"Yo!"

"Get some men and as soon as the injured are removed, wash this deck free of blood. I want it done right, so make it spotless when I see it again." Then turning to Nate, Cromwell said, "If we get a chance before we land, I'd like to get with ya and share a bottle of rye."

Nate grinned and replied, "I'd like that. I'm heading back to my cabin now, but I'm in number seven when you're ready."

"Stay safe, my friend, until we share that bottle."

"Oh, I intend to do just that. Come on, Cotton, I'm worn out and need a drink."

They entered the boat and made their way down the hall to their cabin. Entering, Cotton said, "The bottle is on yer bed."

Nate walked to the bed, picked up the bottle and pulled the cork—it gave a loud pop when removed. His glass was on the dresser, so he added four fingers of the light brown alcohol.

Taking a long sip, he gave a loud sigh, and said, "Man, I needed this. There's something about a fight that takes all the air from my sails."

"What was the reason for this attack?" Cotton asked as he took the bottle and started filling his glass.

"It'd be hard to say, really, because ya know how Injuns are most of the time. Mayhap they're just tired of the white man moving over their lands. Injuns are proud people and they've a right be, because they're as tough as a grizzly bear with a toothache."

"Next time, we ride home. I ain't been this sick in years and then to fight on top of it almost did my ass in. I've never seen a boat attacked before and don't like fightin' on one at all. Hell, there ain't no place to hide 'er nothin'."

"No, not much cover on a boat. But, I think iffen we'd not been on here, they'd have taken the boat and killed every man. It's only our shooting of the canoes in front of the boat that saved the day, or so I think. See, with the crew all gathered on the ass of this thing, the front wasn't defended at all. All the Oto would have had to do was climb on in and then overwhelm the crew."

There was a light tapping on the cabin door.

"Who is it?" Cotton asked.

"It's me, Deacon, and a crippled mountain man called Bear."

Nate chuckled and said, "Let 'em in. We can share our whiskey with 'em."

The two men entered as soon as Cotton opened the door and the first words out of Bears mouth were, "Got two more glasses for some whiskey?" He held up a fresh bottle of rye, not even opened.

"I want both of ya to take a seat, because a light wind will blow either one of ya over." Cotton said.

"We're okay, really, just lost some blood waitin' to get worked on. They sewed my chest together, which beat a hot knife to hell and back, and soaked my finger tip in a glass of whiskey. Then, they wrapped me up and gave me a bottle of panther piss. The captain said we mountain men saved his boat." Bear said and then gave a goofy grin.

Deacon said, "They offered me a bottle too, after sewing my cheek, but I had a couple of glasses as I waited to be treated, now this one, so I'm okay.  Drink has been the ruin of many a good man."

Nate cleared his throat, so Deacon would understand he was preaching again and he'd agreed not to do that, except when asked to do so.  Deacon smiled.

"Well," Cotton asked, "are the two of ya headin' back to the mountains?"

Bear said, "Yep, we sold our furs in Saint Louie and decided to take the boat most of the way back.  I never realized ya two were on here too, until I spotted Nate eatin'."

"I know ya was lookin' fer Coon Turner, so did ya make 'em come?" Deacon asked.

"Nope, he's a slippery one, Coon is, but we'll get 'em.  We heard tell he's headed west and that means sooner or later he'll turn up in our very own parlor, so to speak.  All we have to do is wait."

"What makes ya think he's comin' out west, hell, that'd be stupid of 'em."

"We talked to a man who said he'd bought a herd of mules and was lookin' fer men, or so the jasper thought.  Now, that many mules are only needed out west,  unless he plans to open a livery stable, so he must be goin' back into the tradin' business."

"There is a lot of land out our way, Nate." Deacon said.

"Yep, there surely is, but only a few tribes of Sioux.  The last time he visited, Coon was with old Hump's band, so I figure that's where he'll return.  I plan on being in the village when the man arrives."

Bear laughed and then said, "Hell, ya can't attack or kill the man while he's a guest of Hump's or there will be holy hell to pay.  It's likely the Sioux would tear ya apart."

"Not if I challenge the man.  We're about the same size and there is little the Sioux enjoy more than a good knife fight. Seems I've discussed all of this before."

Deacon said, "I'd think on that a long spell and make sure ya been livin' right for a while before ya challenge him, too.  Knife fights always turn bloody and foul in my view."

"Oh," Nate said with a slight grin, "I don't mind blood and gore, as long as it ain't mine.  But, mark my words, one way or the other, Coon Turner will die iffen he shows."

# CHAPTER 20

The weather was nasty as the men mounted in front of the Dirty Dog Saloon. Dark gray clouds were low overhead and a cold breeze blew from the west. It was a few minutes before dawn and every man recruited had showed up, but not necessarily ready to ride. More than a couple were sitting off center in the saddle as the result of too much whiskey the night before. One man, who looked to be Mexican, leaned over and puked.

"Culp, let's get these drunken fools movin'. Head straight west until I tell ya otherwise. I want horse guards anytime we stop and iffen I catch a guard asleep, I'll personally cut his damned throat." Coon ordered. He glanced at the rough looking men behind him, shook his head and thought, *they ain't much, but there's enough of 'em to keep the Sioux honest.*

"Sure thing, Coon. Alright men, we're movin' west and we're doin' 'er now."

Andy, the cook, grinned and tapped his horse gently in the ribs. He'd placed most of his money in the bank, bought a few clothes, and paid his bills. He'd still had enough money left over to buy a small bottle of whiskey and drink a little the night before. While he'd drank, he felt no ill effects this morning.

The morning passed slowly, especially for those men packing hangovers, but by noon most were feeling better. The wind, while still cold, was blowing with less force and the rain or snow had not shown yet. Glancing up at the sky, Coon said, "Move off the trail about a hundred feet and let's see if these men can stomach any food. Andy, as soon as we stop, start a meal."

"Sure, I can do that. I cooked up a big pot of beans and hog jowl last night. All I'll have to do is warm 'em up a little."

"Smart man!  I can see already you'll be of great help."

"I've some cornbread too, so they'll be eatin' in a few minutes."

"Good, because we'll only stop for an hour.  I intend to ride until about an hour before dusk, but if this weather turns nasty we'll have to hunt a hole."

Culp said, "This time of the year we could get snow or rain, so there ain't no way to tell really.  Except with this wind and as cold as it is, I'd say snow."

"No matter what we get, we're movin' in an hour.  Make sure the men are ready to ride."

Few men had a stomach for food, but Andy kept the leftovers, knowing he'd feed it to the men for supper.  A few more would be able to eat by then, so it'd be unlikely he'd have anything leftover tonight.  But, he'd serve beans and hog meat until the men were out far enough on the plains they could bring him fresh meat - then he'd serve steaks, stews and soups.

An hour later, they were moving in a gently falling snow.  The wind had died, but it still remained cold, just a little below freezing.  While Coon wasn't worried about the men in the least, he kept an eye on the weather for the sake of their horses.  If the snow started piling up or the winds got too high, he'd find shelter for the sake of the animals, not the men.  While he had a large herd of mules and horses, he suspected he'd need every critter he could find with four legs to bring the furs out.  Thousands of dollars were invested and he hoped to at least double his investment on his return.  However, he also knew of the risk he was taking and the danger wasn't just Indians.  The weather, illnesses, wild animals, and accidents could all claim lives.  Besides the obvious problem of keeping the herd of animals he now had from thieving bands of various Indians.

*I'll have to keep a close eye on the herd or some tribe will get every single horse and mule we have,* he thought and then ordered, "Culp, I want a man ridin' point about two hundred yards in front of us, with a second man about a hundred yards behind 'em.  Then, put a man about two hundred yards behind us.  When ya have those three in position, I was two outriders about a hundred yard on each side of us moving parallel to the main group.  Every three hours move the men around.

"I hear ya, Coon and I'll take care of it right now."

Andy, not experienced on the prairie asked, "Coon, I don't know jack shit about these plains, but why do we need those men guardin' us, when we can see for twenty miles? Hell, there ain't a tree to be found right now. I'll bet we could ride all day and still see the town behind us."

Coon gave a light chuckle and replied, "These plains look flat, but they ain't. There are dried stream beds, gullies, and rolling hills that can hide an army. Iffen ya been payin' attention, we've crossed a few gullies already."

"I'll be damned. That never entered my head."

"I'm serious now and mean no disrespect, but start using yer head, or you'll die out here. These prairies are home to a lot of bleached bones of men who thought they knew it all, only they didn't."

"Well, I'll tell ya right up, I don't like it out here worth a shit. I thought the town was bad, but at least wc had a few trees now and again."

"Iffen we live long enough, we'll not see trees until we're almost to the shining mountains. Oh, we'll see a few stunted cottonwoods, but they'll be linin' the streams and rivers."

Glancing at the ground, Coon saw the snow was covering the trail. *If this keeps up like it is, I'll need to stop in a couple of more hours. Only I'll keep pushin' the men as long as I can. I want to make the trade, get out, sell the furs, and move back east. Sooner or later, iffen I'm not smart, some mountain man will corner my ass.*

One of the men riding point, rode to Coon and said, "Pony tracks in the snow, about ten to twelve unshod hosses as near as I can tell. They were movin' south just after the snow started, because the tracks are partly filled with new snow."

"Ride and tell the other point man."

"He held up long enough by the tracks to show 'em to me. He knows."

"Then get back to where ya need to be and do the job now. Culp!"

"Coon?"

"Tonight double the guards on the horses; there are Injuns out."

"In this weather?"

"Why so surprised, hell, we're out in it, ain't we?"

"I thought they stayed in their tee-pees or lodges when bad weather struck."

"These obviously didn't know they were suppose to stay at home, so they're out ridin'. Listen, good or bad weather, we stay ready for a fight, understood?"

"Sure, I understand."

"They may be returnin' home or maybe visitin' another tribe. See, Injuns don't sit in a rockin' chair, by a fire and drink coffee. They are movers and iffen ya remember that, why it might just save yer hair one day. Those braves will try for our horses, iffen they pick up our sign and ya can take that to the bank."

"I see it Coon, but lawdy, we don't need Injun trouble."

"It's part of the job, no more or less a danger than wild animals. Ya got danger workin' any job, so relax. Iffen they see the horses are guarded good, they'll pass us by. Injuns don't want to die either, except they'll take some mighty big risks when it comes to good riding stock."

"Well, I don't like Injuns and they scare the shit out of me."

Coon laughed and then replied, "Good, they should scare ya. Now, I save my last bullet for me and I ain't jokin'. Iffen those braves take a man alive, they give 'em to the women folks and they're pure hell on a white man. I've seen 'em take days to kill a feller and all the while the man was in some serious pain."

Ruth spoke for the first time this day, "Shut the hell up, Coon, with the Injun talk. Yer scarin' me and every man that can hear yer voice. We've all read the papers and heard the tall tales."

The mountain man's eyes narrowed as he said, "By God, they ain't tall tales, but I'll shut up. It ain't smart to be talkin' anyway with those bucks out ridin'."

Toward evening, one of the men up front returned to Coon and said, "Got a sod house about a half mile off to our left. I make out one woman, but no man around that I can see. Do ya want me and some men to check it out?"

"Yep, but go easy with 'em, we don't need to stir up no hornets nest. These settlers are a rough bunch and the women ain't all soft, neither. They'll kill ya in a minute, if ya make 'em mad. Find out iffen she's alone and then one of ya come back and let me know."

"Sure, boss.  One of us will be back in a few minutes."

The men were heard cursing as they waited in the wind, but there were no trees.  Coon thought, *iffen I can overpower the woman, we can use her house and barn fer the men.  It'll beat sleepin' out in the wind and might keep the Injuns off our butts too.*

Twenty minutes later, the man returned, smiled and said, "She's alone, but holding a double-barrel ten gauge like she knows how to use it.  Neither one of us wanted to mess with 'er."

"Lead us there and once we see her, I do all the talkin'."

When they neared the sod home, a woman of middle-age was standing by her open door holding a big shotgun.  It was freezing cold, but all she wore besides her cotton dress was a wool shawl over her shoulders.

Coon said, "Evenin'.  We're passin' through on our way to the mountains and I wondered if my men and I could sleep in yer barn.  It's cold out and we'd greatly appreciate it."

Pointing the big gun at Coon, the woman said, "I'm Sue and I own this place. Now, I want to know who I'm talkin' with."

"Coon Turner is my name."

The woman laughed and replied, "Either yer momma a had great sense of humor or yer a liar, son, 'cause ain't nobody named Coon that I ever heard."

"That's my real name and would ya mind pointing that gun in a different direction?  Iffen it goes off, you'll kill me and half my men."

"Mayhap that's why it's pointed at ya.  See, I'm a woman alone on the frontier, so I have to use caution when strangers ride up to visit.  Until I can trust ya, ole Hank will be pointed at y'all.  Fer all I know, I might have to kill all of ya, but doubt I can get y'all with just two barrels from Hank."

"We just want to sleep in yer barn for the night."  Coon said and then thought, *she's not very trustin' but I don't want to force the issue or some of my men will leave.*

"I reckon not, since I'm alone.  See, iffen I let ya sleep in the barn, I'll have to stay up all night and watch my place."

"Not very trustin', are ya?"

"Nope, I don't trust worth a damn, not since Isaac died a few years back.  Now make tracks mister, before my trigger fin-ger gets jumpy."

"Come on, men, we'll find a place to camp."

"Thank you, Sue, for at least talkin' to me and not shootin'."

"Yes, thank you." Ruth suddenly spoke.

Sue cocked her head to the side and asked, "Is there a woman with ya?"

"My wife." Coon lied.

"Well, it wouldn't be Christian iffen I turned a woman out on a night like this.  I'll tell ya what, ya and yer wife can sleep in the house here, but the men need to go to the barn.  No smokin' in there because of all the loose hay.  Ya burn the place down and I'll turn barnyard ugly on ya."

"Culp, put the men in the barn.  Men, no smokin' in the barn, ya heard the lady.  Ruth, dismount and hand yer reins to Andy.  Andy, put our horses with the others." Coon then un-forked his horse.

"Come on in and warm a spell.  Iffen you'd told me ya had a woman along I wouldn't have been so mean.  But, let me tell ya, I have to be fairly mean just to survive out here."  Sue lowered the shotgun and moved into warmth of the house.

Coon turned and called out, "Andy, feed the men some jerky for tonight."

"I'll do that, boss."

As soon as they entered the home, Sue asked, "Are y'all hungry?  Iffen so, I have some bean patties I can warm up fer ya.  I also have a pot of beans and iffen you'll take 'em out to the barn fer yer men, they can have something hot.  Jerky is okay, except in weather like this a body needs hot food."

Ruth said, "Sounds good to me, because I didn't realize how hungry and cold I was until we walked in here."

Looking around the simple house, Coon thought, *this woman likely ain't got two dimes to rub together.*  His mind shifted, *I'm glad Ruth was along, she got us a warm place to sleep on a cold night.  I might just keep her around a while, since she's provin' to be useful.*

The morning was cold as the men saddled their horses and prepared to leave. The snow had stopped, the wind died, and Coon was in a good mood. Sue had gathered up enough eggs so that each of them in the house had two each, while the men in the barn breakfasted on beef jerky. The frontier woman had sliced some fatback and fried some potatoes to eat as well. Not wanting the men to complain, Coon ordered a shot of whiskey for each man.

Once mounted, Coon ordered, "Same direction as yesterday, but slow the pace. We don't need an injured horse."

"Coon, iffen ya and Ruth are ever back this way, stop and see me." Sue said.

"By golly, we'll just do that. I suspect once my business is done, we'll return this way, God willin'."

"May the good Lord protect ya and ycr men. Ruth, ya be careful with all these men along."

"Thank ya." Coon said.

"Yes, thank ya for the food and for the shelter, too. These are good men, so I'm safe enough." Ruth said and then shivered from the cold.

"Get the point men movin' and let's ride, we're wastin' time." Coon ordered.

The day was cold and long, so by nightfall, the group gathered around the fire to warm up. A quick supper of beans and bacon was behind them and all looked forward to a little sleep.

Culp asked, "What about the guards? I mean, do ya think those Injuns are still out?"

"Keep 'em doubled until we put some miles behind us. I think we're safe, with the weather like it is, but Injuns will always strike when ya least expect 'em to do the job."

"Not a problem. Listen up, fellers, same shifts as the night before last. Ya see anything, try to wake us first, but iffen ya cain't do the job, shoot and we'll get up fast enough."

Coon nodded and then added, "Never try to take out a man sneakin' up on camp with a knife. If he's a better knife fighter and kills ya, we'll never get a warning. Now, let's all get some sleep, mornin' comes early this time of the year."

Coon was awakened by a touch to his ankle and when he opened his eyes, Andy said in a whisper, "Something movin' out there. I ain't sure where the guards are or why they ain't seen it, but something is moving around us."

Andy usually got up at three in the morning, so he'd have breakfast cooked for the men when they woke. As a result, he didn't pull guard duty or any other camp chores.

*It's a damned good thing this feller gets up early, or we might have all been killed,* Coon thought as he rose from his blankets with his rifle in hand. When he glanced at Ruth, laying under the same blankets, she was still sleeping.

Whispering, Coon said, "Wake the men and tell them to prepare for a fight. Send five of 'em over by the horses, where I'll be waiting."

It was still dark and so cold, the mountain man could see his breath in the dim moonlight. Just as he reached the horses, a shot rang out, someone screamed and Coon saw warriors rushing toward the horses. The two guards nearest the horses fired. Coon lined up his sights, took a deep breath and as he released the air, he squeezed the trigger. When the rifle fired, his target fell, shrieking in pain.

Firing erupted from near the center of camp, but fighting off an impulse to join the men there, he started reloading his Hawken. A stray round *zinged* by his head, causing Coon to duck lower. He spotted two braves running toward the herd, so he fired, knocked one man down and heard a second shot from one of the guards. The firing near camp slowed and then stopped, except for an occasional pop as someone fired at a seen or imaginary target.

Finally it grew still, except for the moans, groans, and cries of the wounded and dying.

Coon called out, "Everyone remain where ya are until I say otherwise. They might hit us again."

After almost an hour, the mountain man was unable to stand the cold any longer and called, "They're gone. Someone get a fire started."

Moving toward camp, he yelled, "Culp, I want to know how many dead and wounded we have, so get me a count."

"He cain't do that." A man replied.

"And, why the hell not?"

"He's dead, that's why. He took a ball in the head."

"Andy, are ya okay?"

"Doin' fine.   Do ya want me to count the dead and wounded?"

Nearing the fire, Coon saw Ruth standing with a rifle in her hands.  There was a dead brave beside the fire and she asked, "What kind of Injuns attacked us?"

"Oto and they're a mean bunch, too.  I figure we're lucky to have survived this attack."

"Scared the hell out of me.  I was sound asleep one minute, heard a shot, and then the fight started.  I killed one back by our sleepin' spot."

"Most likely the body is gone."

Andy returned and said, "We've three dead and ten wounded.  All of the wounded are expected to recover and only one man had a somewhat serious injury to his leg."

"So, all of them can ride?"

"Sure, no reason why they cain't."

"Get three men and cut the throats of these Injuns and I mean every single one.  A couple might be playin' possum." Coon said to Andy, then looking at the men near the fire, he walked to the biggest man in the group and asked, "What's yer name?"

"I'm Joseph Wallace, but I answer to Joe."

"Well, Joe, yer pay just went up two dollars a day and yer my new ramrod.  Do ya have the grit to handle men?'

"Hell, yes, fer that kind of money I do."

"Get the gear loaded and the men ready to ride.  We leave in half an hour.  I suspect the Oto will return and I don't want to be here when they get back."

# CHAPTER 21

The weather was rough, with high winds and snow blowing horizontal in front of Nate and his small group. They'd docked the boat as far north as it could go, because any further and the water was too shallow. The boat trip had saved them weeks of rough riding and in all kinds of weather, so once back on shore, Cotton suddenly loved boats.

At their noon camp, Deacon asked, "Ya still moving toward the Sioux to find Coon?"

Nate winked and replied, "Ya bet. He'll be there, too. What about ya two?"

Bear grinned as Deacon said, "We're goin' with ya, iffen ya don't mind. I ain't never seen a man challenged in a village before and it should be interesting doin's in my mind. Bear just wants to see ya skin the man alive."

Nate smiled in return and said, "Sure, ya two can go into cahoots with us. Only before we do this, I have a question for ya, Deacon."

Deacon gave a blank look and said, "Okay, ask."

"What was that yellin' ya was doin' on the boat when we were fightin' the Injuns?"

Bear laughed, as did Deacon. Then Bear said, "Every time he shot one of them he yelled, 'Lord, I ask ya to receive the soul I just sent ya and I'll send ya another in a minute or two. Forgive me fer killin'.' He'd yell something like it each time he killed a warrior."

"What's the purpose of that?" Nate gazed into the deeply religious man's eyes.

"It's my way of askin' God to forgive me. It's simple really, iffen ya give it some thought."

Nate chuckled and then said, "Come on, let's get our horses loaded and get on the tramp."

The day was miserable for the men and horses, so when Nate called it a day a couple of hours before dusk, all the men were glad.

Soon the shelters were up, a fire burning, and supper cooking on the flames. Since the weather was so bad, fresh meat was out of question, so Cotton put a pot of beans and bacon on to cook.

"Do ya think this snow will stop tonight?" Bear asked as he glanced at the low sky.

Nate spat tobacco juice into the snow by his feet and replied, "Yep, I do. The first snow of the season never lasts long. I need to kill Coon and then start trappin' plew before they're all holed up due to weather. Iffen we wait too long, the streams will freeze over."

"Where we trappin' at?" Cotton asked.

"I though near the three rivers area, unless ya have a better idea."

"Naw, that's fine. Hell, I can float a stick there easy enough."

Nate looked at Bear and asked, "And, how about the two of ya?"

"We were discussin' Baldy Mountain."

"Waugh! Have ya lost yer damned minds? That place is crawlin' with Blackfoot."

"Uh-huh, it surely is," Deacon said, "but the beaver are prime and the take will be large."

"I don't know, young pup, iffen I'd go there, but it's yer hair and not mine."

"Bear knows a back way in and out, the Shoshone showed it to 'em, and we'll use that trail."

Nate started to ask a question, but stopped.

Deacon noticed his hesitation and said, "Somethings on your mind, so spit it out."

Turning to Bear he asked, "Can I ask ya personal question and not piss ya off?"

"Sure, we're all friends. I'll tell ya what, iffen I don't want to answer, I'll say so. Ask yer question my friend."

"I heard that ya was married to a Shoshone woman once, but something happened to her.  Is that true?  Now, I'm askin' the question because I think they've the best lookin' women."

Bear nodded, grew sober and replied, "Yep, it's true and she was pregnant at the time, too.  I thought I told ya about this already."

"Mayhap ya did, young coon, but I don't remember well at times, and I'm sorry to bring up bad memories.  I know you'd killed a no account man by the name of Red, but couldn't remember the details."

"It's okay, because I'm not as broken up about it now as I was back then.  Her name was Falling Leaf and I loved her more than my own life.  The short of it is, she was killed by white men looking for the source of some gold the Indians traded us.  She didn't know where the gold was found, none of us knew.  Her death, the death of Jeb and our revenge trail almost drove me insane."

"Now, back to Shoshone women, they're some, they are." Cotton added.  *This young pup don't need any bad memories just before bed.*

"I like 'em, too."  Nate replied and then remembered he'd heard most of Bear's sad tail before.  *I need to think more before I start asking men questions like that.  Waugh, what a fool thing to ask a man.*

Deacon said, "Find one ya like, Nate, and I'll marry ya up white man style, iffen ya want."

Everyone broke out laughing and when it quieted, Nate said, "I ain't got a hankerin' to get married, but iffen I did, we'd do the job right.  I mean we'd be married proper in the eyes of the Lord, don't ya know?"

Staring into the dancing flames of the fire, Bear said, "Leaf and I were married by Deacon, but not this one.  The feller that married us is dead now and he was much older.  I never touched that woman before our weddin' night, as badly as I wanted to, because I knew to do so would be a sin in the eyes of God."

Cotton, stirring the beans said, "Amen to that.  Most men just take a quick roll in the robes and never give thought to a child comin' from it or the woman, much less God.  Then again, they don't think of the risk of the French pox either."

"Man," Deacon said, "is more or less just an animal that can talk. We do many things like animals and mating is a prime example. The big difference between us and critters, besides we can speak, is God. Now, that's all I'm goin' to say about the subject fer right now." Standing and then stretching he added, "I'm callin' it a night and turnin' in. Wake me when it's my turn to guard."

One-by-one the men headed to their robes, except for Cotton, who had the first guard shift. He moved off away from the group, near the horses, and pulled his buffalo robe up and over his head. It was still snowing to beat the band, so he suspected he'd see nothing moving in this weather. His shift, while boring, was uneventful and few hours later he woke Bear and turned in for the night.

A couple of hours before dawn, Nate felt a hand on his ankle. Opening his eyes he saw the snow had stopped and a clear sky was overhead. Since he'd already pulled guard duty, he suspected trouble. Deacon signed in the faint moonlight, "Riders, many."

Two of the mountain men moved to the horses, while the other two stayed near the camp. It was well below zero and it hurt Nate's lungs to breathe. Removing a long piece of cotton cloth he wrapped it over his nose and mouth, so only his eyes were uncovered. All were wearing winter gear, which meant buffalo coats and mittens, along with elk moccasins with the fur turned inside. This clothing kept a man fairly warm most of the time, but laying in snow soon chilled them, especially with this wind.

From the darkness a heavily accented voice called out in English, "Why no fire, white men? Do the Oto scare you? Make a fire, white eyes, and we will share it with you."

"Go to hell. I know who ya are, Bloody Wolf, and I'll share no fire with the murdering Oto!" Nate replied and then moved about twenty feet to his left.

"So, white men know my name. This is good to know, Big Raven Man, so you may fear me. I know your name, too. You take the one who swims."

Silence.

"It is cold, Big Raven Man, make a fire so we can all warm up, or my warriors will take your camp and make our own fire."

Bloody Wolf said, and then laughed as he taunted the white men.

"You can take our camp, but many Oto lodges will mourn the deaths of your braves." Nate said and moved once more. He knew the warriors would key in on position by his voice. If they attacked, some would come for him.

No response from the Oto.

Nate was freezing and in the dim light he watched little white snow devils swirl around him. Finally, after about an hour, he called out, "All but the guard return to camp. We need a fire and need one now. The Oto are gone."

Soon, at camp, flames danced and flickered in the wind as the men hunkered near the warmth and tried to warm up. Cotton put on a pot of coffee and then said, "We need to get some miles between us and the Oto today."

"I figure to do just that, because I don't trust Bloody Wolf not to come lookin' fer us. He's one coldblooded sumbitch and has killed many a white man."

"Why didn't they just attack us?" Bear asked.

Nate shrugged and replied, "Mayhap he didn't have a good count on us or he didn't have many warriors with him. Then again, it's pretty damned cold out, so he likely just stopped to talk a spell so we'd know he's out and about."

Cotton said, "I'd love to get that bastard lined up in my Hawken's sights, just once."

"He'll take a lot of killin', so don't think he'll go under easy like."

Bear said, "Hit anybody square with a big fifty and his ass will go down."

Nate stood and said, "Gather up our gear and let's get the horses loaded. I want to be on the trail within the hour."

Butterfield walked out on the porch of his trading post as Nate and his small group tied their horses to the hitching post. He held a double-barrel shotgun in his hands, as usual, but smiled when he spotted Nate.

"Come on in boys, the first drink is on me."

"I think we'll pass on whiskey, since it's not even seven in the mornin' yet, Butterfield." Nate said.

"Do as ya like, I'm gonna spike my coffee."

The men laughed and followed the old trader into the warm building. An old cast iron stove was glowing red on both sides and after being out in the cold for so long, the room felt sizzling hot. As soon as they removed their coats and sat, Butterfield placed a coffee pot and five cups in the center of the table. He then walked to his counter and returned with a bottle of rye.

Cotton said, "Add about an inch of that rye to my cup, just to take the chill from me."

Bear held his cup out for some whiskey as well.

Deacon and Nate, poured coffee into their cups and passed on the alcohol. "Too early fer me to drink whiskey, but I'll take that free drink this evening." Nate said.

Cotton took a sip of his spiked coffee, looked over the rim of the tin cup and asked, "Is old Hump and his band camped over in the greasy grass again this year?"

"Hell, I ain't got no idea, but they usually winter there every year, so why wouldn't they be out that way this year?"

"Just askin', so we don't ride all the way to the place for nothin'."

"All men are creatures of habit. They've been winterin' there fer as long as I've known 'em, so I see no reason for 'em to be elsewhere."

Nate said, "We'll try there first, because I suspect we'll find 'em there."

"Ain't ya goin' fer plew this year?"

"Maybe and then again, maybe not. We didn't catch Coon in Saint Louie and he's come back out here again. Since he traded guns with Hump the first time, I suspect he'll do 'er again. See, he knows the chief and the Injuns know him. He'll feel safe with 'em."

"He will be safe enough. Hell, ya kill 'em while he's a guest of Hump's, why them Sioux will tear everyone of ya to bits.

Guests are protected and ya should know that by now, 'cause ya ain't no damned greenhorn."

Nate smile and replied, "I can challenge him."

Butterfield blinked a few times, grinned and said, "Well, now, that might work. But, it'll be pretty dangerous. Iffen ya challenge him, only one of ya will live when yer done. Now, most of the time the Sioux will make ya fight with knives, but I've heard tell of spears bein' used too, or war clubs."

Downing his coffee, Nate said, "It doesn't matter to me what we fight with, because I'm meaner than he is on all counts."

"I'd love to see the fight. Hell, to see two big men fightin' would be some, it surely would." Butterfield said, stood, and then made his way behind his counter. He returned a few min-utes later and handed Nate a long knife.

"Son, iffen yer gonna fight the likes of Coon, yer gonna need every advantage ya can get. This knife has a special blade, only made in Damascus or so I heard, and the steel is super strong. Now, I ain't got the foggiest idea where in the hell Damascus is, but they make a really good knife. See them wavy lines on the blade? That's done by some secret process they use to strengthen the steel. Take it and best of luck to ya."

"By God, it's pretty enough, ain't it?"

"It was made only to kill a man with, and you can tell by how the tip is shaped to a point and the narrow blade. That ain't no huntin' knife. Only one purpose for a knife designed like that and she'll be deadly in a fight."

"Thanks, Butterfield." Nate said as he tested the balance of the knife, then the feel of the handle in his massive hand. *This is one hell of a fine blade, he thought.*

"No problem with the knife and I have a leather sheath for it behind the counter. Ya just make sure ya win the battle or Coon will have a new knife to add to his collection."

Nate grinned and then asked, "Can ya get us some supplies in a bit, Butterfield? We'll leave for the Sioux in an hour." The big man placed a piece of paper on the table.

Butterfield picked the paper up, read the list and said, "I've got all of this, even the hot peppers, but they're dried."

Cotton quickly replied, "They'll do fine."

Standing the old trader said, "Give me a few minutes to gather and weigh some of this stuff and you'll be ready to go."

"Oh, add a pint of laudanum to the list too, because I for-got."

Four days later they rode over a slight rise in the plains and could see the Sioux village along side the river.  The village was huge, well over a hundred lodges and that meant close to four hundred men and women called the place home.

"Dog soldier approachin' from the left," Deacon said.

Nate said, "They've been followin' us for the better part of the day.  They know who we are, so relax.  Iffen they wanted us dead, we'd be dead already.  Keep yer hands away from yer guns."

The warrior was not a big man, only about five feet and four inches, maybe a hundred and fifty pounds, but even in the cold he wore no shirt.  The scars of the Sun Dance were clearly seen on his chest.  His ink-black hair held six coup feathers and his eyes were of the same color.

*"Big Raven Man has returned."* The warrior said.

*"Yes, I have come to see my real family, Sharp Knife.  Is my father well?"*

*"Hump is well and so are The People.  Come, we will go to the village."*

While the weather was warmer than it had been for weeks, the day was still chilly, and few people were seen outside their lodges.  The drying racks were bare, meaning all the meat for the moons of hunger was dried and packed away.  No skins were pegged out to be scraped and no women were seen cook-ing outside.

They rode to Hump's lodge, where the warrior slid grace-fully from his horse, as only an Indian can do, and walked to the entrance.  Once the brave saw the white men were dis-mounted, he coughed and scratched the hanging hide.

*"Enter."*

They entered and Nate saw Hump sitting beside the fire, leaning on his backrest.  Hump pointed to his right for the white men to sit and then said, *"Sharp Knife, you will stay."*

Sharp Knife sat on the chief's left.

Pulling his pipe, Hump filled the bowl with tobacco, pulled a brand from the fire and lighted his pipe.  He puffed a few times to get it burning well.  He moved the pipe in the directions of the sacred four corners and then up and down to signify heaven and earth.  He passed the pipe to Nate, who did the same. Once the pipe made the complete circle, Hump knocked the ash into the small fire.

*"It makes my heart happy to see my son once more."*  The old chief said.

*"I am happy as well.  It is good to see those we have missed."* Nate replied.

*"Is there a reason for your visit, or do you return because your heart has missed us?"*

*"Both, father.  I have missed The People and I think the man called Coon will soon come to trade with you."*

*"The white man is coming, but he will not be here for two fingers of suns.  He is far from our village.  He comes with many men and has many things for my people."*

*"He will have many guns, the burning dirt, and the soft rock.  We will trade with him and become stronger against our enemies the Oto and Blackfoot."* Sharp Knife said.

Nate thought for a second, and then said, *"The trader of guns has killed some of my people."*

Hump looked dumbfounded at the thought someone would murder their own people. He asked, *"What is to happen to this trader?  Is he to be banished from the lands of all white men?"*

*"He is to die, father.  He was once a mountain man, as we are, and a taker of the one who swims.  Then, one sun, he murdered his friends and took their furs as his own."*

*"Why would a man do that?  It makes me confused.  Furs are to be found everywhere, but friends have great value.  Has this trader lost his thinking?  Has the Great Spirit touched him?"*

*"He has not been touched, my father, so he must die."* Nate replied and then added, *"I have come to The People to chal-*

*lenge him, according to the laws of the Sioux people.  One of us will die."*

# CHAPTER 22

Coon and his men cursed the weather as they rode, and the small river they'd crossed about a half a mile back was freezing cold.  The mountain man could see ice forming on the leather pants of some of the men.  "When ice forms on your pants and boots, knock it off with yer fists."  He ordered.

"We need to stop and warm up a bit, or we'll start to lose men." Joe said from beside Coon.

"I don't like it, but I hear ya.  Move off to the left and get a fire started.  Andy, while the fires burnin' get some hot food in these men, too.  Hell, it's a couple of hours early,  but we'll take our noonin' now."

"Yo!  I've still got some stew leftover from last night."

"Cody!"

"Yea, boss?"

"I want ya to check all the horses and make sure that ice on the river didn't cause any injuries to any of them.  Get some old wool blankets from Andy and wipe the horses down real good, too."

"I'll take care of 'em, so relax."  Cody replied and he would. He had babied every single horse and mule in the herd, as if they belonged to him.  Like all the men, he had no idea that Coon was carrying guns and whiskey or he'd not come along. He'd had a few close brushes with the law when younger, but those days were over for him.  He'd hired on because he loved horses and needed a job.

"Andy," Coon said as he dismounted, "once the men eat, give each one a double shot of panther piss, but that's it.  I think it's cold enough to warrant a strong drink."  The big man then pulled a silver flask from his coat pocket and took a healthy drink.  He then handed the flask to Ruth.

The meal was done quickly and the whiskey issued. It took Cody almost an hour to care for the horses and soon they were back on the trail. *Colder than a New York City banker's heart,* Coon thought as he lowered his hat against a light wind from the north. *Within a week or so I should have a mountain of furs and be on my way back to the city by the big muddy river. Then, I'll head down to New Orleans and find me a couple of beautiful young women. Hell, I might as well buy a house there and settle down. I'll have more than enough money to do the job.*

Cody rode up beside Coon and said, "I just spotted an Injun off our right and he looked to me to be Sioux."

"Ya know yer Injuns, now do ya?"

"I used to hunt for eatin' places in Independence and ran into a few off and on over the years. They're good people to those they call friend."

Coon laughed and replied, "As long as they trade me all the furs they got, they can call me what they want."

"What do ya want us to do?" Joe asked.

"Keep ridin'. When they want to talk, they'll let us know."

Ruth said, "I don't like this shit at all. What's to keep them from just killing all of us and taking your supplies?"

"Greed, my dear, simple greed. They want what I have and they'll want more in the future, too. The red man is not all that much different than his white cousin when it comes to bein' grabby."

"I hope yer right or a lot of us might die."

"No, iffen I'm wrong, all of us will die. Now, close your mouth and keep it that way."

The rest of the day and night were uneventful and the Sioux were not seen, but Coon knew they were still around. From his days as a mountain man, he had a sense he'd picked up about Indians and right now it was stronger than ever. *They're out there and will be seen when they finally decide to talk.*

Just as they were preparing to mount after breakfast, Cody neared and said, "Look to the left. I count twenty of 'em."

Coon looked and said, "Sioux."

"Are we gonna have to fight?" Andy asked and his fear was clearly heard.

"No, not today.  Iffen they wanted to fight, we'd already be fightin'.  They're in a talkin' mood is my guess."

"What do we do now?" Andy asked.

Turning to Cody, Coon said, "Mount and we'll ride about half way to them and wait.  Iffen they want to talk they'll send a man or two."

"Sure, but I don't speak Sioux."

"You don't have to speak the language, because I do.  Can ya read sign language?"

"I'm fair at sign."

"Then while I talk with 'em, ya keep an eye on their sign. But, for God's sake, don't even think about pullin' a gun.  Now, lets ride."

The two men rode about half the way to the Indians and waited.  A few minutes later two warriors broke from the group and moved toward Coon.

The braves stopped about ten feet from Coon and Cody.

Coon asked, *"Do my brothers have hunger?"*

Long minutes passed before the younger of the two Sioux replied, *"We have no hunger.  Why are you on Sioux lands?"*

*"I wish to trade with your people and I bring many things."*

*"What things do you bring to trade us?"*

*"I have guns, powder and lead to make the Sioux more powerful over their enemies."*

*"How many guns do you have to trade us?"*

*"Too many hands of guns.  I also have the water of fire."*

*"You have firewater?"*

Cody, suddenly realizing what was being said by watching the sign said, "Coon, yer about a lyin' sumbitch, do ya know that?"

"Hush and I mean now.  We'll talk about this later once we have a camp established.  This is not the place."

*"Yes, I have much firewater for the Sioux."*

The older warrior now spoke, *"You will not trade the firewater here or in the village.  Hump does not like it and it will be done as on your last visit to us, white man."*

*"I understand and will do as you have asked."*

Glaring, the old Sioux replied, *"Good, or your scalp will hang on my lodge pole."*

*"Come,"* the younger brave said, *"you may travel with us."*

*"I must return and speak with my men, then we will join you."*

*"We will wait over the next ridge."* The young warrior pointed to the other Sioux.

Pulling his horse around, Coon whispered, "Don't say shit when we get back or yer a dead man."

Cody laughed and said, "Better men than you have tried, but I'm still kicking horse apples around."

About half way back to the men, Coon considered pulling his pistol and shooting Cody, but knew it would just cause problems. *Hell,* he thought, *they would've found out about the guns and whiskey sooner or later.*

Once back to the men, Cody said, "I want out and now. I didn't sign on to sell guns and whiskey to Injuns. Hell, Coon, that's a Federal offense and the army will come after ya. Ya lied to us, ya sumbitch!"

"I lied to no man. Did any of ya ask what I carried to trade? No, not a damned one of ya asked. If any of ya want to leave, go now, but iffen ya stay I'll double yer pay."

Andy said, "I'm leavin'. I don't need no damned army problems in my life."

"I'm goin' too, and for the same reasons." Cody said.

Two other men wanted to leave as well, only Coon said nothing.

Cody said, "I want my pay to date before I leave. I want nothing to do with ya in the future either and iffen I see ya again I might decide just to kill yer ass."

Pulling a buckskin bag from his coat, Coon pulled out a thick wad of bills and paid the men—all the while he glared at Cody with narrow eyes. *I'll kill yer ass fer this one day.*

Folding his money and placing it in his coat pocket, Cody said, "Let's ride men, and see iffen we can put some distance between us and Mister Coon Turner."

As the men left, Coon smiled and said, "I thank ya men for havin' the guts to stay."

A man called Stump said, "Oh, we stayed, but only for the money. Now, I cain't speak fer every man here, but iffen yer lyin' to us, I'll personally cut yer damned throat."

Wanting to move to the warriors, Coon said, "I'll pay. Now, let's get the pack horses and move to the Sioux."

The day passed slowly with most of the white men scared shitless. About two hours before dusk, as they rode across what looked to be flat land, another group of Indians rode up out of the ground. Coon knew they'd walked their horses up a dry stream bed and the illusion was frightening to the white men.

"Coon," Ruth asked, "those warriors aren't Sioux, are they?"

"No, they're Cheyenne and we're in fer a fight in a few minutes. Right now the Cheyenne are seeing if they can scare the Sioux."

"I don't know about the Sioux, but I'm pretty damned scared."

Suddenly, from in front of the Sioux warriors came a loud war whoop and a large group of Cheyenne approached riding hard. Rifles began to pop and men started to fall. The Cheyenne on the side of the Sioux abruptly rode into the Sioux braves and a fight started.

Aiming at a big warrior that had attacked from the side, Coon smiled when his gun fired and the big man fell. Taking a glancing blow from a war club, the mountain man was knocked flat on his back in the grass. While Coon sat still dazed, a young Cheyenne jumped from his horse and ran to the downed white man. He grabbed the white man's hair and when his neck came back, the Cheyenne's knife moved for the throat. There sounded a rifle shot and the young brave fell to the ground with half of his head missing. His body quivered and jerked violently as it shut down.

Coon stood and was immediately struck a hard blow to his back. When he turned, a warrior on horse back was about ten feet away and laughing. In the braves hand, was a coup stick.

"Count coup on me, ya sumbitch," Coon screamed in anger as he raised his pistol and fired. The ball struck the Cheyenne in the center of his chest and bone, blood, and gore exploded out his back. He was knocked off his horse, Coon ran to the man, and pulling his knife, cut his throat. As the brave choked on his own blood, the mountain man scalped him alive.

Climbing on the horse of the dead man, he quickly reloaded his pistol, looked for his rifle, but didn't see it. He heard a scream and when he looked in that direction, two warriors were attempting to steal Ruth.  He almost let them take her, but finally rode toward the men, firing his pistol at one and the man went down unmoving.  Leaping from his horse, he struck the other warrior hard and they both fell to the ground.  Over and over they rolled, until finally Coon was on the bottom.  As he watched, the sharp tip of the knife in the Cheyenne's hand started for his chest.  He tried to buck the man off, but it didn't work.

Suddenly, the warrior stiffened and then gave a warbling cry.  A couple of seconds later the man grew limp and fell from Coon.  Glancing at the man, he saw a knife stuck in the middle of his back. Looking around wildly, he saw Ruth standing beside her horse reloading her rifle.

There came a shot and Ruth was knocked back hard and fell to the long buffalo grasses.  Coon moved toward her at a run.  As he ran, he noticed the Cheyenne were leaving and the area had bodies scattered all around.  He suddenly stopped and looked for his mules carrying the guns.  He saw no mules or horses.  Well over half of his men were down, but the supplies were not to be seen.  Oh, Lord, don't let them bastards have my guns and whiskey!  I have thousands of dollars invested and all this will have been for nothin'.

Seeing Stump moving around with a light wound to his left arm, Coon called out, "Did they get all of our supplies?"

"Them Injuns took the whole shebang, includin' yer horse and mule herd."

"Sumbitch!" The mountain man bellowed in anger.  He then moved to where Ruth lay.  The bullet wound was to her chest and blood would bubble from the hole each time she breathed.  He squatted beside her and said, "Yer hit in the lights, Ruth, and will go under."

She looked at him, her eyes filled with both pain and fear and said, "Coon, I . . . hurt."

"Hell, I'd guess so, a big 50 caliber done hit yer ass dead center in yer chest, but I can't help ya, the supplies are all gone.  I'd give ya some laudanum for the pain, but it was with the stores and we ain't got even a little whiskey."  He lied, because he kept a bottle of the drug in his coat pocket.

"Help . . . me . . . Coon, please."

"Oh, I'm fixin' to do just that."  He pulled his pistol and pulled the hammer back with a loud click.

Ruth's eyes grew large as she pleaded, "No . . . please.  Help . . . me!"

Coon grinned and asked, "Do ya want the bullet in the head or yer chest?"

Anger filled her eyes as she replied, "Coon . . . yer . . . a worthless . . .sumb—"

The pistol shot was loud and the bullet took the farmer's wife almost between her eyes.  The grass behind her head was spattered with bone, blood, and brains.  As Coon watched, her body jerked once and then lay still, he thought damn, *I hated to do that.  I suspect these Sioux would have given a lot of plew for her worthless ass.*

A Sioux warrior walked to him and said, *"We have many dead and injured.  What do you wish to do?  I saw the Cheyenne take your guns and supplies."*

Coon thought for a minute and said, *"We'll go with you.  My men need rest and some are injured.  I can speak to Hump about bring more guns of thunder and other things the Sioux want."*

The Sioux didn't reply and walked off.

Walking to one of his men, Coon said, "Get me a count of the number of injured and dead.  What's yer name?"

"Watkins."

"Watkins, yer now the ramrod and yer pay has just went up."

Watkins spat a long line of brown tobacco juice and then said, "Hell, what good's money iffen a man cain't live long enough to enjoy what it buys?"  He then walked off to do his counting.

Coon walked among the men noticing many of the injuries were severe and not sure what to do with them.  He had no doctor, but realized he couldn't start shooting men.  Finally seeking a Sioux he asked, *"What am I to do with my wounded?"*

*"Wounded white men are a problem you must deal with, white eyes.  We have our own wounded."*

Walking back to his horse, Coon mounted and heard his name called; it was Watkins.  He rode to the man asked, "What's the count?"

"We got fifteen dead and six hurt.  Four of the six won't last the night, gut shot, head wounds, or hit in the spine.  We ain't got a single mount left.  What do ya want to do?"

"Get a fire started and we'll camp here.  There is no use to go to the Sioux now, we've lost everything."  Coon dismounted and shook his head in anger.

A young Sioux brave approached holding a fresh scalp in his left hand and the rope leading a mule in the other.  He smiled and said, *"This is yours.  I found a wounded Cheyenne, but he is now on the other side.  On this day, I became a man."*

*"Thank you for bringing me my animal."*

*"It is nothing."* The young man walked away.

"Watkins, unpack the load on this mule and let's see what we have.  I hope there might be some laudanum in the pack, so we can kill the pain for some of these men."

Coon sat in the grass, mad as all hell.  He'd started out with exactly forty men and now he was down to twelve and no trading supplies.

"Here's some laudanum."  Watkins said, which broke Coon's train of thought.  He held a pint bottle in his hands.

"Give it to me and I'll give it to the men.  This will be tricky without a spoon, because if I give too much it'll kill 'em."

"Hell, they're dying anyway, boss, but I understand."

Squatting beside each man and turning his back so no one could see him giving the drug, he poured double doses into each mouth, knowing he'd kill the men.  They would just hold him back and he had an idea on how to make at least a little money out of the trip.  He'd buy or take supplies from Butterfield's Trading Post and then return to the Sioux.

Over coffee that was found in the supplies, the men discussed the fight and their roles in the whole affair.  Coon thought most of it was bullshit, but said nothing.

Finally, Watkins said, "I need to check on the wounded. They all looked rough the last time I looked."

Coon had just taken a swallow of coffee when Watkins said, "Boss, ya need to come over here."

The mountain man knew what to expect, but moved to the man anyway and asked, "Are they any better?"

"No.  Every damned one of 'em is dead.  I don't know iffen it was the laudanum or their injuries that killed 'em."

"It doesn't matter much, because the good Lord knows we did the best we could with what we had.  Cover their faces."

"Men, in a few minutes, after our coffee we're going to start walking.  Due west of us, maybe twenty or twenty-five miles is a trading post.  Iffen we can get there, I'll get some horses, more supplies and we'll come back out to trade."

Watkins said, "Ya heard the man and it's not like we have a choice.  It's the closest place to go for help and it's our only chance."

One man stood and said, "Ya better pray them damn Cheyenne don't come back or they'll run over us in a heartbeat.  And, twenty miles on foot, over rolling plains, will feel like fifty by the time we get there, if we make the trip."

Coon asked, "What's yer name?"

"Jack and that, by God, is all ya need to know.  I want to make it clear, when we get to this traders place, I ain't coming back out here.  In my eyes, yer a lyin' bastard and while ya admitted that a while back, I stayed on fer the money.  Well, in my mind, ya ain't payin' Injun fightin' wages.  When we get to the trading post, you'll pay me what I'm due."

Coon reached into his coat pocket pulled out a wad of bills and handed money due Jack.  Then with a casual wave of his hand he said, "Get out and do the job now.  I'll have no cowards ridin' with me."

Jack's face grew white as he said, "If ya make me leave now I won't last a day, and ya know it too.  I'll just tag along to the traders."

"I said, get the hell out and I mean now."

Jack went for his gun, but Coon had expected it and pulled his pistol first.  Jack was still clawing wildly for his in his belt.  Taking careful aim, Coon fire and saw bone fragments fly from the man's right arm, just above the elbow.  Knocked to the grass, Jack began to cry.

"Jack, I could have killed you, but I didn't.  Now, do any of the rest of you want to pull iron on me?"

Silence follow for many long minutes.

"Good, Watkins, ya lead the mule, and the rest of ya come with me.  We should be at the traders in a few days.  Oh, and be sure to leave Jack, he's no longer an employee of mine."

# CHAPTER 23

"*What? The white men left you just a few miles from the village?*" Nate was confused why that would happen, especially since Coon had wounded men.

"*The Cheyenne took the white man's thunder sticks, burning dirt and soft rocks. He had nothing left to trade. He had many men killed and injured. His men were poor fighters.*" The warrior said.

Glancing at Bear, Nate asked, "What do ya think he'll do now?"

"The way I see it is this, he only has two choices. He can return to Missouri, then this trip is a total loss for him, or he can try to gather up enough trinkets and stuff to at least make a few dollars before he returns east."

"Hell," said Cotton, "the only place he can get trade goods is at Butterfield's."

Nate thought for a minute or two and then said, "Mount up, we're goin' to Butterfield's."

Within minutes they were riding in the cold fall air, but not a man complained. All four of them knew mountain man justice had to be served and they were just the men to see it done. Like most mountain men, they always completed what they started, from running a trap line to hunting down killers.

As they rode, Nate said, "This will be a forced ride. I'll only stop to rest the horses. I'm afraid if Butterfield confronts Coon, and I damned sure suspect he will, we'll be short a trader. Coon won't hesitate to kill and all of us know he'll do the job in a Mississippi minute, too. I suggest we all pray we get to Butterfield's before Coon does, but I suspect we will."

"What makes ya so sure we'll get there first?" Deacon asked.

"Coon and his men are on foot, so it'll take 'em a sight longer to get there than us.  I think if Butterfield is killed, Coon will loot the store and take it all to the Sioux.  Hell, he's got nothin' to lose doin' the job."

Bear said, "The Sioux warrior told me that Coon had some serious wounded with 'em as well.  He'll not be able to move until they grow stronger."

Cotton laughed and replied, "You can bet yer ass the seriously wounded are dead by now.  The man won't be held back by anything, and I'm sure of that much."

Nate scanned the countryside and then added, "According to Broken Lance, Coon is down to about a dozen men, so that's only three each fer us, if I decide to share."

Light chuckles were heard and then Cotton said, "Ya know most of the men ridin' with 'em ain't killers, but lazy no accounts that usually hang around saloons lookin' fer easy money."

Nate's eyes grew narrow as he said, "If they ride for the brand, they'll fight for the brand.  Now the only one we really want is Coon.  Nonetheless, I'm tellin' all of ya right now, iffen one of those men fires at us, kill the whole damned lot of 'em."

"I'll ride point for a while and I suggest Bear take drag.  It's the only safe way to travel with the Oto and Cheyenne out." Deacon said.

Pulling his horse around, Bear said, "I've got our rear covered."

The day passed slowly, due to low temperature, and it was close to dusk when Cotton, who'd been riding point, returned. "I picked up sign of about a dozen men on foot."

"Injuns or white men?" Deacon asked.

"Whites, by the boot prints.  One man was wearin' moccasins, so that's likely Coon."

Cotton said, "Wait here for Nate, he'll not be long and I'll move forward and see iffen I can discover where these men are camped.  Once I find their camp, I'll come back."

"I think that would be smart.  I suspect Nate might want to visit the boys later this evenin'" Deacon said.

Cotton pulled his horse to the left and rode to where he'd seen the sign.  It was two miles later, just as he started over a rolling hill, that he spotted a fire in the valley below.  The mountain man knew the fire was made by white men, because it was too large and in a poor position. Mountain men and Indians had small fires and usually made them in hard to spot locations. *It's likely these yahoos think they're safe, since they number about a dozen, but they ain't,* Cotton thought as he dismounted. Pulling a picket pin from his saddle-bags, he pushed it deep into the hard loam, and then tied his horse. Checking the countryside for movement, but seeing nothing, he moved toward the fire slowly.

It was growing dark and Cotton stayed in the shadows as much as possible, and even moved down a dry gully to get near the men. Finally, when he came out of the dry stream bed he crawled toward the fire. Moving to within ten feet of the closest man, Cotton listened.

"Stop yer damna bitchin', LeRoy, every man here would like a shot of whiskey, but we ain't got none."

"Well, damn it to hell and back, I hurt. I took an arrow through my thigh and it pains me a mite."

Coon, who Cotton recognized, tossed the man a bottle and said, "Sip this and yer pain will go away and fast, too. It's laudanum, so take just a small sip. Iffen ya take too much, it'll kill ya dead as hell. Watkins, do we have any food at all?"

"There is enough jerky for every man to get one piece, but that's it. Ya know, iffen we dumped the guns, powder horns and knives we collected from our dead, we'd have room on the mule fer LeRoy to ride."

"No, all of that will stay with us, because they're worth more in plew than our man LeRoy is, so he'll continue to ride shank's mare. I want two men on guard all night and for God's sake, keep an eye on our mule. Iffen we lose it, we'll have to pack the extra guns and supplies we have on our backs. Get that jerky handed out and then we'll all get some sleep."

Cotton moved away from the group and grinned when his feet slid into the dry gully. He moved quickly now and just a few minutes later he was mounted, and moving toward Nate and the rest.

"By God, we'll end this whole affair tonight." Nate said just before he took a big bite of buffalo meat.

"I hope so," Cotton said, "because I'm tired of headin' off to Saint Louis, leavin' Saint Louis, and then doin' the job again a few months later. He's provin' to be a hard man to nail in one place fer very long."

"What time do ya intend to hit 'em then?"

"We'll strike in the middle of the night, because Coon is smart enough to have the men up and ready before dawn. That's when most Injuns attack and he's been up the river and down a few mountains."

"Don't forget the guards will be doubled, but I ain't sure how many that means." Cotton said and then placed a big cut of meat skewered on a stick near the fire.

Deacon laughed and said, "They ain't got no ridin' stock and only one mule, so I'd think no more than two guards. Let me and Bear take out the guards and then ya two can start the dance."

"We'll do 'er that way then. As soon as we all finish eatin', let's get some sleep, and I want the guard to wake us all at midnight."

A little after one in the morning, Nate and his small group approached Coon and his men. Dim light was provided by a full moon overhead. It was well below zero and each mountain man was wearing his winter coat of buffalo. A roaring fire was burning in the center of Coon's camp and Nate noticed the men had no blankets or heavy coats. *Must be cold doin's to sleep like that, and it explains the big fire*, he thought as he watched from the gully.

He spotted two guards, positioned on opposite sides of the fire, and from what he could tell, they were both asleep. While each guard was sitting upright, their chins were resting on their chests, which usually indicated they were asleep. Watching closely, Nate saw Deacon and Bear nearing the camp from the far side. They both crawled to within a few feet of the guards and then came to their feet and quickly moved behind the men.

Nate watched as knife blades flashed, reflecting the firelight, and both guards were held tightly as blood spurted from their severed throats. Boots kicked wildly and fingers clawed at the forearms holding them for a few minutes, then the guards grew still, and were lowered to the ground. Deacon and Bear melted into the darkness.

Ten minutes later, Deacon and Bear joined the two mountain men in the gully. So far, things were going as planned, except, Nate didn't see the mule. He motioned his men forward and they quickly surrounded the sleeping men.

Nate's booming deep voice said, "Wake up ya sumbitches, ya have some talkin' to do!"

One man pulled a pistol, but Deacon's rifle spat lead and the man was thrown back to the ground. The other men looked around in confusion as they sat up.

"Nate," Cotton said, "I ain't real good at countin' and such, but there are only ten men here, when I counted eleven of 'em earlier."

"I don't see Coon in this group." Nate replied and then asked, "Where's Coon Turner?"

Watkins said, "The sumbitch left us high and dry last night a little before midnight. He took the mule and skedaddled, leavin' us with nothin'."

"Any idea where he's headed?" Nate asked, but already suspected the answer.

"He told us he'd ride to Butterfield's Tradin' Post, get some hosses, and then come back fer us. Hell, he won't come back."

Nate felt a sudden fear deep in his gut for Butterfield. Coon would murder the man as sure as shit, because killing meant nothing to the man. "Boys, we're gonna let y'all go, but if we ever see hide or hair of any of ya, yer dead men."

"What about Hank? He's the one ya shot with the rifle. He's bleedin' like a stuck hog and we ain't got nothin' in the way of medical supplies." Watkins asked.

Deacon replied, "Hank pulled a gun on me, so he deserved what he got. Now, I usually don't miss, which means there is a better than average chance medical supplies won't change the outcome. Hank is a dead man, only he hasn't given up the ghost yet. May the Lord have mercy on his soul."

"Come on fellers, we need to rush to Butterfield's place and stop the nayjabberin'. While we're talkin', Coon is gettin' close to a friend of mine." Cotton said and then started walking toward his horse over the ridge line.

As the four moved for their horses, Watkins and his group could be heard pleading for help and making all kinds of promises to Nate and God, but the mountain men kept walking. They'd grown hard now, and death was the only way to soften their feelings.

The ride was cold, but they'd all ridden in cold weather before, so they pulled their hats down low and proceeded to move. An hour after sunup they were on a rise and could see the trading post in the valley below. No horses or mules were seen near any buildings.

"Either he's placed the mule in the barn, killed Butterfield already and left, or we passed him on the way here." Nate said and noticed he could see his breath as he spoke.

"Hell, Nate, he might be in there or behind us, but he ain't had the time to take what he wanted and leave yet. I think the man is behind us, because he didn't have a heavy coat and it's colder than a well diggers ass out here. It's more than likely he had to stop and warm up, or freeze to death." Bear said.

Cotton rubbed his beard and asked, "Nate, how do we do this? I mean, he could be in the building."

Nate thought for a minute or two and they said, "We can't kick the front door open, because it's too strong and well built. I think we'll ride up as usual, but leave Deacon with the horses on the side of the building. Once at the door, Bear, ya check to see if it's open or not. Butterfield is an early riser, so iffen he's awake the door isn't barred. If the door is not barred, I want Bear to jerk the door open and we'll move inside. Once inside, Cotton, ya move to the left and I'll take the right."

"What about me?" Bear asked.

"Young pup, ya come right behind us and go straight up the middle."

Cotton blinked a few times and then said, "Let's ride. I'm freezin' my ass off out here."

They rode to the side of the log structure and dismounted. Handing their reins to Deacon, the three men moved for the door. Once at the door, Bear lifted the latch and smiled; it was unsecured. He looked at Nate and Cotton. Bear mouthed on three, one, two, three! He pushed the door open wide and watched as Nate and then Cotton moved inside.

Butterfield had just pulled a pan of biscuits from his stove and when the door swung open wide and the men entered, he dropped his bread and moved for the shotgun beside the stove. Then, seeing it was Nate, he turned to cussing.

Nate and Cotton, followed by Bear, scanned the inside of the trading post, but saw nothing out of place. Finally, Nate said, "Sorry about they way we entered, but we thought Coon was here."

"Coon? Iffen he was here there'd be a body."

Cotton said, "I'll move our horses into the barn and send Deacon in. It's too damned cold to leave that young pup out long."

"Ya do that, Cotton. Yep, Butterfield, we ran into some of Coon's men on the plains and they claimed he was headed this way. I suspect he's behind us then."

"Don't ya ever do that shit again, by God ya scared five years off my life. Bargin' in this place like that is a good way to get yer asses shot off, too." Butterfield said as he picked his pan of bis-cuits form the floor.

Deacon enter and asked, "Butterfield, do ya have any whiskey?"

"Has a rooster got a pecker? Ya bet I do, son. Do ya want a shot?"

"No, I don't want a shot of whiskey. I want a bottle, and of good stuff, brought to a table. I think all of us need a few shots of panther piss to warm us up. Now, I don't hold to drunks and usually drink, if at all, in moderation, but it's so cold out there the bears are wearin' capotes."

"Pull up some chairs and I'll get yer bottle."

Cotton entered a few minutes later and said, "I put the horses up, so iffen Coon comes he'll not see 'em. Hell, I think our mounts would freeze iffen left out in the open anyway."

Bringing tin cups and a bottle to the table, Butterfield sat, and asked, "How are you goin' to handle Coon when he gets here? I'd just as soon ya shoot the sumbitch the minute he walks through the door."

Nate gazed into the old traders eyes and replied, "Ya know me better than that. Oh, I plan to kill the man, but he'll have a fightin' chance."

"Don't destroy the inside of this place, okay?"

"I intend to fight the man outside, iffen he'll go along with the idea."

"Have ya lost yer mind?" Cotton asked.

"No, or at least I don't think I have."

"It's too cold to fight outside." Cotton said.

"I won't tear up the inside of this place just to get a piece of Coon's ass. We'll fight outside and that's the end of it, unless he pulls iron in here. In that case, all five of us can have a shot at the man. I have a gut feelin' Coon will take the fight outside once he hears my terms."

"And," asked Butterfield, "what are yer terms?"

"Knives, until one of us is dead. If he lives, he'll walk from here a free man. Iffen I win, justice will have been served."

# CHAPTER 24

Coon was colder than he'd ever been in his life. Taking this damned mule may have been a big mistake, because at least the men have a warm fire, he thought. He'd decided to leave the group, go to the trading post, kill Butterfield, and then loot the supplies. He knew the old trader kept a dozen or so horses and mules in his barn, which he sold or traded from time to time, so Coon would have a way to transport the supplies to the Indians. His biggest desire was whiskey and guns, which he knew Butterfield carried, and the Sioux wanted. It'd been easy to promise the men he'd return with mounts, but he'd never had the intention of returning for them. Besides, they were spineless and didn't have the guts to challenge him on the issue. But, right now, he knew he'd be lucky to survive this ride.

His first strike at the flint failed to start his fire and his fingers no longer had feeling in them, but he was growing *comfortable*. The arctic-like air no longer cut through him like a knife. *Start fire, or I'm a dead man*, his slow mind screamed. He struck the flint once more and this time his scorched rag ignited.

As the flames ate at the wood like a hungry cancer, Coon added gradually larger pieces of wood to the flickering flames. Warming up brought pain to his whole body and his feet, hands and ears throbbed with each beat of his heart. *Damn pain is killin' me*, he thought and then pulled the bottle of laudanum. He took a small sip and then waited impatiently for the pain to disappear.

As he waited, he opened his possibles bag, after a few fumbled attempts, and pulled out a strip of jerky and a tin cup. Reaching behind him, he scooped up some loose snow in the cup and placed it near the flames. He tore a few pieces of jerky from the strip and dropped them into the tin cup. He felt nothing when his fingers moved and worried if it was from the drug or the cold. When the snow in the cup melted, he added more.

After close to three hours, he began to feel somewhat normal again, but his ears and feet were still numb. His hands had thawed with a gut wrenching pain, which had made him reach for the laudanum once more. *I got to go easy with the drug, or I'll end up needin' the shit everyday. Hell, I'd much rather be knifed or shot than frozen. Good God, the pain is unreal.*

He sipped on the jerky water off and on most of the night and when the sun came up, he saw the mule was dead. Coon moved to the animal and cut a large chunk of meat from a rear quarter and returned to his fire. He cut small pieces from the meat and let it boil in his cup. He then stuck a chunk of meat on a green stick and leaned it near the flames. As the meat cooked, his stomach growled in anticipation of hot food, and Coon smiled. *I'll survive now. I'll go and kill old man Butterfield, steal his goods and then go to the Sioux, once it warms up some. It won't be easy walkin' to his place, 'cause it's around five miles if I remember right.*

There came a loud crack and when Coon glanced in the direction, a tree limb fell from one of the larger cottonwoods. *Sumbitch, it's so cold that limb fell due to the weather. Iffen it's cold enough to do that to a tree, I can't leave here until it warms up a might. I have food and fire, so I'll make 'er.* He took a long sip of his mule broth.

A few minutes later, Coon pulled his knife and moved toward the mule. The animal had been dead for less than an hour, but the carcass was already starting to freeze. He gutted and skinned the animal, so he'd at least have a skin to sleep on, but he needed another one to cover him. He knew all larger animals were way down south or hibernating in this weather, so he'd have to make do with what he had on hand. He quartered the meat and placed it near his camp, because eventually small animals would come for the meat.

He moved into the small grove of trees and found one stunted cedar tree, and he cut enough limbs from it to insulate the ground where he slept. He also pried a few clumps of pitch from the tree bark and placed it in his possibles bag. He knew the pitch would burn like coal oil if exposed to a flame. The next time he needed a fast fire, the pitch would provide the source.

Using his tomahawk, he started constructing a primitive shelter, using limbs and brush. His finished product was crude, even by mountain man standards, but would help if the snow started again or if the winds blew.  Each time he chilled while working, he'd move to his fire and warm up before tackling his task again.  It was a slow process, but he was in no hurry.  His primary goal at the moment was to survive the weather and come what may, he was determined to live.

Adding another log to his fire, Coon thought, *I'll bet the boys are all dead by now, but iffen they ain't, they will be iffen they keep waitin' on me.*  He chuckled, *I wonder how long those fools will stay there, expecting horses to be brought to 'em?  They'll die, iffen they ain't already, because not a one of 'em has any damned sense.*

Moving back into the trees, he peeled the tough outer bark from trees and then removed the softer inner bark.  He'd add it to his mule soup to flavor it up a bit.  He looked for a pine tree, but saw none.  Spotting a birch tree a ways from his camp he made his way to the tree and removed a long wide strip of bark, knowing he could fashion it into a container to boil his soup.  As long as he kept the direct flames from touching the bark and the inside filled with water, the container would work fine.

In less than three hours after sunrise, Coon's day was looking up, or it was until his visitor arrived.  He'd just added another log to the constantly hungry fire, when he heard a low growl.  Turning toward the remains of the mule, he spotted a badger feeding on the entrails of the dead animal.  Not many animals scared Coon, but grizzly bears and badgers did, for damned sure.  He knew both to be mean, ill-tempered, and aggressive.  They both took a lot of killing, too, and rarely dropped with just one shot.

Pulling his rifle up, Coon sighted right where the heart should be on the mean little bastard, took a deep breath, and as he released it he gently squeezed the trigger.  He heard the rifle shot, but smoke blocked his view.  Moving slightly to his left, he could see the area, but not the badger.  Quickly reloading his rifle, he moved toward the carcass of the mule with caution, praying he'd not just injured the mean thing.  If so, he'd soon have one hell of a fight on his hands.

Blood covered the snow and tracks indicated the small animal had moved into the trees. Swallowing his fear, Coon moved slowly forward, following the tracks. *I can't let this thing get away hurt, because sooner or later he'll come for me. Now is the time to end this. Meanest little sumbitches on earth, pound fer pound a badger is, and this one needs to die.*

He'd just stepped over a log when he caught movement in the corner of his left eye. Suddenly, his left leg was attacked by teeth and claws. Blood began to run into his moccasin and pain was radiating up the entire leg as he attempted to draw a rifle bead on the small beast. Unable to shoot, without inflicting injury to himself, he dropped the rifle and pulled his pistol. Leaning over the badger, Coon fired and saw his bullet hit the animal solid, in the middle of the back, but hungry teeth still chewed at his leg.

Not hearing his own screams of pain, Coon pulled his knife and frantically reached for the badger. When the man's hand was close, the little badgers head came up and the animal's teeth attacked the mountain man. Pain instantly shot up his hand to his shoulder and blood flew into the air, as Coon stabbed and stabbed the critter. Finally, the badger died, his teeth still buried in the mountain man's hand. Quickly severing the badgers head, Coon sheathed his knife, picked up his rifle and made his way back to camp.

Once by the flames, Coon pulled the bottle of laudanum and thought, *that little bastard almost killed me, I'm bleeding like a stuck pig. I need some of this for the pain and I need to doctor these injuries up and do the job now.* He took a sip of the powerful drug.

As soon as the pain died, Coon had to remove the jaws of the critter with his skinning knife. He tossed the head and lower jaw over his shoulder, into the snow behind him. Blood was flowing freely and he looked around in desperation for something to use to dress his injuries. All he could see was the skin from the mule.

It was as he was cutting strips from the mule hide that fear struck him in the center of his belly, and he asked aloud, *"Good Lord, what iffen that damned thing had hydrophobia."*

*I don't need to worry about that right now, because iffen I don't get this bleedin' stopped I'll be dead way before I go mad.*

He discovered a long rip in his calf muscle, numerous bites and scratches on the leg, the tip of his left little finger was missing.  He knew he'd have to cauterize his more severe injuries on his own and that was going to be rough, because beyond a doubt he'd pass out, laudanum or no.  He suddenly remembered the flask of whiskey he carried in his inside coat pocket.  He poured a little on his scratches and leg bites, but only just a little.  Coon then placed the flask back in his pocket.  He wanted to save enough of the alcohol to clean his injuries after he applied the hot knife.

Coon placed his knife blade in the dancing flames of his fire, and took one more sip of laudanum as he waited for the knife to turn red-hot.  He desperately wanted a strong drink of the alcohol, but would save it for his injuries.  He turned the drug bottle around and read the contents, and then grinned.  The drug contained seventy percent alcohol, so he felt it could be used to treat his cuts, need be.  Glancing at the knife blade, he knew it was time to start the dance.

Coon picked up the hot blade, pressed it against the stub of his little finger and gave a wobbling cry of pain.  He quickly dropped the knife to the snow, his world grew gray and then faded into darkness.

Later, he had no idea how long he'd been out, but he added more wood to his fire and placed the blade back into the flames.  He sipped a little of the drug and then as he waited for the blade to change color, he thought, *only one more bad hurt to treat.  This one won't be as easy and I need to smear the flesh on my calf together before I pass out.  Iffen I don't, I'll have to keep burnin' myself until the job is done right.  I don't know iffen I can do this again but iffen I don't, I'll bleed to death.  Damn me, what a choice.*

Once the blade was red, Coon pulled his trouser leg up, pulled the knife from the fire, and gritting his teeth against the coming pain.  He didn't hesitate as he placed the flat of the blade against the muscle, groaned loudly and smeared his flesh together as well as he could.  Again, he passed out.

When he awoke, he glanced at his leg, smiled and pulled the whiskey flask from his coat.  He poured a little of the strong drink on his finger and then on his calf.  He felt pain, but it was not nearly as intense as the burning had been, and he remained conscious.  He placed a crude bandage of mule skin against his leg and tied it using strips of mule hide.  He then grinned at his primitive efforts.  *It's rough, but should do the job, unless the critter was hydrophobic, then I'm a dead man.*

Coon spent the remainder of the day resting and drinking mule soup.  It was still lung stinging cold, but the snow seemed to have moved east.  Log after log was burned, the heat providing the difference between life and death.

At dusk, he had a fever and after taking a small sip of laudanum, he fell asleep, only to awaken hours later, cold and shaking violently.  A quick glance at the stars indicated it was about two in the morning and his fire had burned down to only red coals.  Fear started building up inside of him as he added some small twigs and prayed the wood would burn.  *I can't sleep that long with the cold like it is, or I'll wake up dead.  Only I feel flushed and sick.  It's the wounds.*  Then his heart began to quicken as he thought of the badger and the dangers of hydrophobia.  *It's too soon for any sickness from the badger, so it must be from the scratches and bites.  It's normal for men that have been under a hot knife to get a fever.*

For the rest of the night he sat by the fire feeding the flames wood, but occasionally he'd nod off and then awaken when his head would drop to his chest.  It was the longest stretch of his life and it only lasted for about five hours.  *After I kill Butterfield, I'm goin' to sleep fer a week.*

He'd just placed more snow in his mule soup, when he heard a voice call out, "Hello the camp!  I'm a friendly old coon and white.  Can I share yer fire a spell?"

Pulling his rifle to the ready position, he replied, "Who are ya and where are ya headed?"

"My given name is Henson Jackson, but I go by Hen.  I'm a mountain man headed to Butterfield's and smelt yer smoke."

"Come, but keep yer rifle in yer left hand and over yer head.  Move slowly, now, or I'll put a bullet in yer breadbasket."

"Yer like me, when it comes to trustin' others and that's good.  I'm comin' in now and I'll be leadin' my horses."

A small man, looking close to a hundred years old and moving slowly in the deep snow, approached.  His hair and beard were both auburn, but white streaked, and his eyes a deep blue, Coon noticed his his teeth even and white when the man said, "Lawdy, where'd all that blood come from?"

"I fit with a badger a day or so back. I can't recollect for sure when it happened, but I think yesterday."

"Well, let me tie my hosses and I'll take a look at ya. Ya look like shit warmed over, in case ya wondered and I know ya have a high fever. Ya got blood all over the snow too, so have ya been hurt pretty bad?" Hen asked.

"That critter tore part of my calf to hell and back and bit off my little finger to boot. I had to cauterize the injury alone and that was some rough doin's. I'm hot and feel weak."

"Hell, I reckon ya do. Did the damned thing kill yer mule, too?"

"No, the first night I was here the cold killed my mule. There was nothin' I could do about it either. See, the Cheyenne caught me and the boys out on the plains and I was the only one to make 'er out alive."

Hen's right eyebrow came up as his eyes narrowed and he said, "I ain't sure ya was the only one to live. I come across four men about ten miles back and they was frozen as hard as rocks. I looked 'em over pretty good, but didn't know none of 'em and I didn't see no arrows in 'em."

"When the fight started there was an even dozen of us. We had four men with the horses and mules, and then things went to hell fast. I was in the main group of eight or so, and I couldn't tell shit after a few minutes. The Cheyenne were all over us, and I mean in no time, and most of the mounts were gone by then. When a mule neared, I jumped on his ass and here I am. As I rode away, I saw about two dozen of the Injuns overrun my men."

With a questioning look in his eyes, Hen asked, "Yer men? I thought y'all were company men. Hell, I know all the free trappers, or thought I did." *Something about this story ain't on the up and up,* Hen thought, *but I cain't put my finger on what yet. I'll let him talk some more, but I damned sure won't trust 'em none.*

"I trapped out here the last two years, as a free trapper with some mountain men known as Johnson, Hanks, Burrows, Possum, and a new man named Williams. Mayhap ya know one 'er more of them. They was killed by Blackfoot earlier this year."

"I knew Johnson, Hanks and old Possum. They were some, they really were."

"Yep, good men, all of 'em.  But, the Blackfoot kill a good man as fast as they do a poor one.

Tilting his head to the side, Hen asked, "And why wasn't ya killed then, too?"

"I was out runnin' my trap line.  I come back and every swinging dick was dead, scalped and our plew gone."

Sitting on a buffalo robe he pulled from his packhorse, Hen said, "Well, now, ain't ya about a lucky sumbitch.  Here we have two massacrees and ya survived 'em both, and as the only survivor.  God must value ya highly, young pup, to show ya such personal attention."

"My name is Whiskey, Whiskey Jones."

*Yer a damned liar, Coon, because yer the one who killed yer trappin' partners.  Butterfield told me how Cotton Top and Nate Grisham were on the tramp after yer ass.  Won't they be surprised when they find out I caught yer useless ass,* Hen thought, but chuckled and said,  "Is Whiskey a nickname or yer given name?"

"Nickname, I don't use my old handle much these days."

Standing, Hen said, "Whiskey, let me get some good grub and some robes from my horse.  Once we get ya fixed up better and get some good food in ya, ya'll be able to rest a mite.  It must have been rough to use the hot knife on yerself and keep a fire burnin' all night, with ya hurtin' like ya was.  Ya can relax now and I'll see ya get what ya need to mend."

*I could just shoot his ass now and take his stuff as mine, but I can't do that.  I'll wait until we get to Butterfield's, then shoot 'em on the front porch or something.  Right now he can help me heal faster and take care of me.  I can think on this some more after I've healed a mite,* Coon thought.  He then said, "I'm not thinkin' real clearly right now, so iffen I'm a mite slow, it's 'cause of the fever and the fact I'm just worn out."

"Not a problem and it's expected.  Hell, yer lucky to be alive.  Mule makes a tough meal and I know because I've had 'er before, so I think even my nasty cookin' will bring a smile.  Just relax and let me take care of ya and the fire."

As he removed supplies from his horse, Hen thought, *I'll get yer ass drunk as a dog and then take ya to Butterfield's.  There we can have a trial, iffen we can find enough trappers.  I'm sure we can lock ya in the storehouse until we need ya fer a hangin'.*

*Hell, ain't no way out of that storehouse and she's built strong, too.*

Laying a buffalo robe inside the shelter, Hen said, "Ya crawl on top of that robe, I got another one to cover ya with, and get some sleep. Here in a couple of hours I'll wake ya up to feed ya."

"I thank ya kindly fer carin' fer me, Hen. I'll make it good one day. I figure I owe ya." Coon moved toward the shelter.

"Huh-uh, we mountain men take care of each other and ya don't owe me a damned thing. Hell, one day ya might help me out of a mess like this."

"Maybe," Coon said and took a pull of his laudanum.

"Ya'd better back off the painkiller or you'll get hooked on 'er and not be worth a shit to yourself and anybody else. It gets to be a habit." Hen picked up one of his two clay jugs and one of his tin cups. He poured one cup full and took it to Coon, along with the jug. "Drink this and as much of it as you can. It'll kill yer pain and help ya sleep. It's better fer ya in the long run than the painkiller. The jug will be beside ya as ya rest."

Coon downed the cup of raw alcohol in two drinks and then poured another one. He felt feverish, weak, and light headed. Before he'd finished the second cup, he was asleep.

# CHAPTER 25

Cotton and the small group were still at Butterfield's. They were relaxed, well rested, eating better than they had in months, and getting a daily shot or two of good quality whiskey. They'd been there for four days when Cotton asked, "Where's Coon?"

"Ya in a hurry to see a gal friend 'er something?" Butterfield asked with a grin.

Nate met his friends eyes, shook his big head and said, "It's been well below freezing this whole time, and I suspect his ass is holed up someplace waiting fer a break in the weather. Then again, ya know as well as I do, he might have been killed or injured. I think he'll be here, but not for a few more days."

Deacon nodded and said, "I agree with Nate on this. Ain't no man or critter with any sense that'd be out in this weather."

"We can go lookin' fer 'em, cain't we?" Bear asked.

Deacons eyes grew large at the thought of riding in sub-zero weather for days and he started to speak, but changed his mind and stayed quiet. *Ain't no way I'd meander out in this cold fer days and mayhap still not find Coon.*

"And leave Butterfield without help?" Nate snapped instantly.

"By damn, I can take care of my own self and don't need a damned nurse maid."

"I'll tell ya what, Cotton, iffen yer gettin' the urge to travel, just ride on out, son, because I suspect he'll come along directly. It's too cold for my butt to be out in this weather lookin' fer bad men." Nate said.

"By God, I'll do that. I don't mind waitin', but we ain't even sure iffen he's comin' here or not. Fer all we know, he might have headed to Fort Atkinson or Saint Louis. I'll scout around for about five miles out and see if I can turn up any sign. If he's around, I'll find 'em. Anyone else want to ride with me?"

"Mayhap ya will find 'em, but I think not." Nate said and then added, "See, our boy is a greedy man. He come out here to make money and it ain't likely he wants to ride home empty handed. The only place within a weeks ride is right here, but iffen ya want to freeze your balls off out there, by golly saddle up and ride."

When no one else agreed to ride with him, Cotton left the building alone and moved for the barn.

As soon as Cotton left, Butterfield asked, "Who put a burr under his saddle?"

"He's always like that. He's a damned fine mountain man, the best friend any man could have, but he lacks patience. Ain't never been a time when someone was riding our asses hard that he didn't want to take the fight to them, just to end it. His lack of patience might end up killin' 'em one day."

Pulling the cork from a bottle of rye, Butterfield said, "It might just be today because it's colder than my first wife out there."

"First wife? I never knew ya was married."

"Hell, Butterfield," Bear said, "I ain't seen no wife here in the years I've known ya."

"Pawnee she was, and hotter than a midday sun in August before we married. Once we was hitched up, she lost all interest in our robes. Instead of goin' to bed with a hot woman, she turned colder than a judge at a hangin'."

Nate and the others laughed. After Butterfield added some whiskey to his cup, Deacon said, "I ain't never had a full-time wife, but I was close once. I fell in love with a Shoshone woman and her name, Talks Much, got me to thinkin'. So, I called the weddin' off."

Butterfield broke into a loud laugh and then said, "Bullshit."

Just after dawn this morning Cotton smelled smoke. It was cold enough limbs would crack and fall, but not cold enough to make rocks explode. He was in a cranky mood, hungry and cursing for leaving the warmth of the trading post. Tying his horse to a small cedar tree, he injuned up on the camp. He immediately spotted Coon sitting by the fire drinking something from a tin cup and the man looked like holy hell. Another man, who Cotton knew as Hen, a mountain man with the bark on 'em, was placing wood near the fire.

When Hen entered the woods once again to pick up dead wood, Cotton moved to the man. Once near, he whispered, "Hen, it's me, Cotton Top. Come with me, we need to talk."

Hen had pulled a pistol and cocked it in one smooth motion, but when he saw Cotton, he released the hammer and placed it back in his belt. As Cotton moved away from the camp, Hen followed.

After he covered about a hundred yards, Cotton stopped and said, "Ya have Coon Turner and he's the man who killed Possum's trappin' partners."

"I know all of that, and I was goin' to bring 'em to Butterfield's for a trial. He told me some bullshit story about the Blackfoot rubbin' the group out and takin' their plew, but Injuns ain't got no use fer furs, hell, they got nothin' but fur all around 'em."

"Why is the man loose?"

"He thinks I believe his story and I figured it'd make it easier to travel with 'em. Now, I have an idea. Let me get back, get 'em drunk and then ya can just walk in and tie his ass up. Don't worry none, because I'll cover yer every move. He's hooked on laudanum a little and as sore as a whore the day after payday. He fit a badger and won in the end, but he took a beatin' to win, let me tell ya. Lost a finger and the muscle on his calf was torn off. I'll check his injures in a bit, tell 'em the calf is startin' to fester and have him drink some of his drug. Then, as I heat up a knife, I'll feed 'em a bunch of whiskey. Once he's good and drunk, I'll start to sing. Then, ya rush in and we'll hog tie his ass."

"He armed?"

"Has two pistols he never takes out of his belt."

"Ya keep 'em away from the pistols or Nate might be short a ridin' partner come mornin'."

"He'll be roostered and I'll watch for his guns.  Iffen I have to do the job, I'll just shoot his ass."

"Okay, get back now and let's get this started."

Cotton walked with Hen as close to the camp as he dared and then squatted in the cottonwoods.  He gave a man a few minutes to enter camp and then moved up close.

Throwing a few logs he'd found on his return to camp, Hen said, "I need to change the bandage on yer leg and check yer finger."

"Have at it," Coon said and extended his hand.  As Hen looked him over, he picked up his tin cup and sipped a little whiskey.

"Yer finger looks good."

"I imagine, 'cause it don't hurt much."

Squatting, the mountain man unwrapped the leg, gave a loud sigh and said, "Legs startin' to fester, so I need to scrape 'er clean, wash it out good with some drink, and cauterize it again." The strange fact was, the injury was turning sour.

"Shit, I was afraid of that.  It's been painin' me off and on all day.  It started hurtin' me late last night."

Hen stuck his knife blade in the flames and said, "Drink up and when yer good and drunk, I'll do the job.  Iffen ya got any laudanum left, now would be the best time to drink a bit.  I'm gonna have to hurt ya, old coon."

Taking a swig of the powerful drug, Coon finished his whiskey and poured another one.  Hen watched as the man's eyes slowly glazed over and then asked, "Ya about ready?"

Throwing back one more cup of whiskey, Coon said, "Yep, do 'er now."

Pulling Coon's knife from the ground, he placed the knife edge against the thin scab and with one quick movement, brought the blade down the length of the injury.  Coon screamed, his eyes rolled back in his head, and he passed out.

"Cotton, get yer ass in heah, he's passed out!"

As Hen waited, he reached into Coon's belt and pulled his pistols, and threw them and the knife to the other side of the fire.  Cotton moved to his side, his face beet red from the cold. Hen tied Coon's hands behind his back, looked at Cotton and said, "Hell, his leg really is festered.  Do ya want me to clean 'em up?"

"Pour some whiskey on it then burn 'er shut.  We'll leave shortly.  Can I get a bit of that whiskey?  I about froze my ass off out there waiting for ya to start singing."

"I didn't have to sing, he passed out.  He's got a laudanum and whiskey problem now, or will have for the short period he has left on this earth.  Sure, pour us both a cup of panther piss."

Picking up the laudanum bottle, Cotton poured it into the flames and as the fire flared up, from the high alcohol content of the drug mixture, he said, "His drug problem just went away.  We'll keep his ass drunk on the way back to make him easier to handle, not to kill his pain."

"When are we leavin'?"

"Just as soon as you place that red-hot blade against his injury and wrap 'em up.  We'll be at the tradin' post in a little under two hours."

"Hell, he won't be in any shape to sit in a saddle."

Cotton smiled and replied, "I don't really give a damn what kind of condition he's in when we ride.  He'll be thrown over a saddle and tied to the horse.  He'll be movin', even iffen if kills 'em."

It was right after dusk when they rode to the hitching post at Butterfield's.  Coon was as drunk as he could get and not pass out.  He was still tied belly down over a saddle and he'd cursed and sang songs most of the trip.

Just as Cotton was tying the horses, Butterfield stepped out holding a lantern high, with a shotgun in his other hand, and asked, "Who in the hell are ya?"

"It's me, Cotton.  I have Hen with me and Coon's hogtied to a horse."

Looking over his shoulder, Butterfield yelled out, "Boys, it's Cotton Top and he has Coon."

As Nate moved toward the door, Butterfield moved to the horse, grabbed Coon's hair lifted his head so he could see his face clearly.  "Yep, that's the murderin' sumbitch.  Let me get the keys to the storehouse and we'll lock his nasty ass up. There's a stove off in one of the rooms, and it keeps the place just a little above freezin'."

Nate stood on the porch, looked at Coon and said, "By God, Cotton, ya done did good, ole son. I can't believe this." Then seeing Hen, he extended his hand and added, "Good to see ya again, Hen. How'd ya end up with Coon Turner?"

Hen explained the situation and Nate laughed. After a few minutes he said, "Well, he should be called whiskey now, because he's totally shit-faced."

"Let me get some blankets fer 'em and we'll lock 'em up in the storeroom." Butterfield said and then walked back into the trading post.

"Gonna have a trial?" Hen asked.

"Yep, to make the hangin' legal." Nate replied.

"You'd better do the job quick, because his leg is festered and he was torn up pretty good by a badger."

"They'll tear a man a new butt, iffen he ain't careful. But, we have Deacon and Bear inside, so we've enough men to conduct a trial in the mornin'."

"Here, I have the blankets. Cotton, ya and Hen go in and have a couple of drinks while Nate and I take care of Mister Turner. Tell the boys we'll be back in directly."

"By golly, I can do that." Cotton said.

"Let's go, Cotton, I'm cold as hell," Hen said and then added, "Ya two watch yer asses now, because he's drunk."

"Ya two have done enough, we've got the man now." Nate said as he untied the reins and moved toward the storehouse.

At the door to the storehouse, Butterfield unlocked the door, and held it open as Nate pulled Coon from the horse. He threw the man over his shoulder and packed him inside the roughly made building, and lowered him to the hay. Nate took the blankets from the trader and gently covered the man. He then stood and looked the room over, but saw no way Coon could escape, except through the doorway. There was a small window, about twelve inches wide and twice that in length, but too narrow for Coon to get out of due to his size.

As they walked outside again, Butterfield closed the door, locked it and then lowered a metal bar to further secure the door. Noticing Nate watching him, he said, "When mountain men have too much to drink and start to raise hell, this is where we keep 'em until they sober up. Coon will still be here come mornin'"

"I'm sure he will."

"Ya head on back, I've a fire to start in another room of the building and I'll join y'all in a few minutes. Now, there ain't no other door available to Coon, so he cain't get at me. Ya don't need to worry none, 'cause I'll be okay."

Nate turned and made his way to the trading post, glad justice would be served in a few days.

The next morning, the trading post had been converted into a courtroom of sorts, with tables pushed to the side, a row of chairs for the jury, and one chair for Nate, who would be the judge. They'd just started to fetch Coon, when the door opened and in stepped a man none of them had ever seen before.

"I need some help. I was in a fight with Cheyenne a few days back and shot in the arm. It's soured on me, or so I think. My name is Jack."

"Well, Jack," Butterfield said, "come in a sit at the table. I'll fetch some whiskey and we'll take a good look at yer arm."

Hen asked, "Jack, was ya ridin' with Coon Turner when ya fit the Injuns?"

Lowering his head, Jack replied, "Yep, I was, but we didn't know what the man planned to trade guns to the Sioux, until after the attack."

Hen said, "He told me all the white men were killed and he was a lone survivor. Now, I come across four other men who'd frozen as solid as rocks just before I met Coon and now ya show up. Something about all of this makes no sense to my mountain man mind."

Lying, Jack said, "Five of us left Coon after the attack, because he told us what he was carryin'. Not a one of us wanted problems with the army, not over guns and whiskey. At first we were all together, but once we learned about the guns, we ran Coon off. When the others stopped for the day durin' the cold weather, I kept walkin'. I knew the only safety close by was this tradin' post."

As the men talked, Butterfield took a knife and cut Jacks shirt off and when he saw the injury he grimaced as he said, "Jack, this arm will have to come off."

"Ain't there no way to save it?"

"Look at the arm. Do ya see those red and purple lines movin' up and down? That's poison in yer system. Iffen we don't remove the arm, you'll die within a week and a hard death it'll be too, son."

Cotton said, "There are bone fragments and dirt in yer arm, so I think ya need to give Butterfield's words some serious thought, young coon."

After about a minute, Jack said, "Take 'er off then. Only I'll need a bottle of whiskey and I ain't got any money."

"Son, don't worry about money, but whiskey I have and some laudanum."

Deacon asked, "What about Coon?"

Butterfield gave him a nasty look and said, "Injured folks come first. Coon ain't goin' no place, except to hell when we hang 'em. When I checked earlier, he was one mad sumbitch. I tossed a bottle of cheap whiskey in the room with 'em, but he wants his drug."

Nate asked, "Do ya want me to do the doctorin'?"

"Yer likely the best at the job and I'll help ya out." Butterfield said and then stood. He made his way to the counter, pulled out a bottle of laudanum and a jug of traders whiskey."

Walking to Jack, the trader poured some of the drug into a rough cast pewter spoon and said, "Drink this. I know it has a nasty-assed taste, but it'll kill yer pain. Then, start on the whiskey. After ya pass out we'll remove the arm."

Three hours later, Jack was in bed with his arm off about eight inches above the elbow. He was pale and still unconscious, but his heartbeat was regular and his breathing was good. The stub had been cauterized and cleaned with whiskey before bandaging.

Bear asked, "What's his chances?"

"Not real good, to be honest. Oh, not because of the poison in his system, but he's weak and ain't been eatin' good. Come to think on it, what has he been eatin'? All game has gone to lower elevations and he didn't mention a horse or nothin'." Nate replied.

At that point, Deacon entered the room holding a partially chewed on hand. Glancing around the room he said, "I found this in his possibles bag. I pray to God he's not been doin' what I think he has, because it's a sin."

Nate sat on the edge of the bed and said, "Take the hand out and toss 'er into the woods. If Jack has been eatin' people, do ya think he left his friends before or after they died?"

Hen said, "Look, when I found those bodies frozen, they was whole and wasn't cut up 'er nothin'. Iffen I was starvin' and my buddies died, by God, I'd eat 'em, iffen that's what it took to survive."

"I think," Deacon said, "God might view it differently if the men were already dead. But iffen he killed 'em to eat, then that's murder."

Cotton had been thinking, so he finally said, "These woods and plains ain't filled with folks like back east, so I suspect he found the same dead men Hen found. Since they were dead and he was hungry, well, ya can figure it out from there."

Nate stood from the bed and said, "We can talk all day on this and it won't change a thing. We'll wait fer Jack to come around and then have us a talk."

"What do they call men like that, the ones who eat people?"

"Cannibals?" Deacon said, unsure of the word.

Nate, who read a great deal said, "Uh-huh, that's the word fer 'em. I can tell ya one damned thing, Jack will find it hard as hell from now on to find a man who'll ride with 'em."

Butterfield was moving for the door when he said, "Shit, I'd guess so. I wouldn't ride with the man fer all the money in Saint Louis."

# CHAPTER 26

Two weeks later, Coon had recovered a bit, but he was acting strange and he was slobbering all the time. He refused to eat or drink and complained of flu symptoms constantly. When asked about how he felt, he'd turn aggressive and try to attack the speaker. Nate knew immediately what the problem was and called the men together one evening after supper.

"Fellers, our man Coon has hydrophobia and I think he got it from the badger that attacked him. Iffen ya notice he's droolin' all the time, won't eat or drink at all. Hell, when I opened the door this mornin' to feed 'em, he growled at me like a damned animal."

"Good Lord." Deacon said, his voice barely above a whisper.

Cotton poured some whiskey into his cup and said, "Ain't no cure and he's a danger to us, too."

Nodding, Nate said, "Yep, he's a danger, but he owes us a life."

"I say we have court in the mornin', with Coon kept locked up, and decide what we're goin' to do about this. Hell, while we're at it, we can do Jack at the same time." Butterfield said.

Nate took a drink of whiskey and then wiped his mouth off before he said, "Okay, we'll do 'em both in the mornin', but I don't see where Jack did anything wrong."

Bear said, "Maybe he didn't, or maybe he did, it's hard to say. I do know he won't talk about it and that, to me, means he's hidin' something from us."

Morning came with the trading post turned once again into a courtroom with the tables and chairs moved around. Nate was sitting alone, as the Judge, while Cotton, Deacon, Hen, and Bear were the jury. Butterfield would argue for both defendants.

Jack was sitting a chair and appeared scared shitless.

They opened the proceedings by telling all they knew of Coon's crimes and killings, and Butterfield made an honest attempt at fighting the charges. Each man told of the searching of Coon and every small detail they could remember.

Finally, after almost an hour, Nate stood, walked to the bar and pour four fingers of rye into his cup. He gulped it down and then returned to his chair with the cup and bottle. He turned to face the jury and asked, "Have ya reached a decision?"

"Uh-huh," Cotton stood and replied, "we find Coon Turner guilty of murder, bein' a thief, tradin' guns and whiskey to the Sioux, and then runnin' from it all."

Banging on the table in front of him with the butt of his pistol, he said, "Coon Turner, who we all know is locked up in the storehouse because of havin' hydrophobia, I have reached a decision on yer punishment. The Good Lord wants ya dead as badly as we do, which is why yer sick and dyin' right now. It is my order, as the judge at Butterfield's Tradin' Post, that ya be confined to the storehouse until hydrophobia kills ya dead, dead, dead. Yer not to be fed or given water to prolong yer life. Let God's will be done. Upon yer death, ya'll be taken into the woods and hanged. You'll hang, Coon Turner, until yer flesh and bones fall to the ground or the rope rots, whichever comes first. Your remains will not be buried. May God have mercy on yer soul, because I will not. All monies, guns and gear of Coon Turner will be divided among members of this court, to pay for the time lost this season hunting for his worthless ass."

Butterfield took a big gulp of his whiskey and said, "The next case is Jack, who is charged with eatin' his dead partners who froze to death durin' a bad snowstorm. Jack is in the courtroom."

Nate looked up and said, "Jack, move to the chair and repeat after Butterfield."

Butterfield walked to the man holding a new Bible. He said, "Place yer hand on the good Book and—"

"What's the problem, Butterfield?" Nate asked when the trader stopped talking.

"Jack ain't got but one hand, so he cain't put a hand on the Bible and then raise the other hand. I ain't ran into this problem before."

Nate asked Jack, "Since we can't swear ya in normal like, do ya promise to tell the absolute truth, so help ya God.  Now, I want ya to remember, He is listenin' to every word ya say."

"I do."

"Now," Nate ordered, "tell us what happened out there in the snow and cold.  Remember, too, the good Lord is listenin' to every word ya say."

Jack lowered his head and spoke of the Indian attack, being shot by Coon, and how he'd been forced to leave the group.  The first night he'd sat by a fire and fed it wood as his hunger grew.  The next day, as he stumbled toward the trading post, he'd ran into the men, but Coon was gone, along with the mule.  The men expected Coon to return, but Jack thought better.

"When did ya get something to eat?" Butterfield asked.

"The first night they shared a bite of jerky with me, but that was all we had."

"What happened next?" Nate asked and then took a drink of rye.

"I was too scared to sleep, because if the fire went out I'd freeze to death and knew it.  We all had light jackets, but no coats.  We really needed blankets, which we didn't have, so I fed the fire all night.  When the sun came up, three of those men were dead as hell and frozen like rocks."

"Is that when ya started eatin' 'em?" Butterfield asked.

"No, Green was still alive, and we moved our camp over a bit from the bodies.  I'd say a good hundred feet or so.  We took to boilin' tree bark and limbs, but they made us sick and we puked it all up."

"Keep talkin'." Nate ordered.

"It was about then that Hen came through and saw the bodies.  Blowing snow had filled our tracks in, but me and Green watched 'em as he checked the men.  Ain't no way he could tell we was around. Well, after Hen left, we went to the dead men to remove their clothes, hoping they'd keep us warmer.  Ya have to understand how cold it was.  Well, me and Green started arguing over some coats, so I pulled a pistol and shot his ass right then and there."

"Did Green have a pistol?  Now, tell me the truth, because God is listenin' to yer every word."

"No, he was unarmed and his gun was back at camp. Only I'd already decided to kill the sumbitch anyway."

"Why?" Butterfield asked.

"I come to understand the only way to survive was to eat a dead man. The other men were frozen hard and it would be almost impossible fer me to cut their flesh. Green now, I could shoot him, butcher 'em up while he was still warm, and not have to worry about cutting him into food later. Don't ya see, I killed him to survive! I had to kill the man, because his body was still warm, and I had no choice." Jack broke into a sob.

Silence, except for Jack's weeping.

Finally, after many long minutes, Nate asked, "Is there more ya need to say, Jack?"

"No, that's . . . all that . . . matters."

Turning to the jury, Nate said, "The three of ya go to the counter and share a few drinks of rye while ya talk this over. Once ya decide iffen Jack's guilty of murder and cannibalism, come back and tell me what y'all decided."

Fifteen minutes later the men were back in their chairs and all wore grins. Nate noticed Hen's cheeks were flushed.

"Members of the jury, have y'all reached a decision on Jack yet?"

Cotton stood and said, "Oh, that didn't take but a minute 'er two, but Bear and Hen wanted a few shots of whiskey, so we waited."

Shaking his head, then takin' a gulp of his whiskey, Nate asked, "What is yer decision?"

"We find Jack guilty of killin' Green so he could eat the man. He's guilty of both murder and cannibalism and admitted as much."

Nate banged the table once more with his gun butt and said, "Jack stand as I tell ya my decision on yer worthless ass."

Jack stood on trembling legs and then lowered his head. The men heard him crying softly.

"Jack, yer a sorry excuse fer a man and about the lowest form of life to be found on both sides of the Mississippi River right now. Iffen I had all the say, I'd turn ya loose and let ya live the rest of yer life haunted by the ghost of Green. I know you'd never have a minute of peace after what ya did to the man. How-some-ever, this court is governed by the Good Book and the mountain man creed, both of which tell me I can't let ya live. The Bible speaks of an eye for an eye and the mountain man creed demands vengeance for any murder. Do ya have anything to say before I tell ya the sentence?"

Raising his head, both cheeks stained with tears, Jack said, "Death doesn't scare me and I thought of killin' myself more than once, but that would be a sin. I've—"

Butterfield, who'd been in his bottle much more than the other men blurted out, "Sin? Why ya filthy man eatin' sumbitch! Ya ain't got the balls to kill yerself is the problem. Hell, ain't no bastard that'll eat a partner that's worried about sin!" The old trader exploded from his chair.

Nate, suspecting the old trader was going to whip Jack's ass, yelled, "Sit back down, Butterfield, and let the man talk. Here in about twenty minutes his days of talkin' will be over."

Butterfield remained standing, his hands balled into fists and his face red with anger.

"John Butterfield, ya either sit yer ass back in that chair or I'll get up and pound ya to the floor. The choice is yers." Nate stood, his huge form intimidating to all in the courtroom, and then continued, "Sit, John, this is a legal court of law, not a sa-loon. Have respect for the law, which is based on the Holy Bible, my friend."

Butterfield sat and poured another cup of whiskey, but glared hatefully at Jack.

"Sorry about that, Jack, now finish what was on yer mind about dyin'."

"I've prayed to God about my sin, and He has forgiven me. I'm promised in the Bible iffen I ask the Lord for forgiveness, he'll give it to me, and he has. I know my crime was a terrible one, but don't ya see, if ya kill me, you'll be doin' me a favor. I can't unkill Green, there ain't no way. Only now, I can't sin again by killin' myself. I know, beyond any doubt, I'll be re-ceived by God into heaven and he'll wrap his lovin' arms around me. I've done a terrible thing, Nate Grisham, I truly have and I'm more sorry for it than you'll ever realize. So, go on and tell me when I'll hang. The Lord waits for me."

Deacon stood, deeply touched by the condemned man's simple words and said, "I am a man of God, Jack, so if you've re-ally asked for forgiveness, it was given. If ya want, once Nate passes judgment, we can pray together until it's time."

"I . . . I'd . . . like that, Deacon."

Banging on the table again, Nate said, "Son, I wish to hell I didn't have to pass judgment on ya, I really do, only ya have to pay fer what ya did to Green.  Turning religious is a great thing and I'm happy fer ya, but it only means once ya die you'll go to heaven and not hell.  That doesn't really sound right, I guess, except what it really means is, in order to get to heaven ya have to stretch some hemp rope first.  I didn't mean to make it sound like goin' to heaven ain't important, when it's the goal of every man in this room."

Butterfield blurted out a drunken, "Amen, Brother Nate."

Ignoring the drunk trader, Nate said, "Jack, it is my sentence that ya be placed on the back of a horse, led to the big oak tree on the edge of the barnyard and there ya will be hanged by the neck until dead, dead, dead.  Once hanging, you'll remain on the rope for a period of two hours.  At the end of that time, you'll be given a Christian burial by Deacon and your remains will be buried and marked.  This sentence is to be carried out immediately and since I passed judgment, I'll do the job."

Every man in the room saw Jack smile.

"Bear, get a rope and Cotton, ya go get a horse ready, but don't worry about a saddle.  Deacon, ya stay with Jack until we come for him, and I'd suggest y'all pray.  Hen, meet me by the oak tree."

"What about me?" Butterfield asked.

"Meet us at the tree in a few minutes."

Ten minutes later, Jack was sitting on a roan with a roughly tied noose around his neck.  He was no longer grinning, but his tears were gone.

Deacon said, "Let us pray.  Lord, Jack here has done some terrible things to his fellow man and knows in his heart he was wrong.  He has asked ya for forgiveness and we know ya have forgiven him. Please welcome Jack Patterson into heaven, Lord, and let him sit at yer feet for eternity."

As the other men said "Amen", Deacon slapped the horse hard on the ass and turned his head away as the animal ran out from under the condemned man.  A loud snap was heard and when Deacon looked back, Jack's body was jerking and quivering as it shut down.  The rope, with the body on it, was still swinging wildly from side-to-side.

"Deacon, why'd ya do that?  I said I'd do that." Nate asked.

"It was his last request, Nate.  He wanted a man of God to send him home."

A week later Coon died in the storehouse and his body was re-moved by Nate and hanged from a large oak about a hundred yards from the trading post. Before he left the man, the big man took the twenty dollar coin he'd taken from the bartender in Saint Louis and placed it in Coon's shirt pocket. "It's fer a job that wasn't done back in the city."

Nate made his way back to the building and was having a drink at a table when Butterfield asked, "I don't see the point in hangin' the man, hell, he was already dead."

Nate grew sober and gazed into the old traders eyes as he said, "The court said he'd hang until his body or the rope rotted. See, John, I had no choice.  A sentence passed will be carried out, or our laws are useless."

"I guess yer right." Butterfield replied and then shook his head.

Standing, and his chair screeching as it moved over the un-finished wood, Nate said, "Cotton, pack 'er all up, son.  It's time we head to the mountains."

*The End*

# ABOUT THE AUTHORS

 **W.R Benton**, a pen name, is a retired U.S. military senior Non-commissioned Officer with over twenty-six years of active duty service. He grew up in the Missouri Ozark Mtns., where hunting, trapping, camping, and other outdoor activities were the norm. Additionally, he spent more than twelve years teaching survival and parachuting procedures to U.S. Air Force personnel as a Life Support instructor.  Mister Benton has an Associate's Degree in Search and Rescue, Survival Operations, a Bachelors Degree in Occupational Safety and Health, and a Masters Degree in Psychology near completion.

Mister Benton is a member of the America Authors Association (AAA).  You can visit W.R. Benton online at http://www.wrbenton.net or his War Paint Site at http://www.warpaint.info.

Visit him on Facebook at
www.facebook.com/wrbenton01

**Grady Clark**, pen name for Melanie C. Benton, is a retired respiratory care practitioner who now works with her first loves, photography and writing. While running a successful photography business for years, she only recently turned to writing a novel through the urging of Western Fiction Writer W.R. Benton, her husband. Melanie's photography has appeared on the covers of a number of W.R. Benton's books. Her first book, "*A Southern Moon Rising*," was released in 2008 and was recently released as an eBook. Her second book, "The Widow Nancy Buck," was released this year. She's also the co-author of *Nate Grisham, Black Mountain Man.*

An avid outdoors-woman, she enjoys acting, deer hunting, fishing, camping, and outdoor photography. She prefers the smell of wood smoke, the crackling of a fire late at night, and the serenity of nature, to a fast-paced life in a big city. Born and raised in Mississippi, most of it on a farm, she is a true Southern Belle.

Contact Melanie at www.melaniedcalvert.com
or on Facebook:
www.facebook.com/melanie.c.benton

# The NEW WORLD ORDER series
## 'A political-thriller uncomfortably close to today's headlines'

As the rich and elite of the world move to put the new world order in place across the globe, they understand they must move quickly.  At times just as rich and exciting in content as real American history — this is a series of heroism, valor, patriotism, greed, blackmail, sex, traitors, and death, as normal day-to-day Americans make a valiant stand against the takeover.

*Available at Amazon in both ebook and paperback*

**Mark of the Beast, Vol. 1** - the rich and elite move quickly to take complete control of the world and all governments. They attempt to place the whole world under the control of one leader, unidentified, with a totalitarian world government.  They hope to have one world bank, one currency, one government, and they promise comfortable lives for all citizens of the world. Countries are invaded by UN troops and martial law is declared, a few weapons are gathered, food is suddenly strictly rationed, no cars, no gas, and no utilities for anyone who is not wealthy and a part of the New World Order.

**California Invasion, Vol. 2** - In Volume 2 of the New World Order series, the Order shows a new U.S. President what will happen if he doesn't do their bidding. These shadowy puppet-masters will sacrifice anyone, even elites in the upper circles of power, and they prove that to the new President in vivid detail. Individual lives mean nothing when their objective is so close they can taste it.

www.ingramcontent.com/pod-product-compliance
Lightning Source LLC
Chambersburg PA
CBHW071753190726
48292CB00003B/969